I0675141

RIO DESPERADO AND TOP GUN

Two Full Length Western Novels

GORDON D. SHIRREFFS

WOLFPACK
PUBLISHING
— EST 2013 —

Rio Desperado and Top Gun
Paperback Edition
© Copyright 2022 (As Revised) Gordon D. Shirreffs

Wolfpack Publishing
5130 S. Fort Apache Rd. 215-380
Las Vegas, NV 89148

wolfpackpublishing.com

Paperback ISBN 978-1-63977-860-7
eBook ISBN 978-1-63977-861-4

RIO DESPERADO AND TOP GUN

RIO DESPERADO

CHAPTER ONE

The gaunt, wind-tortured tree at the top of the pass bore strange and gruesome fruit. Burke Dane slid from his saddle and walked toward the tree. Behind him, down a long and twisted road, was the valley of the Little Bonito, fully concealed by the low hanging mists of that cold and rainy day. Beyond the pass, hidden from sight by more mist, was the valley of the Rio Desperado. To certain men, the top of the pass was the point of no return. To the blue-faced man whose body hung in the whining wind of those heights it had been the end of the trail.

Burke stopped ten feet from the lynched man and slowly rolled a cigarette. There was no expression on his lean and angular face. The blue eyes were as hard as glacier ice. He read the crudely lettered placard that had been fastened to the soaked cowhide vest of the dead man. "Rustler," said Burke Dane in a low voice. He spat to one side before he lighted his cigarette. His lips drew back to one side as he looked down toward the misty valley of the Rio Desperado. Then he looked back at the hanging man. "Charley," he said quietly, "I've come to take you home."

There was "no haste as Burke cut down the stiffened

corpse and placed it on a flat slab of rock. He worked the taut noose loose from the deep groove it had dug into the cold flesh. He made no attempt to straighten the grotesquely crooked neck and head. He bound the body first in a blanket and then in a rectangle of tarpaulin and carried it to the big dun. The dun shied and blowed as Burke placed the corpse across the saddle and lashed it in place.

Burke walked back to the tree and picked up the rope. It was a fine reata, handmade as far as he could tell, and braided by an expert. Four-stranded and made of rawhide. An expensive rope for a vaquero to buy. Most of them carried a *grass* rope made of Manila hemp. Burke slowly coiled the rope and carried it back to the dun. He led the big horse back down the trail toward the valley of the Little Bonito.

The rain began to beat down on his slicker and on the tarpaulin that covered and protected the lynched body of Charley Mayo—younger half-brother of Burke Dane.

———

THE RANCH LAND spread along both sides of the Big Bonito as far as the eye could see. The log buildings were well built, though not large. They were designed to be practical as well as beautiful. Charley Mayo's tastes had always revealed his two prime characteristics of business-like workmanship and love of the beautiful country in which he was born and raised. No man could have selected a better place in the Territory of New Mexico to build a ranch and a future.

It was just turning dusk as Burke Dane's dun clattered across the log bridge that spanned the rushing river. He tugged at the halter rope of the stray burro he had roped in the valley of the Little Bonito, miles to the west, to carry the body of Charley Mayo home to its final resting place. The rain that had been holding off all day continued to patter down, dappling the dark waters of the Big Bonito and slanting in leaden colored veils down through the tops of the forest clearings to further soak the wet ground.

Through the rain, the yellow lighted windows of the ranch house appeared. A thread of smoke rose from the big fieldstone chimney, only to be beaten down by the cold rain. The wind shifted and with it came the tempting odor of roasting meat. Hungry as Burke Dane was, for he had not eaten all that day, the thought of food did not appeal to him. He took the wet cigarette butt from his tight lips and flipped it into the water.

He led the dun to the side of the corral and ground-reined it. He walked back to the burro and its bundled burden, and for the first time since he had found his brother, a trace of wetness showed in the hard blue eyes. It was not grief for Charley, that was already buried deep —though not forgotten, within the lean body of Burke Dane; it was grief for the young woman in the house, and for her little brood. The young woman who had sent a message to El Paso to find the older half-brother of Charley, so that he would look for his missing brother. It was the one thing that could have brought Burke back to the country of the Big Bonito.

Burke shook his head. He led the burro to a lean-to, took off the soaked tarpaulin and its contents. He placed the body atop a pile of hay and felt for the makings. Then he stopped. There was no use in stalling. He'd have to face Marion with the truth. He walked toward the house and onto the wide front porch that had such a pleasing. vista of the valley and the river. Burke heard her voice in the kitchen. He closed his eyes and prayed for strength. He had not prayed or anything in years, for Burke Dane, by thought and deed, was hardly a man of God.

Burke slammed a hard fist sideways against the wet door, then peeled off his slicker. Feet pattered on the puncheon floor and the door swung open to emit a flood of warm light and the mingled odors of a finely cooked meal. A small girl stood there looking up at the big man whose face was shaded by the brim of his hat. The little lady smiled and ran forward to wrap her tiny arms about his knees. "Mama!" she screamed. "It's Uncle Burke!"

A dish clattered to the kitchen floor and Burke heard the sound of hurried footsteps. In a moment she was there, framed in the kitchen doorway, wiping her slim hands on her apron while she looked eagerly at Burke.

"Burke!" she said, "You found him?"

He opened his mouth and then shut it.

"Burke?" She came forward into the room, tucking away a stray wisp of her lovely brown hair. Her gray eyes searching his weathered and bristly face. "Burke?" Her voice faltered a little. "Did you find him?"

He nodded. "I found him, Marion," he said at last. He gently disengaged little Dolly's arms from his legs and led her toward her mother. He kicked the door shut behind him. "He's outside in the lean-to," he said quickly, for want of anything better to say.

She eyed him closely and then she knew. "How did it happen, Burke?" she asked in a low voice.

He reached out an awkward hand and rested it on her shoulder. "Now, Marion," he said gently.

"Tell me!" she insisted.

He looked down at the little girl.

"She doesn't understand, Burke," said Marion.

Burke looked at Marion. Without a word he took the soggy placard from within his coat and held it out to her. She stared at the almost illegible word written on it, then at Burke.

"I don't understand," she said quietly. Then her eyes widened. "Not that, Burke! Not *that!*" she almost screamed.

He nodded and looked away from her. "I found him at the top of Windy Pass," he said. "Right beside the trail.

He was there several days at least." He caught her swiftly as she fell.

"Mama asleep, Uncle Burke?" asked little Dolly.

"Mama asleep," said Burke mechanically as he carried her to her room. He covered her with a quilt, then closed the door behind him. He hurried to the kitchen and inspected the meal, doing what had to be done. He knew then and there that she had expected the both of them, for the meal was one of Charley's favorites, and on top of the stove shelf were three berry pies, all favorites of Burke Dane. He walked into the living room and peeled off his damp coat. Dolly came to him and he picked her up, then walked to place his back against the fireplace to feel the grateful drying heat of the fire. A door creaked open and Print Campbell, Marion's father stood there, staring unseeingly toward Burke. "That you, Charley?" he asked.

"It's Burke Dane, Print," said Burke quietly.

A strange look fled across the sightless face. "Where's Charley?"

"Charley is dead, Print."

The wall clock ticked along and then Print spoke again. "How did it happen?"

"They lynched him atop Windy Pass, Print. Some days ago, from the looks of him."

"Who did it, Burke?"

"*Quién sabe?*"

Print felt his way to a chair and sat down heavily. "I told him to stay out of the Rio Desperado country, Burke. He wouldn't listen. You know how he was, Burke."

"Yes."

"Leastways he could have taken some of his own boys with him. No! He had to hire men over in that hellhole. Charley thought a lot of his ability to take care of himself, Burke."

"It runs in the family, Print."

The strange look fled across the face again. "Yeah.

But Charley was a good man, Burke. Don't you misunderstand me. He took care of me, Burke." Print passed a hand across his sightless eyes. "You'd have thought *this* would have warned him to stay away from that damned Rio Desperado country."

Burke looked away although he knew the old man could not see him. Print Campbell had lost his sight in the Rio Desperado country years ago and had almost lost his life along with it. A load of birdshot at close range had done the job. Print Campbell, so the story goes, knew too much about certain men. Not only did the incident close his eyes forever, but it sealed his lips as well, for if Print Campbell talked, quite a few men, still riding free and easy in the Rio Desperado country would have long since had the same fate as that of Charley Mayo. Although they would have had the benefit of law and a trial to boot.

Footsteps sounded in the hallway and Marion Mayo came into the room. Her eyes were red and swollen but her voice was steady as she spoke.

"You're cold, wet and hungry, Burke. Change your clothes. Some of Charley's things will fit you. By the time you've changed, supper will be on the table. Father, take care of Dolly. The baby is asleep, Burke. You can see him when he wakes up."

Burke handed Dolly to her grandfather. He nodded. It was the way of the women of that country. Marion Campbell had filled the gap in Charley Mayo's life seven years ago. She had satisfied his two prime characteristics. She was a practical and beautiful woman; a fine wife and a loving mother. Now Charley was gone, never to return to this earth, and her other menfolk needed to be fed and taken care of in the best way she knew how. It was as simple as that.

Burke went hesitantly into the bedroom. The lamp was lit and the quilt was neatly folded and placed at the foot of the bed. Marion Mayo's grief was oceans deep, but her discipline would carry her through in safety.

Burke swiftly changed his clothes. He carried his wet things into the kitchen to dry and hung his damp gun belt behind the stove to slowly dry out. He withdrew his Colt, emptied it, wiped it carefully, tested the action, then placed it on a shelf. It wasn't until he was done with that automatic task that he realized that both Marion and her father were looking at him. They had heard the spinning of the cylinder, the crisp metallic clicking of the hand-honed action. His face hardened a little. Neither of them had ever believed in gunplay, at least the sort Burke Dane was known to practice.

Marion silently served them, then turned away from the table. "There are more biscuits in the warming oven," she said. She reached for her rain cape.

"No," said Burke quickly. He stood up from the table. His knife dropped to the floor.

She smiled gently. 'I'll have to see him sometime, Burke," she said.

He passed a hand across his face. "Well, that is, I don't know *what* to say."

She walked to the kitchen door. "I'll be all right," she said.

He withdrew his clasp knife and walked to her. "The lashings are wet. Cut them," he said. He took a lantern from the shelf beside the door and lighted it for her. She took it silently and walked into the darkness. He watched her cross to the lean-to through the pattering rain and a great sickness came up within him. He walked back to the table.

"You couldn't stop her," said Print quietly.

"No."

The blind man shoved back his plate. "Can't hardly eat, Burke. I was only eaten' to please her."

"Me too. Smoke?"

"Please."

Burke rolled two cigarettes, placed one in the old man's mouth and lighted it. "She's lovelier than ever, Print," he said. "Breaks a man's heart to look at her."

Print blew out a mouthful of smoke. "You still love her, Burke?"

"I'd rather not talk about it, Print."

The old man leaned forward and looked directly at Burke, almost as though he could really see him. "Maybe we got to talk about it, Burke. She's got no one but me now and I ain't no use to her. She's got those two kids to take care of. She can't run this ranch, man! *You* can."

"Just what are you driving at?"

Print took the cigarette from his dry lips. "You're all she's got now to take care of her, Burke."

"Hell of a time to talk about that now!"

"Maybe Charley would have wanted it that way."

"Yeah," said Burke dryly. "You and Marion, and Charley. Maybe that time was seven years ago, Print. You know damned well why I left the Big Bonito country, man."

Print shrugged. "It was your decision. Charley was still here. He was a lot like you, Burke. She was lonely. Charley was good to her."

"She loved him, didn't she?"

A piece of firewood snapped in the big range. The rain slashed suddenly against the misted windows. Little Dolly scraped her plate and looked curiously at the two big men on each side of her. The wind moaned down the chimney.

"Yes," said the old man at last. "She *grew* to love him I think, Burke. It wasn't hard." He stared sightlessly at Burke. "But she never forgot *you,* Burke."

Burke got up and rolled another cigarette. He laughed dryly. "Same old Print," he said in a hard voice. "Looking out for his own. You'd tell me that just to make damned good and sure I'd stick around and take care of my brother's wife and *his* kids. Well, I don't buy that, Print! I'm leaving here before dawn." An odd feeling fled over Burke. He turned slowly to see Marion standing in the open doorway, the rain dripping from her cape. She was looking directly at him with her lovely and tragic eyes. *How much had she heard?*

She put out the lantern, removed her cape and hung it up, closed the door and crossed to the stove. "Hot berry pie for dessert," she said quietly.

Burke's face tightened. Damn the old man and his ways! Seven years ago he had made it well known he wanted no part of Burke Dane as a son-in-law and in those days Print Campbell's word was pretty near law in the valley of the Big Bonito. That was before he had found a tougher law in the valley of the Rio Desperado and had paid for it with his sight.

"I'll take Charley into the spare room," said Burke. He walked into the living room and got his slicker. He left the house and stomped across to the lean-to. He picked up the body of his brother and carried it back to the house, shielding the blue face from the rain with his hat. He took the body in the back way and into the little spare room at the rear of the house. He placed it on the bed in the darkness and closed the door behind him.

They were waiting for him in the living room. Marion and her father, with little Dolly playing on the floor, and the baby boy, Alan, cradled in his grandfather's arms. "I'll be leaving before dawn, as I said," spoke Burke as he lighted a cigarette.

"Back to El Paso?" asked Print tonelessly.

"No, Print. Back over Windy Pass and into Arizona Territory."

"But that's the Rio Desperado country!" said Marion. Her hand crept up to her throat.

Burke nodded.

"But why?" asked Marion.

Burke leaned against the fireplace. "My brother went over there to buy cattle. You said at supper he was carrying a thousand dollars with him for that purpose. Charley didn't get the cattle and the money is gone. Charley was murdered. I'm going back to get the man, or *men* who did the job, and I'm bringing back the cattle or the money for you, Marion."

She" stood up and slowly shook her head. "They'll kill you too!"

Burke shrugged. "They can try. I don't think anyone over there knows I am Charley's brother. I haven't been around here for seven years. I think I've changed considerably in those seven years, haven't I?"

There was no need for them to answer him, the answer was plain on their faces.

"This is no time for that," said Print slowly. His face hardened. "You've got to show respect for your dead brother, Burke. Aren't you going to stay for the funeral?"

"The best respect I can show for Charley is to do exactly what I said I intend to do."

"It ain't right!" snapped Print. "You're going to stay here until Charley is properly buried! You hear me?"

Burke looked at Marion. "I can't stay here, Marion," he said. "No one knows I'm back in this country. If I stay for the funeral and word gets around who I am, my chances of running down his murderers will be gone when I reach the top of Windy Pass." He smiled crookedly. "I might end up the way Charley did."

"I understand that," she said quietly. "But I don't understand *why* you have to go. It isn't worth it, Burke. Not to me, it isn't."

He straightened up. "It is to *me,*" he said. "I've got to go, Marion."

"Damned fool!" snapped Print Campbell.

Burke eyed him. "It's said you know a lot more about those people over there than anyone around here, Print."

"I don't know anything!"

"Yes you do," said Marion. She looked at her father. "You'll have to tell him, Father."

Print's face worked. "All right," he said at last. "It really doesn't matter anymore. I'm old and helpless now. A burden on you, Marion."

"I didn't mean -it that way," she said quickly.

"I know." He smiled. "Well, maybe if I was all right, I'd do as Burke is going to do. I'll tell you all I can, Burke, though God alone knows if it is of any value."

The fire was almost dead, and Marion had long ago gone to bed, when at last Print Campbell finished filling in Burke Dane with all he knew, from actual experience or from hearsay about the Rio Desperado country.

Burke stood up and stretched. He was dead weary and ready for bed. "Say good-bye to Marion for me," he said quietly. He took out his wallet and separated five one hundred dollar bills from the money within it. "Give this to Marion. She can pay me when I bring back the money Charley lost over there."

"Yen," said Print quietly. "Thanks, Burke." "You don't think I'll be back then?" The old man looked up at him. "No. Do you?" Burke put out the lamp. "I don't know, Print. I don't know. But there is one think I am sure of: I'll ram my navel into the sand trying!" "Amen," said Print Campbell.

The wind whipped along the valley of the Big Bonito, on its way to lonely and haunted Windy Pass, to plunge into the valley of the Rio Desperado far to west, almost gleefully, as though to spread the news that Burke Dane was on his way and that death would be a close rider of the big man from El Paso.

CHAPTER TWO

Burke Dane, through no choice of his own, was ascending Windy Pass from the valley of the Little Bonito in the howling darkness of a wind and rain storm that had begun in the late afternoon. Lightning crackled and snapped along the rimrock, etching the fanged peaks against an eerie sky while in the canyons and through the wind-swept passes the thunder drums rolled in mad fury. There would be no shelter on the eastern side of Windy Pass that night, nor indeed within the pass itself, for the rain-laden wind swept through it as though it was a gigantic funnel lashing and bending the tortured trees and stripping them of their leaves.

He hunched within his slicker trying to light a quirly but it was no use. There would be no solace of tobacco for him until he descended the pass into the valley of the Rio Desperado. The thought of trying to camp out that night even on the more sheltered side of the mountains was hardly tempting.

The top of the pass was deep in wet darkness when he reached it at last, hoping to God he could pass through and not see the scene of his brother's horrible death, but such a break was not allowed him that night.

The lighting shafted repeatedly through the streaming skies, marking the lone tree in its twisted nakedness. The memory of what he had seen there was etched on his mind no matter how hard he tried to think of other subjects.

The dun stumbled at the top of the pass and immediately began to favor a leg. Burke spat a curse into the night and slid from the saddle to examine the left fore hoof of the dun. It was then that he heard something crying eerily above the mad howling of the wind. A cold feeling swept over him as he straightened up, but he could not bring himself to look at that damned tree as though afraid of what he might see there; something not of this earth, but familiar enough to him.

The crying came again, distorted by the wind. Burke peered down the western side of the pass as the lightning flashed with almost stunning force above the peaks. There was a gap in the narrow roadway with a small area close to the mountain side where he would pass. There had been a slide and a big one. It was not there when he found Charley's body. He led the dun down the streaming roadway to stop at the gap. The lightning seared through the sky and he saw something white far below, a faint movement. Then the area was plunged again into darkness. But there had been just enough time to know that it was a man down there, clinging for dear life to a rock.

Burke stepped back from the edge and took his reata from the wet saddle. He knew it was too far for the rope to reach, so he took the gruesome relic of his brother's death from a saddlebag and linked the two reatas together. Stones and rocks slid from beneath his boots as he moved toward the edge and he threw himself backwards. A voice rose above the clattering of the fall. "Take it easy, for God's sake!"

Burke led the dun back and tethered him to a tree; made the end of the line fast to the saddle horn, then he coiled the linked lines and held them in his left hand.

The lightning gave him enough illumination to allow him to pick his way partly down the treacherous slope. It also showed him that beyond the base of the slide there was nothing except a sheer drop of hundreds of feet into the wet woods below.

He hung onto the line with his right hand and eased himself down. Now and then loose rock slid from beneath his dug-in feet. Despite the cold wetness of the night, he was sweating profusely. Halfway down the slope the lightning lanced through the skies to stab into a naked and towering butte on the far side of the pass. He saw then that the man was farther down than before and that his legs were dangling into space.

There was no use in trying to drop a noose over the man. There was nothing to do but inch down that treacherous slope, hoping that the sliding rock wouldn't push him over the brink, or stun him into letting go his weak hold. Further and further he descended until he was within two yards of the man. He could see the strained face, the wide eyes, the sickness within him. "Keep a mane holt!" he yelled as he shifted the coil to his right hand and the line to his left. A foot slipped and his full weight was held by die taut line.

"I'm going!" screamed the man.

Burke slid down the line. One foot went over the edge. He held the line with a grip of steel and dropped the coil, trying to get it around the man, but it slid over the edge and dangled into darkness.

"Oh God!" screamed the man.

Burke lunged and gripped a handful of wet cloth in his left hand, twisting it to get a better grip, while he hooked his left-leg about the man. Rock and dirt cascaded down both sides of them and then Burke felt that the man's full weight was dangling. *If that line broke!*

He worked a leg about the man. The strain was telling on his right arm. "Grab the line, damn you!" he yelled.

The weight was dead on him now as the man gripped the line, slipped and gripped it again. "Got it!" he said.

Burke gritted his teeth. "Get a leg up," he said.

The man raised a leg and seemed to find a footing. Burke slowly and steadily dug in his left boot, hoping to God he didn't break loose, for if the weight of the man became full on his right leg breaking his grip, he knew the man would be doomed, and maybe Burke, too.

Inch by inch the man worked his way up until he could wrap his arms about Burke. His eyes were close to Burke's. "What now, *amigo?*" he said. He managed a faint grin.

Burke swallowed hard. "Ring for the operator to take us up the shaft," he said.

"Not bad." The man looked up that steep slope. "Guess he's gone for a beer," he said.

Burke began to dig in his heels. "I'll use both hands on the line," he said. "Hang on!"

"I wasn't thinking of letting go."

It seemed to Burke Dane that they were not moving at all. It was almost as though the wet and rough surface of the earth beneath them was moving as they fought their way up, like squirrels in a turning cage. His hands were raw from contact with the wet rope and the flesh of his knees was ripped and torn by the cruel ground.

The lightning flamed coldly through the skies and thunder pealed in the gorges when, at last, Burke got a leg over the edge and threw his body over. The rescued man released his grip and rolled over and over on the rough ground until he was far from the ragged rim of the gorge. He pressed his wet face hard against the ground and his body shook spasmodically.

Burke got slowly to his feet and coiled up the lines. He walked to the dun and rested his head against the wet leather of the saddle. He felt weak as water. He raised his head and opened a saddlebag to take out a bottle. He pulled the cork with his teeth and walked slowly back to the man whose life he had saved. He tapped him on the shoulder and handed him the bottle.

"Take a slug," he said.

"*Gracias.*" The bottle was upended. The man coughed. "Jesus! That's good! Mescal?"

Burke nodded. "Baconora." He raised the bottle and downed a good belt of the warming stuff. He sat down on a rock and felt the cold rain seep through his ripped slicker. "I ought to ask you how it happened," he said.

The man sat up and shoved back his hat. "The road was all right when I come up to the top of the pass. It was the way down that threw me, *amigo*. The whole damned road seemed to sink under me. The sorrel dropped right from under me, I tell you. I got hold on a bush but it broke loose. I grabbed a rock but it slid with me. I was just about to let go when I saw you up there like a rescuing angel."

Burke grinned. "With a couple of days' stubble on my dirty face? Some angel!"

The man reached for the bottle and downed a drink. "The name is Jesse Lester." He grinned at Burke. "Didn't quite feel like introducing myself down there."

"Burke Dane." Burke gripped a wet hand, then corked the bottle. "We might need the rest of this later on. Looks like a long, cold night, Jesse."

"Yen." Lester stood up. He looked down the pass. "You think we can make it?"

"I ain't about to go back."

"Yen. You come from the east?"

"Big Bonito country."

Lester looked quickly at Burke. "You live there?"

"No, just passed through. Not much work there."

"No."

Burk untethered the dun and slung the linked reatas over the pommel. "Figure I better lead him past the slide," he said.

Burke led the way, foot by foot, one hand against the

rock face, listening to the irregular clattering of rock far below as the dun's hoofs displaced them. He was a good hundred yards down the road when the lightning plainly lighted it and he could see that it was solid enough, to the sight at least.

Lester came up beside him. "Not much shelter before we reach the East Fork of the Desperado," he said.

"Might as well go on then."

They were far down the pass when the odd thought came to Burke. Lester had said the road was all right when he had come to the *top* of the pass but it was the way *down* that had thrown him. He couldn't have been hanging there long, so he must have come up the pass after dusk. Why would a man ride up that exposed pass on such a night, only to turn back again rather than to descend the other side of it?

Burke glanced back at Lester. He was young, hardly more than in his early twenties, blonde and gray-eyed, and damned handsome to boot. He didn't look much like the rough and tumble type of cowpoke common to the Bio Desperado country.

There was a sagging shack not far from the bridge that spanned the rushing East Fork. While Burke took care of the dun in the lean-to, Lester went inside the shack and started a fire in the stove. Burke came in after him and shut the door. Lester had lighted the stub of a candle in the neck of a wax encrusted bottle. "Ain't much," he said cheerfully, "but we call it home, Burke."

Burke stripped off his slicker and coat. He shivered. "Poke up the fire," he said. "I see a can of Arbuckle's on the shelf. Anything in it?"

Lester grinned. "Just enough coffee for a potful."

The grateful warmth began to flow about them. Lester began to prepare the coffee. It was then that Burke noticed that the kid wore twin holsters hung from a buscadero belt. One of the holsters was empty, but the other revealed an ivory gun butt. Lester saw Burke looking at the empty sheath. "Lost it down the mountainside," he said. "Matched pair too. Cost me plenty to replace it."

"No problem for me," said Burke dryly. "I've only got one."

The kid placed the pot on the table. "Got 'ta get some water," he said.

"That shouldn't be any problem. Hold it under that leak in the corner." Burke grinned.

While the coffee was brewing the kid pulled off his fine boots and placed them near the stove. "You aiming to stay in this country, Burke?"

"Depends."

"What's your line?"

Burke grinned. "Well, I ain't a whiskey drummer, kid."

Jesse flushed. "Well, I meant do you do anything besides work cattle?"

"What else is there to do?"

Lester peeled off his wet socks. "You look like you know how to use that six-shooter."

Burke narrowed his eyes. "What do you mean?"

"A man who can handle guns can get work a helluva lot faster in the Rio Desperado country than just a plain vaquero, *amigo*."

"I've heard that," said Burke. "I ain't a gunfighter, Jesse."

The kid's gray eyes studied Burke. "Now you ain't pulling my leg are you, Burke?"

Burke reached for his tobacco sack. "Why should I?" he said. The kid was probing too damned much. Maybe he knew something about Burke. Something he didn't let on. What the hell *had* he been doing up in that pass anyway?

"I've seen your breed too many times to get fooled," said the kid.

"Maybe this time you are wrong."

The kid got two cups from a dusty shelf and wiped

them out with his silk scarf. "I ain't usually wrong," he said. "You see, Burke, it's my business to know people like you."

"Meaning?"

Lester filled the two cups and placed one before Burke, then accepted one of the two quirlies Burke had fashioned. He lighted it and eyed Burke through the swirling smoke. "You don't think I poke cows for a living, do you?"

Burke grinned. "With *two* guns hanging in the way?"

He glanced at the kid's clothing. And in *that* fancy rig?"

Jesse Lester flushed a little. "I like good clothes," he said softly, "and good guns, fine horseflesh and plenty of money."

"No offense, Kid."

Lester blew out a smoke ring. "That's why I was up in the pass tonight. I suppose you were wondering about that too?"

Burke blew out a cloud of smoke to hide the expression on his face. "No," he said.

"Happens I was looking for something I lost up there."

"Such as?"

"A damned good rawhide reata. Made by Jorge Sanchez of Holbrook. Best man in the business."

Burke slowly took the cigarette from his lips. The rain was slashing down the pass and pattering steadily against the shack. The river was roaring along in flood. A gust of wind flung open the door. The kid darted to it and fought it closed.

Burke's hand dropped to his Colt. It would be so easy. He withdrew his hand before the kid turned. *Not yet...*

"Did you find the reata?" asked Burke quietly.

"No, dammit!"

"How'd you happen to lose it up there, of all places?"

The kid refilled his coffee cup. "One of my *amigos*

borrowed it from me some time ago, then lost the damned thing. It was worth a trip up there to try and find it. Like I said; I like good things and that reata was one of them."

"You have no idea where he left it?" asked Burke softly. His hard eyes studied the kid.

"No."

"You'd know it if you saw it?"

"I think so. Why?"

Burke shrugged. "Isn't an easy thing to identify."

"You'd know Jorge's work if you saw it."

"Yeh," said Burke. He rolled another cigarette and passed the makings to Jesse. "Who do you work for, kid?"

"Ben Hinch." Jesse glanced quickly at Burke.

Burke lighted his cigarette. There was no expression on his face.

"You never heard of him?" asked Jesse.

"Can't say that I have, Kid."

"He's about the *biggest* man in this country, *amigo*."

"So?" Burke had always prided himself on his poker face and this time he surely needed it. Print Campbell had told him aplenty about Ben Hinch, and none of it to Hinch's credit.

"I can put in a good word for you, Burke," said Jesse.

Burke drained his coffee cup. "I said I wasn't a gunfighter, Kid."

"What makes you think Ben Hinch needs gunfighters? You just said you never heard of him."

Burke looked at the kid. "You said you didn't poke cows for a living. With two guns hanging on you, I figured you were a gunfighter. So, I figured Ben Hinch, whoever he is, has need of gunfighters. It's as simple as that." Burke smiled easily.

"Are you looking for work?" asked the kid flatly.

"I ain't sure. What difference does it make?"

Jesse got up and poked the fire. He dumped in more

wood. "Ben Hinch usually likes to know what strangers are doing in this country," he said over his shoulder.

"I mind my own business."

The kid turned and his gray eyes were as hard as steel. "You might be able to fool some people, Burke. You aren't a saddle tramp. You aren't a common cowpoke. What are you? Gambler? Gunfighter? *Lawman?*"

Burke leaned forward. "I mind my own business, Kid," he said quietly, and his eyes were as hard as Lester's. "Maybe you ought to try it."

For a long moment the kid stood there, and then he smiled. "Forget it, *amigo*. I was only trying to pay you back for saving my life up there. Thought I'd help you along the way. You mind your own business and I'll mind mine. Keno?"

"Keno." Burke stood up. "I got a blanket roll on the dun. I'll bring it in. We might as well hole up here until dawn."

Burke closed the door behind him and hurried to the dun. He took the linked lines, hastily coiled his grass rope and fastened it to the saddle, then coiled the rawhide reata and placed it in the bottom of his saddlebag, beneath his extra gear. He took the blanket roll back into the shack. He gave Jesse one of the blankets. The kid bedded down on the floor, letting Burke take the bunk. Burke blew out the candle and lay with his arms behind his head, staring up at the ceiling.

He wasn't so sure of himself now. Ben Hinch ran the Rio Desperado country and Jesse Lester was one of his boys. The rawhide reata was the only clue Burke had to help him find the man, or men who had lynched Charley, and he was quite sure in his mind that Jesse Lester owned that fine reata. Jesse was curious, perhaps downright suspicious of Burke, despite the fact that Burke had saved his life. Evidently the Rio Desperado country was the kind of place where a man had to take sides, because there was no neutral ground.

The wind moaned about the shack. A spit of icy rain came through a crack in the wall and touched Burke's face. The kid turned restlessly on the floor. The river roared steadily and the trees thrashed. It promised to be a wild night.

Burke closed eyes. He was dead beat; but too full of confused thought to sleep. It was going to be a long night for him.

The kid moved. "Burke?" he said.

"Yes?"

"So long as you're a friend of Jesse Lester," he said, "you don't have to worry too much about Ben Hinch."

"Thanks, Kid."

"Forget it, *amigo*." Jesse rolled over and pulled the blanket over his head.

Burke wet his lips. As long as he was a friend of Jesse Lester's he wouldn't have to worry too much about Ben Hinch. But supposing Jesse had lied about that reata business? Supposing he had gone up there to retrieve his prized reata from the neck of a man he helped lynch?

The wind howled in diabolical glee down Windy Pass, almost as though anticipating the events that would take place when Burke Dane tried to find the murderers of his brother in the valley of the Rio Desperado.

CHAPTER THREE

"That's the West Fork of the Desperado," said Jesse Lester over Burke's shoulder. "Piñon is just beyond those trees there. You can see the smoke. Maybe Piñon ain't much, but we call it home."

Burke nodded sourly. A cup of last night's rank coffee, laced with bacanora, was hardly enough breakfast to hold a man on a twenty mile ride in the cold morning light. Besides, he had not slept well, and the thought of riding double a good part of that twenty miles with a man who might have put the noose about Charley's neck was hardly conducive to pleasant thought.

Piñon was pleasant enough in the watery sunlight. It spread along both sides of the road from Windy Pass, which became a little more dignified, as well as wider, to form the main street of Pirion. The town was larger than Burke had anticipated it would be, with new false-fronted buildings between older log structures. Somewhere beyond the town was the sawmill, with the resinous odor of freshly cut pine drifting on the morning breeze mingling with the raveled smoke.

"We'd better get some breakfast before we go to see Ben Hinch," said Jesse. He slid from behind Burke and stretched, then walked beside the tired dun to a hitching rail in front of a combination saloon and restaurant. "The Mecca," said Jesse. He grinned. "Some Mecca. But the food is good."

"I ain't fussy," said Burke. He dismounted. The dun hung his head and Burke patted it. "Thanks, *amigo*." He turned to join Jesse.

The kid was eyeing a rangy gray that was tethered farther down the rail. His eyes were half closed. He drew his Colt and twirled the cylinder to check the loads. He sheathed the fine handgun.

"What's wrong, Kid?" asked Burke quietly. "Trouble?"

"Nothing I can't handle."

"We can go somewhere else."

The kid turned slowly to face Burke. "I said it was nothing that I couldn't handle," he said sharply.

"I ain't hungry enough to go looking for trouble," said Burke. He knew the signs.

"It ain't your fight, *if* it comes to a fight."

Burke shrugged. He took out the makings and rolled a cigarette. "I thought this was Ben Hinch's town," he said casually.

"It is."

"You're a Hinch man, Jesse."

Jesse jerked his head toward the gray. "The man that owns that gray, is, or rather *was,* a Hinch man."

"So?"

Jesse shrugged. "I cost him his job. He won't forget it. He's been warned to stay away from Piñon. Guess he doesn't warn easy."

Burke lighted the cigarette. "Wouldn't it be just as easy to eat somewhere else?"

"You skirt?"

Burke walked up to the boardwalk and across it to the double doors of the saloon. He opened one of them and walked in. The kid grinned, then followed him.

Burke sat down at a table near the window. The bartender glanced at him. "Jenny," he called out. Then he turned to see Jesse framed in the doorway and his fat face paled a little. He glanced quickly at a man who stood at the far end of the bar facing the doorway. The man was tall and dark. His right hand held a whiskey glass and his eyes were fixed on Jesse.

"Hello, Moss," said Jesse easily.

Moss put down the whiskey glass. He stared at Jesse.

The waitress bustled out of the kitchen towards Burke's table, then she saw Jesse. She smiled quickly, and the smile faded as she glanced back over a plump shoulder toward Moss.

"I spoke to you, Moss," said Jesse.

"I heard you," said the tall man.

Burke quietly moved his chair back. He looked up at the waitress and jerked his head toward the kitchen. She turned slowly and walked toward the kitchen with her plump bottom waggling a little, wanting to run, but too afraid to start.

"I was looking for you last night," said Moss to Jesse.

"I wasn't here, Moss."

"Yen. I thought for a while you just might have taken off over Windy Pass to get away from me, Lester."

"You know better than that, Moss."

"Yen." The tall man smiled a little, but there was no mirth in his dark eyes. "I had a feeling you'd be back. Windy Pass ain't no place for a man like you if he has any conscience at all."

"Oh my God," said the bartender. His hands shook a little. "Look, fellas, I'll buy."

Jesse slowly shook his head. "Maybe *Mister* Moss needs a drink. I don't. *Mister* Moss is doing a lot of talking this morning. Maybe a drink will loosen his tongue a little more."

Burke wanted to get out there, but he didn't want to precipitate anything by standing up. It was likely that the man named Moss didn't know that Burke was with Jesse Lester, but if he did, he'd probably think Burke was going to side Jesse if six-shooter talk started. Burke eased his hand to his Colt and traced his dry lips with the tip of his tongue. He wished to God he had taken his hunch and stayed out of the place, but it was too late now. He could almost sniff the foul, cold smell of death in the air.

The kid was walking toward the man named Moss, supreme in his youth and his strong confidence in his skill and courage. Burke moved a little. "Sit still, you!" said Moss harshly to Burke.

"Leave him out of this," said Jesse.

Moss smiled crookedly. "You Hinch boys usually got *someone* to side you. Who's this one, Lester? Maybe he's going to replace *me,* eh?"

"That wouldn't be hard," said the kid easily. "I swear to God, Jenny back there in the kitchen could replace *you,* Moss."

Burke stood up. "This isn't my fight, Moss," he said.

Again the crooked smile. "You mean you're going to let this brave little man fight *alone?*"

Jesse leaned on the bar and he was between Burke and Moss. "Get me a glass, Dan," he said to the bartender.

Dan slid a glass along the bar. Jesse smiled at Moss. "With your permission, Mister Moss," he said. He poured himself a drink. "You're not drinking with me?"

Moss reached for the bottle. In a second, swift action began, almost too quickly for the human eye to follow. Jesse threw the whiskey from his glass at Moss' face, but the tall man was fast too. He bent his head to one side and hurled the bottle with all his strength at the cocky young face in front of him. Jesse tried to bend his head to one side but his foot slipped on the sanded floor. The thick base of the bottle caught him on the left temple and he fell sideways against a table, clawing for his Colt.

Moss grinned coldly as he jumped from behind the end of the bar and slapped leather. He crouched and aimed from the waist at the kid's bleeding head. A shot cracked flatly. Moss slowly fell forward. His gun roared from reflex action of fingers on trigger and the slug buried itself in the floor inches from Jesse's head. Moss struck the floor and lay still. Blood flowed from his body and formed a widening pool; sucked up greedily by the sand. Powder smoke swirled in the draft and then flowed in rifted layers toward the windows.

The bartender looked with wide eyes at Burke Dane. "For the love of God," he said in a low, tense voice. "That was impossible!" He looked at the smoking Colt in Burke's hand, then up at the hard blue eyes, and he did not like what he saw. He fumbled beneath the bar and got a glass. He filled it with rye and downed it swiftly. Beads of sweat formed on his fat face.

"Pour me one, too," said Burke. He sheathed his Colt. It was then that he saw the broad-shouldered man standing framed in the doorway. Burke hesitated.

"It's all right," said Dan. "It's Matt Foxx, Ben Hinch's foreman."

Foxx nodded at Burke. "I saw what happened," he said. "I knew Moss was in here waiting for the Kid. When I saw you and the Kid come in here I came right over. Almost too late at that." Foxx eyed Burke. "If it hadn't been for you, Moss would have killed the Kid." Foxx grinned a little. "Of course you would' a killed him right after, eh?"

Burke walked to the bar and looked down at the man he had just killed. "No," he said quietly. "It would have been to late then. I would have let the law take care of Mister Moss."

"Yen," said Dan dryly. "The *law*."

Foxx shot a hard look at the bartender. "Send a man over to the undertaker, Dan. Get that stiff out of here."

Burke downed his drink, then refilled the glass. He knelt beside Jesse. The kid opened his eyes. "I saw Moss aiming for me, Burke," he said weakly. "Couldn't do a damned thing about it. Passed out. Thanks again, Burke."

Foxx was standing beside them. "What do you mean *again,* Jesse?" he asked curiously.

Jesse gripped Burke by the shoulder and pulled himself up into a sitting position. "Mister Dane has a habit of saving my life, Matt. Second time in twenty-four hours."

Burke stood up. "You couldn't help the first time, Jesse," he said quietly. "You walked into this one. Damned fool stunt if I ever saw one."

Jesse's eyes narrowed. "There was no way out of it, Burke," he said.

"You could have stayed out of here."

The kid got shakily to his feet and touched the swelling on his forehead. "You don't know me very well."

"Amen," said Matt.

"You'd better not move the body until the sheriff gets here," said Burke. A pounding, stabbing headache suddenly began to lance through his skull. It had been a long hard trail, and an uncomfortable night, climaxed with a killing; a killing by Burke Dane, who had been soul weary of killing, for this was not the first man he had killed, nor, he thought, would it be the last if he kept following the devious and bloody trail he had embarked upon.

"It's all right," said Matt. "It was self-defense, wasn't it?"

"Not for me," said Burke. He looked at the stocky foreman. "It wasn't my fight."

"Justifiable homicide then," said Foxx.

"You talk like a lawyer," said Burke. "I still think you ought to get the sheriff."

The kid grinned. "Matt is the deputy-sheriff in these parts," he said.

"I thought he was foreman for Ben Hinch," said Burke.

"He does that too," said Dan the bartender.

Burke wet his lips and reached for the rye bottle. "Very convenient," he said.

"What do you mean by that?" asked Matt Foxx after a pause.

Burke looked up into the man's hard green eyes. A tension had suddenly come into the drafty barroom.

"Well, mister?" demanded Foxx.

Burke looked away. "Nothing, mister. Nothing at all." But he knew well enough he hadn't put Matt Foxx off the track. It had been a damn fool thing for Burke to say, but then he had a reputation for doing just such things. He'd have to watch that tendency in the Valley of the Rio Desperado.

"Let's eat," said the kid suddenly.

Burke turned slowly. "With *that* on the floor?" he asked.

Jesse grinned. "You act like you never seen a dead man before."

"I've seen a few here and there," said Burke.

"Jenny!" called out Jesse. "Ham and eggs for two! Get us started with a pot of jamoke!"

Matt Foxx poured himself a drink. "Don't forget Moss had a couple of good *companeros,* Kid," he said.

"No."

"They haven't done anything that would make Ben Hinch fire them like he fired Moss," said the foreman.

"Keno," said Jesse easily.

The green eyes probed at Jesse, "Just keep it in mind, Kid."

"I will."

The foreman left and Jesse walked to a table and sat down.

Burke rolled a smoke and sat down across from the Kid. He handed him the makings and watched the Kid deftly roll a quirly. "What did he mean, Jesse?" asked Burke.

"Curly Carter and Larry Newman. They were *amigos*

with Joe Moss there. Fact is, Larry was his cousin." - "Great, oh great," said Burke.

"They don't like me either," said the Kid.

"I wonder why?" asked Burke softly. "Why did Joe Moss lose his job with Hinch?"

"He got fresh with my sister, Burke."

"So he loses a job and then he gets killed."

The Kid quickly pulled the draw string of the tobacco bag with his even white teeth but his gray eyes were fixed on Burke. "I'll kill any man who gets fresh with Belle," he said quietly. He lighted his cigarette. "Anyone. *Comprende?*"

Burke shrugged and then nodded. "I wasn't figuring on getting fresh with any woman," he said.

Jenny bustled in and placed the coffee pot on the table. She filled two cups. Her wide hip brushed against Jesse. His hand moved swiftly. She jerked a little and her face reddened. "Now, Mister Lester," she said chidingly, but it didn't seem as though her heart was in it. Then she jerked again. "*Mister* Lester! You ain't no gentleman!"

The Kid grinned. "Can't help it Jenny. When I see a target I just got to try a shot at it."

"Mister Lester!" She marched off, her hips waggling defiantly.

"Ain't you the one," said Burke dryly. "A few minutes ago a man died because he got fresh with *your* sister."

Jesse sipped at his coffee. "Jenny likes it," he said.

"Your sister must be pretty lonely."

"Why do you say that?"

"Hellsfire, a man would be loco to chase after her with you hanging around in the background breathing fire and smoke."

"Wait'll you see Belle," said the Kid. "Just wait."

The stiffening body was removed before the two of them were served, for which Burke was duly grateful. It didn't seem to matter one way or another to the Kid.

"Let's go home and clean up," said the Kid. He paid

for the meal and winked at Jenny. She giggled, but kept her tempting hips away from his quick hands.

Burke untethered the dun and led him along the street. Here and there men watched them and Burke sensed a definite feeling of hostility emanating from some of them. It didn't seem to bother Jesse Lester though. He walked easily, with a cigarette dangling from the corner of his mouth, trading look for look with every man, and it was the others who looked away first. Then Burke remembered some of the information told to him by blind Print Campbell. Benn Hinch ran that country like a feudal lord, but there were men who hated his guts because of it. Trouble was, Ben had the money, the power, and the fighting guns to back him up.

Jesse turned down a side street and stopped in front of a pretty little frame cottage, fenced in with pickets and with window boxes in the windows. "Home," he said. He glanced at Burke. "This is your home as long as you stick around, Burke."

"I wasn't figuring on leaving right away," said Burke, "but I don't aim to wear out my welcome."

Burke tethered the dun to the fence and followed the Kid up the walk to the porch. He opened the door. "Belle!" he called out. "I'm home! Got company!"

Burke walked into the neat little living room and looked about. If Belle Lester kept a place like this she'd make a good wife for some staid businessman, or maybe a sky pilot. Then he saw her, framed in the doorway to the kitchen, and he knew right then and there that the Kid had not been joshing when he had said, "Wait'll you see Belle. Just wait."

There wasn't any doubt that she was Jesse Lester's sister. Her coloring was the same, and she had the same fine blonde hair and clear "gray eyes. She looked enough like Jesse to be his twin, except she must be some years older, but still a young woman. She wore a split riding skirt, white shirt open at the throat, a short leather jacket, and small figured boots. A hat hung at her back, from a leather strap about her shapely neck. She was a beauty. Burke wasn't quite sure he had ever seen one quite like her. He had seen lovelier women of course, but the combination of her coloring, her features and configuration was enough to make any man stop and look at her.

"You can close your mouth now, Burke," said Jesse with a sly grin. "This is my sister Belle. Belle, this is Mister Burke Dane."

Burke was acutely conscious of his unshaven face and general trail dirtiness as he took off his Stetson and bowed his head. "Mighty pleased, Miss Lester," he said.

There was a slight iciness in her expression as she nodded her lovely head. "Mister Dane," she said in a voice that seemed to have the ringing quality of a silver bell. She looked at Jesse. "I was just about to leave for Windy Pass, Jesse. Why didn't you come back last night?"

"Seems as though I ran out of road, sis."

"What do you mean?"

Jesse quickly explained what had happened. There was a softer look about Belle now. She thanked Burke warmly. "Jesse insisted on going up there yesterday after that silly rope of his. I can't understand why he couldn't get another one."

Evidence, thought Burke. Evidence that he had hung one man and might yet put a rope about Jesse Lester's own neck.

She looked at her brother. "Joe Moss' came back to Piñon last night," she said quietly. "I wanted to warn you about him, Jesse."

"You're a little late," he said.

She eyed him closely. "What do you mean, Jesse?"

"We already ran into him."

Her lovely eyes nickered toward the swelling on his forehead. "He was saying that he'd kill you on sight, Jesse."

"He meant to," said the Kid.

She glanced at Burke and then back at her brother. "Where is he now, Jesse?" she demanded.

Jesse dropped into a chair and thrust his slim legs out in front of him. "Mister Farrier, our esteemed mortician, has "him in charge, sis. "

She paled a little. "You *killed* him, Jesse?"

"Not *me*. My partner Burke did the job. Saved my life twice in twenty-four hours."

Burke flushed. "He would have killed your brother in cold blood, ma'am," he said. The look on her face repelled him, but he was game. "Don't you see? I had to kill him."

"I see all right," she said quietly. "I see killing all the time in this country. Where will it end? Those who live by the sword . . ."

"Your brother is safe," said Burke dryly. "It was him or Joe Moss."

She glanced down at the tied-down six-gun and at the brown capable hand of Burke Dane, then looked up into his bitter blue eyes. "Who are you?" she asked suddenly. "Why have you come here? What have you to do with my brother?"

Burke had the eerie feeling that she was seeing right through him, as though she knew something; *something that Jesse Lester did not know.* He picked up his hat. "I'll be seeing you, Jesse," he said. "Happy to have met you, ma'am."

"You're staying here with us until I get you a job with Ben Hinch," said Jesse quickly.

"No," said Burke. "I'll find my own place here in Piñon."

"You might find a place to stay, you won't get nothing but a two-bit job unless you work for Ben Hinch."

"I'll chance it," said Burke.

"You're driving him away, Belle!" said Jesse angrily.

She came closer to Burke. "Thanks for saving my brother's life," she said. "Please stay."

He walked to the door and opened it. "I'm sorry," he said. "See you later, Jesse." He closed the door behind him and walked to the gate. He stepped over it and mounted the dun after untethering it. He kneed the big horse out into the middle of the street and rode back toward the main street of Piñon.

Belle Lester came out onto the porch and looked after Burke. "Who is that man, Jesse?" she said.

"I told you. Burke Dane."

"Where did he come from?"

"*Quién sabe?* From New Mexico Territory is all I know." He eyed her. "Why do you ask?"

She tapped her quirt against the side of her leg. "I don't really know. He isn't any run of the mill saddle tramp. There is something secret about that man."

"Oh, cut it out, sis! Burke is all right. I'll get him a job with Ben Hinch. After what Burke did this morning, Ben won't hesitate to hire Burke. He's fast, Belle! I didn't see him, but Joe Moss had his six-gun out and cocked when Burke fired. Dropped him like nothing."

She walked toward the stable at the rear of the lot. "Faster than *you*, Jesse?" she asked over her shoulder.

He stared at her. "What do you mean?"

She turned. "No one in this valley seems to be quite as fast as you, Jesse. Ben Hinch says that. Everyone said that except Joe Moss. Joe Moss was fast, wasn't he, Jesse?"

"Yes."

"As fast as you?"

"Pretty close, Belle," admitted the Kid.

"And this man, this Burke Dane, from nowhere, drew and killed him when Joe had his gun out and cocked?"

Jesse half closed his eyes. "Yen," he said softly. "Yen. He said he wasn't a gunfighter."

She had saddled her mare and she mounted it and

rode it up beside the porch. "I'll see Ben this morning," she said. "I'm going riding with Clete."

He flushed. "Clete Hinch? Him? He ain't no good, Belle. Ain't there any other men around Piñon you can ride with instead of him?"

She drew on a pair of gloves. "Certainly," she said, "but let's face it, Jesse. We haven't got a clime. The big money in the Rio Desperado country is in the Hinch family, and Ben Hinch won't live forever. Clete is his only man child and his pride and joy as well. I'm like you, Jesse. I like nice things. I'm not a fast gun, nor a man killer like you, but I've got some stock-in-trade." She looked down at her lovely body. "Something Clete Hinch is mighty interested in."

He smashed a fist against the side of the house. "Don't talk like that!" he rasped out.

She smiled, "I'm free, white and over twenty-one. You do your type of man killing and I'll do mine, Jesse." She touched the mare with her heels and set it at the fence, rising gracefully over it. She galloped the mare down the center of the street, a picture of loveliness and grace, enough to turn any man's head. She turned. "It'll take a wedding ring to close the deal, dear brother," she called back, "so don't worry about your sister's virtue!"

There was a sick look on Jesse Lester's face as he watched her turn onto the main street and disappear from sight. He walked into the house and took a full bottle from a cabinet. The bottle was half empty before he fell asleep in the big platform rocker.

Another man had watched Belle Lester ride past. Burke Dane had seen her through the dusty window of a corner saloon. He had the uneasy feeling that Belle Lester had seen through him as he had seen through the streaked window glass. He looked down at his drink and seemed to see her lovely oval face framed in the amber fluid. He downed the drink and placed a coin beside the empty glass. The whiskey seemed to sicken him. "Where can I get a room?" he asked the barkeep.

"Upstairs. Piñon House. Ain't much, but it's better than sleeping in a barn. Not much better though, Mister." The man grinned. "Then there's the Hinch Hotel."

"Owned by Ben Hinch?"

"Yep." The man grinned again. "Happens he owns the Piñon House too."

"And this saloon?"

"I rent the place, Mister. He owns the building."

Burke nodded. "Mister Hinch seems to be the big frog in the puddle around here."

The flat eyes of the bartender studied him. "After what you done this morning, maybe Ben Hinch will own you too, Mister."

Burke shrugged. He walked to the door.

"If he makes you an offer, take it, Mister," called out the bartender.

"And if I *don't?*"

The man picked up the glass, rinsed it and wiped it. He set it neatly atop a group of other glasses. "Then get on your hoss, aim it east, west, north or south and keep again'."

The man's words stuck in Burke's mind as he left the bar and led the tired dun to the livery stable. He signed in at the Piñon House, getting a corner room with a view up and down the main street as well as the street upon which Jesse and Belle Lester lived.

There was one other thing he did before he bathed and shaved; he checked the back entrance to the hotel. A man never knew when he might have sudden and important need of such knowledge.

CHAPTER FOUR

It was dusk when Burke awoke to hear the faint pattering of rain upon the windows. He sat up and shivered in the damp cold. He dressed in fresh clothing and walked to the front window to look down upon the main street. Yellow lamplight shone through the misty rain slanting down upon the town. Lightning flickered against the dark and lowering skies. Burke rolled a cigarette and was just about to light it when he saw the man standing in a doorway across the street—the sixth sense born in a man who lives a hard and dangerous life immediately alerted Burke. He took the cigarette from his lips. He walked to the door and placed an ear against it. There was no sound from the hallway.

He swung his gun belt about his lean waist, buckled it, then checked his Colt. He put on his coat and slicker, placing a double-barreled derringer in his left coat pocket for extra insurance. Burke left the hotel by the back entrance, coming quietly down the long stairway to the muddy alleyway. He squelched through the mud to the eastern end of the alley, cut up the intersection, crossed the main street swiftly and then walked west along the alleyway behind the buildings on the side of the street opposite his hotel until he reached the next intersection.

He walked to the corner and looked at the man in the doorway. The man was too busy watching Burke's hotel window to see the tall, hard-faced man watching him. Burke stepped into a nearby doorway as another man left the saloon across the street and came across to the watcher.

Burke pulled down his hat brim and turned up his slicker collar. The wind was blowing toward him from the two men.

"You see him yet, Harv?" asked the man from the saloon.

"Hell no! He's either dead asleep or dead drunk, Curly."

Curly spat into the gutter. "Jesus, I ain't got a mind to stay here all night waitin' for him to leave that room."

"What's your beef? You been sitting in Garvey's saloon whilst I been standing out here in the wet."

"Yen, well maybe you'd like to try the saloon awhile?"

Harv shook his head. "From what I heard about this *hombre,* I don't want no likker in me if he comes agunnin', Curly."

"Maybe he was just lucky," suggested Curley.

Harv shook his head again. "That's not what Dan Phipps said. Godfrey! Joe Moss had the Kid down on the sawdust, as woozy as a drunk, and Joe had his cutter in his hand, cocked too, when this *hombre* draws and shoots! Joe would' a killed the Kid if it hadn't been for this Dane *hombre.*"

Curly rolled a cigarette while he looked up at the window of Dane's room. "Yen. But it was what he said to Matt Foxx that puzzles me. That was after Matt ast' him if he would' a killed Joe after Joe had killed the Kid. Dane says no, that it would' a been too late then, that he would' a let the law take care of Joe. That proves he ain't no real sidekick of the Kid."

"Who *is?*" asked Harv dryly. "That conceited, swellheaded yearlin' don't want no one siding him. He's too fast! He's too good! He's tough as a boot! Yaaah!"

Curly looked nervously up and down the street. "Well, *I* ain't ascairt of him."

Harv grunted. "Not as long as Larry Newman is between you and the Kid, you ain't!"

Curly eyed the window again. He lighted his cigarette. "Let's give him another twenty minutes, then take a look up there. What the hell does Matt Foxx think we'll find up there? From what I heard, this Dane looks almost like a saddle tramp."

"*Quién sabe?* We got our orders. You want to quit? Then you quit, and you tell Matt. I ain't going to do it!"

Burke faded around the corner, returning the way he had come. He entered the livery stable by the back door. The place was deserted except for half a dozen horses. He patted the dun, then removed Jesse Lester's rope from the saddlebag. He placed the rope beneath his slicker and left the stable the same way he had entered it, to return to his room. He stripped off coat and slicker, then lighted the Argand lamp. Burke rolled a cigarette and puttered about the room, taking as much time as a man would normally take to get dressed. He knew well enough those two men were still watching the window. The rain slashed against the side of the frame building as he put out the lamp and walked into the hall. He knew full well they would examine his belongings once he left the room, but there was nothing there to cast suspicion on him. Nothing more than his dirty trail clothing, personals and other odds and ends any man would carry with him while traveling. The only incriminating thing on him, in the eyes of *those* men, in any case, would be the fine rope he had found about his brother's neck in Windy Pass. It was quite likely they'd also check his horse gear. The cold thought struck him that they might already have done so. He'd risk it; he'd *have* to risk it.

Thinking of the rope gave him an idea. He walked to

the rear entrance and out onto the back porch. A clothes line was strung from post to post. He cut the wet and stiff knots and tied the line across the top of the flight of stairs, about six inches high. "Diabolical," he said with a crooked grin.

Burke re-entered the deserted hotel. The place was as quiet as a cliff-dwelling ruin, and there was no sign of the clerk in his cubbyhole at the bottom of the front stairs. Burke stepped out into the street and lighted another cigarette, spotting Harv and Curly in their doorway across the drizzling street. Burke walked leisurely down the street, like a man looking for a good eating place. He entered a restaurant at the corner, bought a couple of sacks of makings, then left by the side entrance. He walked back to the corner just in time to see Harv and Curly enter the Piñon House.

Burke walked slowly toward the hotel, giving the boys time to get to work. He walked into the entrance and saw the clerk. There was a startled look on the man's face, and Burke knew then and there the man was a willing party to the surreptitious search going on upstairs. "You're back quickly," he said nervously.

"Forgot my wallet," said Burke. "Can't get grub without dinero."

"No need for you to go upstairs," said the clerk hastily. "I can grubstake you, Mister Dane."

"That's right nice of you."

"It's all right.

Burke glanced up the stairs. "On second thought I might want to try the games tonight. I'll need a little gambling money. He started up the stairs.

"Wait!" called out the man. He came around the desk. "How much will you need?"

"A hundred anyway."

"I haven't got that much here but I can get it in the saloon."

Burke turned slowly. "By that time I could have my wallet," he said with a smile.

The man could not meet his gaze. "All right, Mister Dane," he said in a loud, carrying voice. "You have your room key?"

"Yes," said Burke. He trod heavily on the stairs.

He heard the room door swing open and the quick thudding of booted feet on the thinly carpeted flooring of the hall. Just as his head reached the floor level he saw the two shadowy figures at the end of the hall. They tore open the door. There was a loud yell from the first man, followed by an explosive curse from the second man. Something thudded and crashed down the outside stairway and a man screamed harshly.

Burke casually walked into his room and looked about by the light of a match. The dresser drawers gaped open. The mattress was off center. The room stank of candle grease. Burke closed the door behind him and walked down the stairs. "Sounds like a fight back in the alleyway," he said pleasantly to the white-faced clerk who was coming up the stairs, two at a time. "None of my business. Take my advice and stay out of it."

He grinned as he closed the outer door behind him.

Burke took plenty of time to eat and enjoy his dinner. He bought a couple of good cigars, thrust one between his even white teeth and lighted it, then strolled leisurely back toward Garvey's saloon. The rain had stopped and a cold wind swept along the muddy street. He entered the saloon. A drunk sat at a rear table with his head resting on his folded arms. Another man sat in a chair titled back against the rear wall reading a newspaper. There were two more customers in the place and there was no doubt who they were. Harv and Curly stood at the end of the bar. Curly had a wet cloth at the back of his neck and had his head held back. Blood stained his face and scarf. There was a large swelling on his forehead and his lip was split. Harv was nursing his left arm and. his face was swollen on the left side.

"Beer," said Burke easily to the bartender. It was the same man who had served him that morning.

"Comin' up. You get your room all right?"

Burke nodded. He jerked a thumb upward. "Right overhead, on the corner. A little drafty but it has a nice view." He managed to keep a straight face as two pairs of eyes shot suspicious glances at him.

"Like I said," remarked the bartender. "It ain't much, but it's better than sleeping in a barn. You find a job yet?"

"How'd you know I was looking for one?"

The bartender shrugged. "Figured you was. You remember what I told you about any offers."

"You mean Mister Hinch is looking for help?"

Again the two pairs of eyes flicked at him.

"He usually is." Garvey glanced at Harv and Curly. "That right, boys?"

Curly grunted. Harv shrugged. "You'd have to ask Mister Hinch."

Garvey grinned. "Oh, he'll give this fella a job all right." He looked at Curly. "How's your nose?"

"How's yours?" growled Curly.

"The boys fell over some stuff in the alley," said Garvey in a low voice. "At least that's what *they* say." He wiped the bar. "Jesse Lester was in here awhile back, looking for you, Mister Dane. I told him I thought you had a room upstairs. He said he'd meet you down at the bar and grille in the Hindi Hotel."

"Sounds very elegant," said Burke dryly. He downed his beer and walked toward the door just in time to see a tall, lean man walk in, dart a look toward the two sorry looking characters at the far end of the bar, then fix Burke with a hard set look. Burke instantly knew this type. It was the same breed as Joe Moss and in fact the man resembled Joe Moss a little.

"Have a drink, Larry," said Harv.

A cold feeling came over Burke. *Larry*. It must be Larry Newman, Joe Moss' cousin. The hard flat eyes held Burke's almost as though trying to force him to look away. Then Newman stepped aside. "Matt Foxx wants to see you boys," he said to the pair at the end of the bar.

Burke had his hand on the door knob when Newman spoke again. "Wait, you," he said in a low voice.

Burke turned slowly. "Yes?"

"You're Dane, aren't you?"

"Yes."

Newman looked up and down Burke, "A fast gun, eh?"

"Fast enough," said Burke easily. "I'm not anxious to try and prove it."

"Like you did this morning, eh?"

Burke shook his head wearily. "Moss was going to kill the Kid."

"And you killed Moss. *Just like that,* eh?"

"I don't want no trouble in here," said Garvey.

"Shut up!" snapped Newman. He studied Burke. "There won't be no trouble. *Now,* anyway. I don't know who or what you are, Mister Dane, but Joe Moss was my cousin.

The Kid had a gun whipping coming to him. He'll get it yet. He was lucky this morning."

"You seem to forget that it was more than a whipping he was going to get, Newman," said Burke quietly. "Moss was going to kill him, not pistol-whip him."

"Was it any business of yours?"

"I don't like murder."

"Then you come to the wrong place, by Godfrey," said Harv.

"Who are you trying to fool, Dane?" asked Newman. "I know your type. You aren't any saddle tramp looking for twenty-five a month and found. Who are you?"

Burke smiled gently. "How long have you been appointed official nose around here, Newman?"

"Oh my God," said Garvey.

Larry Newman smiled thinly. "I'll remember that too, Dane. Right now I've got things to do. But I won't forget you, Dane. Ever ..."

Burke walked outside and relighted his cigar. Like a damned fool he had jumped into this mess with both feet, and with closed eyes. It would have been easier to drift into town and get any kind of job until he was ready to make his move, but rescuing Jesse Lester in Windy Pass, then saving him from being killed by Joe Moss had put him right in the local limelight, and there wasn't a thing he could do about it. There was no use in back-trailing unless he wanted to forget his mission to get Charley's money and find his killers. That he could not do.

There was one thing he knew for certain. A man was either with Benn Hinch and his *corrida* or he was against them. There was no neutral ground in the Rio Desperado country. Print Campbell had assured him of that in no uncertain terms. Burke wasn't so sure he wanted to ally himself with such men as Jesse Lester, Harv and Curly, and the man he had just faced in Garvey's saloon; the man named Larry Newman. Newman was stiff-legged with the hackles up and it wouldn't take much to trip the hair trigger of his intent to pay off the blood score for the death of his cousin, Joe Moss.

The night life of Piñon was flickering up as Burke walked slowly toward the imposing pile of the Hinch Hotel. One could hardly miss it. The streets were empty of local ranchers and townspeople. The shops were closed but the saloons and gambling halls were flooded with light, thick with tobacco smoke and bursting with the mingled cacophony of player pianos, clinking glass-ware, rattling poker chips, tumbling chuck-a-luck cages and whirring roulette wheels. Patient, hipshot horses stood in rows at the hitching racks; their wet hides glis-tening in the lamplight.

Burke peeled off his worn slicker in a doorway,

wrapped it about Lester's rawhide rope, and stuffed slicker and rope into a hollow area in the ramada shelter above his head in front of a leather goods shop. He walked along the boardwalk to the hotel and saw the side entrance that opened into the bar and grille. He glanced into the big lobby of the hotel. It was well carpeted, filled with overstuffed furniture, lighted by crystal chandeliers and fine table lamps on marble-topped tables. Very elegant.

Burke flipped his cigar butt into the gutter, straightened his string tie and walked into the bar and grille. Ben Hinch had done himself proud in this establishment as well as the rest of the Hinch Hotel. For a moment Burke almost thought he was in one of the plushier joints of Albuquerque, El Paso, or Fort Worth. The two bartenders were replete in white mess jackets, waxed mustaches and varnished hair. The bar itself was a mahogany masterpiece, backed by a full length mirror set with an array of glittering glassware and polished silver utensils. Well, pardon me all to hell, thought Dane as he saw the thick carpeting on the floor and the massive garboons softly reflecting the glow of the many lamps. The light also caressed the naked shoulders of half a dozen women in various booths, and Burke wasn't sure whether they were guests or high class filles working for the house.

Burke hung his hat on a brass hook and walked toward the rear of the establishment followed by the half bold, half coy looks of the women, and the curious, half challenging looks of some of the men. He heard the soft laughter of Jesse Lester and saw him sitting in a booth with a woman who was dressed to the nines in red, and with her dark glossy hair piled up, highlights showing as she moved her head. The Kid grinned as he saw Burke. "You're getting 'way behind, *companero,*" he said. His eyes flashed. He had been playing the bottle that evening. He placed a hand on the naked shoulder of the girl for she was hardly more than that, and looked up at Burke. "Sally, this is Burke Dane, my good friend. Burke, this is Sally Depree, belle of Hindi's Hotel."

Young as the girl was, and lovely in the soft glow of the lamps, there was a hardness in her wide green eyes. "Jesse has been telling me about you," she said, a little breathlessly. She held out a slim hand and as Burke took it he felt the slight pressure that conveyed everything, or *almost* everything he had to know about her. As she moved to look at Jesse the locket she wore about her lovely neck swung and rested in the deep cleft of her high young breasts and Burke Dane's eyes became riveted on it.

"Sit down, Burke," said Jesse. "We're drinking sangarees. What about you?"

Burke nodded. "I'll have the same." He sat down opposite the girl. She flicked those lovely green eyes at him. Burke had been around. He had seen the elephant in many a dive and joint from Fort Worth to Yuma, but he had never seen a lovelier specimen of her shameless breed than this girl.

"Burke Dane," she said musingly. "I'm almost tempted to ask if that is your *real* name, Mister Dane."

"It is as far as we're concerned, Sal," said Jesse.

"Why did you say that?" asked Burke of the girl.

She narrowed her eyes a little. "It sounds almost familiar."

"Jesse has been telling you about me, you said. Maybe too much, Miss Sally. Memory plays strange tricks."

"I suppose you are right." She placed her lovely mouth at the rim of her glass and sipped her sangaree.

But Burke Dane knew he had not put her off. The cold feeling fled through his mind that she might know him from elsewhere, or have heard of him from some of the other girls. Members of her profession traveled widely and knew everyone. He glanced down at the locket, and she smiled, thinking he was studying the fascinating cleft just under the locket. Jesse stood up. "Excuse me," he said a little thickly. He walked toward the rear of the big room.

"You like the locket?" she asked of Dane.

"Yes." It was heart-shaped and set with small diamonds.

"Jesse gave it to me," she said carelessly. "Jesse is always trying to put his brand on me."

"He seems to be doing pretty well."

She leaned toward him and the locket swung forward, tinkling against a water carafe on the table. "I don't belong to anyone," she said softly. "Not *yet* anyway, Mister Dane."

He reached for the locket and pressed the catch. It opened before she could straighten up. Burke found himself looking at the tiny pictures of Dolly Mayo and little Alan Mayo, his niece and nephew. Sally pulled the locket from his fingers. She snapped it shut.

"Relatives?" murmured Burke quietly.

She bit a full lower lip. "I didn't even know there were any pictures in it. I thought it was new!"

Burked leaned back as the waiter placed fresh drinks on the table. He studied the girl. Maybe she *didn't* know where that locket came from. The last thing Marion Mayo had told Burke the night before he had left the valley of the Big Bonito, was that Charley had taken the locket—a wedding gift to Marion from Burke himself—to the Rio Desperado country so that he would have the pictures of the children with him. Now here it was, about the neck of a lovely young honky-tonk girl in Piñon, given to her by Jesse Lester. There was only one way he could have gotten it.

He looked up to see the Kid weaving through the narrow aisles between the tables, waving casually to those he knew and trading bold stares with those who knew him for what he was—a hired killer with a baby face.

Jesse sat down. "Ben Hinch wants to see you, Burke," he said.

Burke grinned. "You talk to him in the men's room?"

"Haw! No, he's in his office, just off the bar back there, between this room and the lobby. Better hurry."

Burke drained his glass, smiled at Sally, though there was cold murder in his heart, then walked easily back through the room toward the wide door of the office.

Curious looks were directed toward him. It didn't take long in a town that size to know who a stranger was and Burke had made himself known the *big* way by killing Joe Moss that very morning.

He tapped on the door and heard a man call out, inviting him in. He opened the door and walked into a big office, paneled in fine wood, carpeted, and lighted with fine lamps. A man sat behind a paper-littered desk eyeing him. "You're Burke Dane?" he said.

"Yes."

The man stood up and held out a hand. "Ben Hinch. Sit down. Cigar?"

Burke accepted a cigar, cut off the end of it in a silver clipper on the desk, lighted it and sat down in a deep leather chair, blowing out a ring of smoke as he did so. Ben Hinch was a medium sized man in his fifties, dark of hair and eye, clean-shaven, and successful looking. Hinch waved a hand at a small table covered with bottles. "Drink?" he said.

"Later, Mister Hinch."

Hinch nodded. "Business first, eh?"

"You're doing the talking, Mister Hinch."

"So I am. I usually do around here."

"So I've heard."

An odd, pleased sort of a look fled across the smooth face. "Jesse Lester has been telling me about you. *And* Matt Foxx, as a matter of fact. Seems as though you saved Jesse's life twice in twenty-four hours."

"Luck," said Burke quietly.

"Maybe. I can use you, Mister Dane."

"In what way, Mister Hinch? You know nothing of my capabilities."

The man leaned back in his chair and smiled coldly. "I can always use a fast gun, Mister Dane."

"That isn't my business."

Again the cold smile. "Listen, Mister Dane, I was born and raised here in the Southwest. I know men. The average cowpoke is an average shot, and far from being fast on the draw. He hasn't got the time nor the money to practice shooting to develop the deadly skill men such as yourself and Jesse Lester have developed. Now, a man with that skill, is most likely a gambler, a lawman, perhaps an outlaw, or a hired gun. Which category do *you* fall into, Mister Dane?"

"I have been a gambler, but I know many gamblers who are not fast guns, Mister Hindi."

"And the other categories?"

Burke smiled. "You leave little room for maneuvering, Mister Hinch."

"So?"

"I'm not a lawman, an outlaw, *or* a hired gun."

"You will be a hired gun if you stay in the Rio Desperado country, Mister Dane." Hinch relighted his cigar. His dark eyes probed into Burke's eyes. "Either that, or get out of this area within twenty-four hours."

"And if I don't?"

"I can't afford to have a free-lance fast gun hanging around my country, Mister Dane. Like all successful men, I have made enemies on my way to the top of the heap. Some of those enemies might just hire a man like you to fight against Ben Hinch. I can't allow that."

Burke inspected the end of his cigar. "I was under the impression I was in the Land of the Free. America, isn't it? Or did I somehow leave the States on the way here?"

Hinch leaned back in his chair. "I like a man with a sense of humor. Like the man who strung a rope across the top of the back stairs of the Piñon House earlier this evening. Rather a rough sense of humor, but justifiable under the circumstances. I might have done the same thing myself, Mister Dane."

Burke's poker face was a tribute to his years of training in the gambling halls of the Southwest.

"Well, is it a deal, Mister Burke Dane?"

Burke looked steadily at Hinch. There was no other way out.

"One hundred and fifty a month. Horses and cartridges at my expense. Frequent bonuses for jobs well done."

"Bounties?" asked Burke.

"Bonuses, Mister Dane. Is it a deal?"

Burke nodded. He gripped Hinch's extended hand. The big man smiled. "One other thing: You never *quit* a job with Ben Hinch. You get *fired,* but you never *quit.*"

Burke stood up. "Very clear," he said.

Hinch waved a hand. "Report to Matt Foxx out at the ranch no later than noon tomorrow. Tonight your drinks are on the house, compliments of Ben Hinch. But be sober when you show up for work tomorrow."

"*Gracias,* Mister Hinch."

Burke walked to the door. He glanced back. Ben Hinch was already working at his papers. It had been a routine job of work for the big man. Hire a fast gun, a professional killer, put the Hinch brand on him so that no one else in the Bio Desperado country could use him, then forget he exists until he is needed. It was as simple and mercenary as that.

CHAPTER FIVE

T he rain was slanting down in a fine silky looking mist as Burke Dane stood in the deep doorway of the Hinch Hotel Bar with a cigarette dangling from the corner of his mouth. The town was quiet, almost too quiet to suit Burke Dane, even if it was three o'clock of a dark and rainy morning. Jesse Lester came out behind Burke and as he did so the door closed and the key turned in the lock.

"The last dog hung?" asked Burke sourly. The kid was just a little drunk, which was a surprise to Burke, for Jesse had been playing the bottle a good part of the night. The only reason Burke had stayed around was to make sure Jesse got home safely. No one but Burke Dane was going to collect the blood debt from the kid.

Jesse hunched his slicker up about his neck. "Where's yours?" he asked.

"Forgot it," said Burke. "We can stay under the ramadas a good part of the way."

Jesse shrugged. They walked around the corner of the hotel and looked down the deserted main street. A lone pony stood hipshot at a rack. Burke and Jesse passed beneath the ramada where Burke had hastily hidden the rawhide reata. Burke's- eyes flicked up and down the street. No one was in sight. They crossed the intersection and passed along the second block, across the street from Burke's hotel, and still there was no sign of life except a dog rooting in a trash pile.

They crossed the intersection at a diagonal. Burke turned and looked back toward Garvey's saloon. The place was in utter darkness. The Kid kept on and had reached the alleyway and was looking for a place to cross the muddy ruts that were running with rain water. Burke's head was beginning to clear from the tobacco smoke of the bar, and the little drinking he had done that evening, while he passed the time in a game of draw for low stakes.

Jesse jumped the ruts and cursed as he went in over his boot tops. Beyond him was the dark shell of a burned out building. Something moved within a pane-less window. Something glistened in the darkness. *Shotgun,* thought Burke. He darted forward and hit the Kid with a shoulder driving him down in the mud, while he himself dropped to his knees and swept up his Colt in an easy and fluid motion. The scattergun roared, both barrels belching smoke flame and leaden death. Something invisible to Burke whipped his Stetson from his head even as he fired twice into the darkness. A man screamed harshly and it seemed to Burke he had heard someone scream like that not too long ago.

"Look out, Burke!" yelled the Kid. "Drop!"

Burke dropped into the cold and clammy mud as Jesse fired over his head. A man staggered across the street and even as he did so he fired his six-gun. The slug rapped into the burned out building. Jesse fired three more times and each of the soft nosed slugs slapped into the doomed man. He pitched face forward into the mud and lay still, smoke arising from the hot muzzle of his gun.

Burke jumped to his feet and whirled as he heard boots thudding in the mud. A man jumped into a doorway just as Burke fired twice, throwing screaming lead inches behind the man. Red flame spouted in the wet darkness but the man was shooting wild. Jesse darted out into the street and slammed two shots into the doorway, but by that time the man had gotten into the building. "Stay back!" warned Burke. He walked slowly forward, pistol at hip level, searching the darkness with slitted eyes.

Jesse was swiftly reloading. He ran up beside Burke and passed him to reach the main street, then whirled and fired three times down the street. A man yelled hoarsely, then hoofs thudded in the mud of the street and faded away into the -night.

Jesse turned and grinned. "Neat," he said. "Too damned bad we didn't get him too. I think I winged him though, Burke."

Burke turned and ran back toward the man lying in the street. A lamp went on in a house and a door slammed on the main street. A man shouted. Burke rolled the man over and looked into the set white face of Harv. Jesse clambered into the building. "It's Curly Carter," he said. "Dead as last night's bottle." He came back. "Let's get out of here," he added.

"Why?" -

The Kid spat. "I ain't in any mood to go to a coroner's inquest on this. It was self-defense, wasn't it?"

Burke stared at the Kid. He had made sense, and Burke was already hock deep in trouble his first day in Pifion. The Kid ran up the alleyway with Burke close at his heels, like two kids fleeing the scene of a Halloween prank. Jesse darted up a passageway between two buildings, scaled a fence, cut across a yard, pushed his way through a thick hedge, and walked into a barn. Burke followed him and the Kid slid the door shut.

"Where are we?" asked Burke.

"My barn," said the Kid. "We're safe here unless Belle

shows us." He grinned. "Sure taught those boys a lesson, eh, Burke?"

Burke took off his hat and eyed the ragged shot holes in it. "Yen," he said quietly. "A *permanent* lesson." He cocked his head to listen to the hoarse shouting down the street as men gathered at the scene of the shooting. "Who was the third *hombre?*"

"*Quién sabe?*"

"If we killed Harv and Curly, it's a cinch the third man must have been Larry Newman."

Jesse shoved back his hat. "Yen," he said. "I wish to God I had gotten him too. He won't never rest now, Burke, until he gets me, and *you,* too, for that matter."

Burke slowly reloaded his Colt. It had been a near thing. If Curly had fired a few seconds faster he would have blown Jesse's head into bloody meat fragments, and quite possibly one of the other two drygulchers, or both, would have gotten in a killing shot or two at Burke.

Jesse reached inside his coat and withdrew a pint bottle. He handed it to Burke, and Burke took a neat slug of the warming contents. Jesse tipped up the bottle and drank deeply. He lowered the bottle, wiped his mouth and then grinned. "By Godfrey," he said. "Nearly busted the bottle when you knocked me down. Thanks again, Burke. That's the third time you saved my life."

"We're even," said Burke quietly. "I saved you, and you saved me. Harv had me cold out there."

"They had the both of us cold," said Jesse. "We got more luck than brains.'

"Now you know why I waited for you."

The Kid nodded, then eyed Burke closely. "I was wondering about that, *amigo.*" -

Burke did not look at him. Even in the darkness it was possible Jesse might see the cold and calculating look in Burke's icy blue eyes; the killing look. "I'm getting out of here," he said. "I'll cut along the next street, then come into the hotel by the back way. I've got to report to the ranch tomorrow, wherever that is."

"Don't worry. I'm going with you."

"Thanks. I can find it."

Jesse smiled. "It ain't that easy, Burke. Ben Hindi told me to make *sure* you got out there."

Burke turned. "What do you mean?"

"I happen to work for Ben Hinch, too, partner. *Remember?*"

Burke nodded. He eased open the door. "Seven o'clock," he said over his shoulder.

"Keno."

Burke faded into the darkness. He cut over to the next street, found it empty, hurried to the next intersection, then down the alleyway, luckily unseen. He saw men grouped about the body in the street and another group standing near the building. He remembered his slicker and walked quickly to the ramada where he had hidden it. His questing hands found nothing. A lighted match revealed that both slicker and rope had vanished. There was a cold feeling within him as he entered his hotel by the back way, and it didn't come from the cold wetness of the night, or the recent close bout with violent death in the street. His name was India-inked under the collar of that slicker.

He made it to his room without being seen, then stripped off his wet and muddy clothing. He wrapped a blanket about his lean, muscular body and looked down into the side street where two men had died in as many minutes. They were carrying the bodies up to the main street. Jesse Lester had used more sense in running from the scene of the killings than Burke had by wanting to stay there. Joe Moss had no longer been with the Hinch corrida when Burke had killed him, so it mattered not to Ben Hinch, but Curly Carter and the man named Harv had still been active in the corrida, and from what Burke had heard of Hinch's methods, he knew the big man did not tolerate gunplay within his private army.

Still, the third of the drygulchers had escaped. That, and the fact that Burke's slicker and the rawhide rope had mysteriously vanished during the night, was enough to warn Burke Dane that he was treading a little too heavily footed on eggs he could not afford to break. Poisonous eggs for Burke Dane.

————

THE MORNING HAD dawned fresh and clear after the rain of the night. Cloud puffs drifted swiftly across the fresh and startling blue of the sky. The drying wind soughed through the trees as Burke Dane and Jesse Lester rode west from Pifion along the West Fork of the Rio Desperado on the way to Ben Hinch's Double Bar H spread.

"That is all Hinch land," said the kid, as he waved an arm toward the land across the rushing river. "The best land in the Rio Desperado country, Burke. Good for cattle, timber and some mining. Ben has his fingers into every money making pie around here, I tell you."

Burke rolled a cigarette. "Hasn't anyone ever put up a fight against him?"

Jesse shrugged. "Now and then. Not as often as they used to. Used to be some pretty bloody fracases when Ben was on his way up, but he got the reins in his hands about five years ago and he hasn't let go of them. When he passes on, I wonder what Clete will do about handling the Hinch properties."

"What do you mean? Isn't Clete like his old man?"

Jesse accepted the makings from Burke. "In some ways," he said.

"Maybe it's the old story about the father making good, pulling himself up by his bootstraps to make a career for himself, only to realize he has to turn it over to a wastrel or weakling."

"This time the story is different, Burke. Clete is no wastrel and no weakling. His big trouble is he's already anxious to take over and the old man doesn't want to let go—*yet* anyways. Once in awhile the two of them go round and round, but the son ain't a big enough man to beat his old man's britches off, I tell you. He's biding his time."

"Is that why Belle is going with Clete?"

The Kid turned slowly to look directly at Burke. "I don't like that kind of talk, Burke." Sorry.

Jesse nodded and lighted his cigarette. "Well, anyway I can't really blame her, Burke. We haven't got a red cent. Hellsfire! I owe every merchant in town, seems like. Sure, there are plenty of other men camping on Belle's hocks, waiting for a chance with her, legal or otherwise, but Belle is smart. 'Shoot for ducks' is her motto. Clete Hinch will be the big man in this country some day and I guess Belle figures she might as well be Mrs. Big as anything else around here."

Burke blew out a puff of smoke. "Well, I have a feeling Belle won't be any tame kitten for a man to have around, even if he *is* Mister Big."

"Keno." Jesse pointed ahead. "There's the ranch now, beyond that timber."

A heavy log bridge spanned the Rio Desperado and beyond it, through the timber, Burke saw a mass of buildings, white-washed, shining in the bright morning sun. Several windmills whirred in the freshening wind. It was quite a spread; in fact, a whale of a spread, thought Burke. It smelled of profit and wealth, and yet there was nothing ostentatious about the place. Its size and layout indicated money, rather than any useless and materialistic trappings.

"Ben keeps adding on," said Jesse as they crossed the bridge. "Any new ideas, tools, blood stock, all end up here, but not for show, I tell you. Ben bleeds money out of everything he gets his hands on, or out it goes."

"Like his gunfighters?"

Jesse looked sideways at Burke. "You're getting the idea fast, *amigo,*" he said dryly.

"What happens when a man doesn't measure up?"

Jesse jerked a thumb toward the distant mountains. "He leaves thataway."

"Or gets buried on Hinch land, is that it?"

Jesse spat into the clear water. "Well, Ben don't charge the deceased's family for the burial plot, if that's what you're driving at. Hawww!"

"You're coming out with a good one now and then," said Burke. He flipped his cigarette butt into the river.

Jesse turned in his saddle. "One thing, Burke: Ben usually requires a new man to prove himself."

"Meaning?"

The Kid's face was expressionless. "A man has to blood himself to prove he rates riding with the Hinch corrida."

"You mean a killing?"

Jesse smiled. "You're getting the idea."

"So Ben has something to hold over his head, is that it?"

"Yes."

Burke shrugged. "I've got two killings against me already. In Pirion at any rate."

"Joe Moss doesn't count. Besides, if Ben knows we killed Curly Carter and Harv last night he won't take it lightly."

"You think that third man will talk?"

"I'm banking he won't. Those three boys weren't waiting for us on Ben's orders, you can bet your boots on that. Ben don't allow any fighting within the corrida.

If that third man is one of Ben's men, he won't likely open his mouth."

"And if he isn't?"

The kid smiled quickly. "Then what difference does it make? He sure as hell ain't going to go around blowing about how he was a party in an attempt to drygulch two of Hindi's boys, is he?"

"You've got something there," said Burke. The thought of the missing slicker and rope fled through his mind. He'd have to sweat that out. It wasn't yet time for him to make any moves.

A tall man came striding from the big ranch house as Jesse and Burke drew rein and dismounted. "Jesse!" he called out. "Mount again! We've got work to do! Who's that with you?"

"Burke Dane, Clete," said Jesse.

The man swung up into the saddle of a fine black. "The new man? Good! We can use another man."

"What's up?" asked Jesse as he mounted.

"Trouble over in the meadow country. The rest of the boys are busy up north. It's up to you and me, and Dane as well. We'll meet Larry Newman at the fine shack by Cold Creek."

"Dandy," said Jesse out of the side of his mouth. "If that *was* Larry who got away last night, he'll be sporting a bullet scratch somewhere, or I miss my guess."

Clete Hindi rode toward them. Burke was struck by his resemblance to his father, although he was a taller and better looking man. Clete eyed Burke up and down. "My father said you were a good man with a gun. Is that right?"

"I can take care of myself, Clete," said Burke quietly.

"You call me Mister Hindi, Dane. Understand?"

Burke nodded and looked at Jesse. Jesse smiled. "Likely Clete and me will be brother-in-laws someday. Clete *allows* me to call him by his first name."

Clete shot an angry glance at Jesse. "I swear to God, Kid, you go too far sometimes!"

Jesse's expression changed. "What's the trouble you spoke about, Clete?"

"Sticky loopers. Larry sent one of the boys back to say he had seen three or four of them working in the timber over against Bald Mountain."

"A good place," said Jesse. "Can't see very far in that timber. They can cut out a few head of cows and run them up a canyon until after dark, then edge them along the base of the mountain until it gets daylight, run them up into another canyon until dark, and so on."

"We'll take care of that this time," said Clete. He smashed a gloved hand down on his saddle horn. "I hope to God we catch 'em cold this time."

Burke rolled another cigarette. "What happens then?" he asked.

Clete looked at him. "We don't give rustlers a second chance in the Bio Desperado country."

"A law unto yourselves, is that it?" asked Burke.

Hinch stared at him. "What the hell do you mean by that?"

Burke smiled. "I heard you gave short shrift to rustlers over here."

"Where do you come from?"

"New Mexico."

"*Where* in New Mexico?"

"All over, Mister Hinch."

"One of that kind, eh?"

Burke nodded. "One of that kind, Mister Hinch."

"You said the Big Bonito country once," said Jesse.

Clete Hinch shot another glance at Burke. "Is that right, Dane?"

Burke shrugged. "I worked around there while drifting west, is all."

"Know a man named Print Campbell?"

Once again Dane's poker framing kept his face impassive. "I've heard of him."

"Charley Mayo?"

It wasn't easy this time for Burke. "I've heard of him," he said casually. "Rancher, isn't he?"

"Was," said Jesse. He grinned.

Burke lighted his cigarette, trying hard to keep control. "Was? What happened to him?"

Clete splashed his black through a rivulet. "Seems as though Charley Mayo was a son-in-law to Print Campbell, Dane."

"So?"

They all reached the far bank of the rivulet. "Mayo got a little out of hand over here not too long ago," said Clete.

"And?"

Clete turned. "I said we didn't give rustlers a second chance in this country."

"There's Larry," said Jesse quickly. He looked at Burke. "Somebody strung Mayo up in Windy Pass. Sort of a warning you might say. We don't cotton to New Mexico men coming over here and stealing Arizona cattle, *amigo*."

"You had the goods on Mayo then?" asked Burke quietly.

Clete forced the black up a cutbank. He turned and looked at Burke. "We never said *we* did the hanging," he said. "But Print Campbell was run out of here long ago, and told to stay away from here."

"Was Mayo hung because he was a rustler or because he was a son-in-law of Print Campbell?" asked Burke.

"What the hell difference does it make?" said Clete.

"None, I guess," said Burke.

Jesse Lester eyed Burke quickly, and an odd expression fled across his handsome face.

Larry Newman was sitting easily in his saddle, a leg hooked around the horn, a cigarette dangling from his lips. He nodded shortly as the three riders approached and drew rein. There was no sign of a wound about the tall man, but Jesse could have scratched his hide somewhere with a bullet and the wound could be well hidden.

"What's up?" asked Clete.

Larry flipped away his cigarette. "They're still over there," he said, jerking his head toward a huge out-thrust shoulder of the towering mountain of almost naked rock. "I've been keeping an eye on them all morning.

"Bold as brass, eh?" said Clete. "In broad daylight."

"They had a lookout," said Larry casually. "I took care of him. They probably still think he's keepin' an eye out for some of our boys."

"Good work, Larry," said Clete. "Lead the way!" He eased his Winchester in its saddle scabbard. "I hope to God we can trap *all* of them!"

Burke eyed the rancher. There was a cold eagerness on Hinch's face that boded no good for the sticky loopers.

The four of them rode toward the thick timber; death in the saddle.

CHAPTER SIX

The three bustlers were working fast, driving twenty head along the wide meadowland toward the thick timber that edged the mountain base. Although it was hard to tell exactly where the canyon opening was against the masses of eroded and splintered rock of the great talus slope, it was obvious that the sticky loopers knew where it was, for they moved confidently toward the timber that shielded the canyon mouth.

"That's all of them," said Newman.

"You're sure?" asked Clete Hinch.

Larry turned a little and there was almost a sarcastic smile on his lean hard face. "No chance of us getting dry-gulched, if that's what you mean, Mister Hinch."

"I wasn't thinking of that," said Clete quickly. "I want all of them. *All*, you understand?" He shot hard looks at his gunfighters.

Jesse shoved back his hat. "Me and Burke can cut along the east side of the meadows. The ground is lower there and hidden by timber. We can get to the canyon mouth before they do."

Clete nodded. "Go on then. Larry and me will keep to

the west, and close in on them if they break back this way."

Jesse set the steel to his bay and rode swiftly to the east, followed by Burke. Burke looked back to see Clete and Larry drawing out their rifles. Then the two of them rode into the timber.

It was a beautiful day. Birds twittered in the timber. Patches of sunlight moved back and forth in the dappled shade. A deer moved silently and swiftly across a glade and disappeared into the woods. A porcupine stood in the trail and did not move as the two horsemen approached him. "Spunky buggers, ain't they?" asked Jesse. He spat at the bristly creature.

It was easy. Burke and Jesse tethered their horses in the timber, took their rifles, and padded quickly through the timber to where they could see the narrow canyon mouth. They reached the area ten minutes before the rustlers. The cattle bawled hoarsely. Now and then the rustlers looked nervously over their shoulders toward the creek in the distance. They hadn't been warned of the approach of the Double Bar H men and they never would be, for the first of them was already dead in the timber.

Jesse shoved back his hat and levered a round into his Winchester. "You any good with the long gun?" he asked casually.

"Fair."

The cattle were now even with Jesse and Burke, and the three drivers were too intent on their work to watch for anyone. Jesse quickly raised his rifle and fired. The sharp report rang up the canyon and the horse of the lead driver went down. The rustler leaped free and ran toward the timber but Jesse had reloaded. He swung the rifle easily and just as he fired, Burke bumped purposely against him. The man staggered as the slug hit him and went down writhing on the damp ground.

The gunsmoke drifted through the timber. The other

two rustlers lashed their mounts, trying to reach the canyon, then saw Burke and Jesse mounting their horses. They turned and raced back along the meadow. A rifle spoke flatly and the lead rider pitched heavily from the saddle while his horse veered off and ran toward Jesse and Burke. The third and last rustler turned his horse and drew out a pistol. He fired wildly at Jesse and Burke. Two rifles cracked together from the west side of the meadow and the rider stiffened in the saddle, then fell sideways, his foot caught in the stirrup. The horse galloped toward the bawling cattle, dragging his rider behind him. The horse vanished in the canyon mouth along with the cattle.

The smoke drifted slowly across that meadow of death. Jesse looked at Burke. "You bump me apurpose?" he asked.

"Maybe. You were going to kill him, weren't you?"

"I didn't see *you* do any shooting."

"I thought he wanted them captured."

Jesse slid his rifle into its sheath. "Sometimes you ain't too bright, *amigo*."

"They got three out of four and saved the cattle. Isn't that enough?"

Jesse rolled a cigarette and shook his head. "Not for Clete Hinch, it ain't. Come on. The second act is about to begin."

Clete and Larry had stopped at the still figure of the man lying in the middle of the meadow. Larry dismounted and hooked a foot under the man, heaving him over on his back. His arms were outflung. Larry looked up at Clete and nodded. The two of them rode toward the wounded man. The four horsemen met together, sitting easily in their saddles, looking down on the sweat damp face of the kid, for he was hardly more than that. His clawed hands ripped steadily at his left shoulder.

"You're getting out of practice, Kid," said Larry.

Jesse spat. "Any time you want a match, Larry, you just say so."

Larry looked at Burke. "No score for the 'Man from New Mexico,' eh?"

"He doesn't know the rules yet," said Jesse.

"He better, by God, learn the rules, and pronto!" snapped Clete.

Burke dismounted and ground-reined his horse. He walked toward the kid on the ground and knelt beside him.

"What the hell!" said Larry.

Burke took the Colt from the kid's holster and tossed it to one side. "Let me take a look at that wound," he said.

"Get up, Dane," said Clete Hinch.

Burke ignored him as he began to free the bloody shirt from the wound.

"Get up, *you*" said Clete once more.

Burke had exposed the wound. He eased the kid back onto the ground. A gun hammer clicked back. Burke looked up into the stony eyes of Clete Hinch and the one cold, black eye of a gun muzzle. "He'll bleed to death, Mister Hinch," he said quietly.

"Up, damn you!"

Burke wiped the blood from his hands and stood up.

"Get that horse, Larry," said Hinch.

The gunfighter rode toward the stray. He led it back toward the waiting men. "Mount," said Clete to the kid.

Sweat trickled down the rustler's face. He got weakly to his feet and fell against the horse. The horse shied and blew at the smell of fresh blood.

"Mount!" snapped Clete Hinch.

The kid got a boot into the stirrup but he couldn't make it into the saddle.

"He can't ride," said Burke harshly to Hinch. "Let me

bandage him and take him up in front of me, Mister Hinch."

"Jesse said you didn't know the rules," said the rancher. "Help him, Larry."

Larry pulled the kid roughly up until he could fork the horse and grip the saddle horn. He looked at Burke. "My name is Jerry Kenna," he said. "From Benson. My maw lives there."

Burke looked curiously at him.

"Now!" yelled Clete.

Larry lashed the kid's horse over the rump with his reins. The horse galloped toward the canyon mouth. Jesse and Larry looked at Clete. "Let Burke have him," said the rancher. He looked at Burke.

"*You* go to hell, *Mister* Hinch," said Burke Dane. "And none of *you* try to get that kid!" It was then he realized that Clete Hinch still held a six-gun aimed at him.

Jesse raised his rifle and looked at Larry. "Ten bucks I get the hoss." His rifle cracked and the horse staggered in its stride. Harry's rifle spoke but he missed. Jesse fired again. The horse went down and the man fell heavily. He staggered to his feet and looked wildly about, then began a slow run toward the timber. Jesse raised his rifle but Larry Newman beat him to the punch. The Winchester rang out and the kid went down with a slug between the shoulder blades.

Again the powder smoke drifted across the quiet meadow as the gunshot echoes died away. Now Burke knew why the kid had told him his name and home. The kid knew more about these men of the Double Bar H than Burke knew. He knew he was doomed.

Clete let down the hammer of his Colt." You've got a lot to learn, Dane," he said. "I should fire you right now."

"You didn't hire me, Mister Hinch," said Burke evenly. "It's up to your father to fire me."

"I can take it upon myself to fire you!" snapped the rancher.

"Go on then,". said Burke easily. "Do that, Mister Hinch."

For a long moment there was pure hell in the man's eyes and his lips worked.

"There's Belle, Clete," said Jesse quickly.

Clete turned in the saddle and saw the lovely young woman riding toward them. "I don't want her to see this mess," he said. He spurred his black toward her.

"Gentle soul, ain't he?" said Burke.

"You work for the Double Bar H, Dane, and you obey the rules," said Newman.

"I don't believe in killing helpless men," said Burke.

"Seems as though you change the rules to suit your-self, eh, Dane?"

Burke eyed the gunfighter. "I can kill when I have to, Newman. You ought to know that."

"Your day will come, Dane." Larry Newman kneed his horse away from the two of them and rode toward the canyon. "We can't get those cows back sitting here talk-ing," he said over his shoulder.

Jesse shook his head as he and Burke rode after Larry. "You're all horns, hoofs and rattles this morning," he said to Burke. "Beats me." He looked back toward Clete. "So help me. You could'a got away with what you said to Ben Hinch, because Ben Hinch, for all his money grabbing and lust for power, secretly admires a man who stands up against him, *if* that man is right."

Burke rolled a cigarette. "Maybe a man like Print Campbell or Charley Mayo, eh?"

Jesse's eyes narrowed. "Why did you say that?"

"I've heard stories. Print Campbell was blinded apur-pose, wasn't he?"

"That was before my time on the Double Bar H. Just what the hell do you know about Charley Mayo?"

"Rumors, Kid, only rumors. Let's go get those cows!"

Jesse hesitated, watching Burke galloping toward the canyon mouth, and his sister's words came back to him on the wind soughing through the pines. *"He isn't any run of the mill saddle tramp. There is something secret about that man."* And again: *"And this man this Burke Dane, from nowhere, drew and killed him when Joe had his gun out and cocked?"*

An uneasy feeling fled through the cocky young mind of Jesse Lester, and he remembered too that very morning, in the dark and wet, when Burke Dane had seen Curly Carter hiding in the ruins with a scattergun in his hands and had saved Jesse's life by driving him to one side. Jesse hadn't seen anything. Jesse owed Dane his life, not once, but maybe three times: first in the pass; then when he had killed Joe Moss; thirdly, when he had saved Jesse from Curly Carter.

He liked and admired Burke Dane, but now something else had crept into his mind. It was a tried and true saying that there was always a better man than you somewhere in the wide world, and that it was inevitable that you would meet him for a showdown. For the first time in his careless young life, Jesse Lester felt the weight of being known as a fast gun and a gunfighter. Such a reputation had to be maintained at any cost. Such a reputation bred enemies; men who only wanted to beat you to prove to the world that they were the fastest gun. These men came from nowhere. Maybe from California or Utah; Colorado or Texas; *or New Mexico...*

It took several hours to round up the spooked cattle. They had found the body of the third rustler up the canyon, his head battered beyond recognition from beating against the rocks as he was dragged by his horse. They drove the cattle back into the meadow, and while Larry stood guard, Jesse and Burke hauled the bodies to the canyon and buried them in a deep rock cleft, filling the cleft with detritus and loose rock.

Everything went with them. Guns and saddles were pitched in. It was Ben Hinch's way. Let their friends and relatives wonder what had happened to the four men who had taken their guts into their dirty hands to rustle cattle from the Double Bar H. The fact that they did not return, and no traces would ever be found of them, made the reputation of Ben Hinch and the Double Bar H corrida just that much more omnipotent and sinister.

CHAPTER SEVEN

The sun was in its zenith when Jesse and Burke rode back to the headquarters of the Double Bar H. Larry Newman had left ahead of them, for he was ramrod under Matt Foxx, and there were other things for him to do. "I wonder if it was him this morning," said Jesse thoughtfully.

"He didn't show any signs of being wounded, Kid. Unless you missed him."

"I can call my shots," said Jesse carelessly. He eyed Burke. "I'd still like to know if it *was* him."

"We can try to find out," said Burke. "What do we do if he was the third man?"

"We'll know how far hell go to even up the score, *amigo.*"

"I think we both know that already.'

"Well, no one else but us besides that third man knows who killed Harv and Curly. We keep our mouths shut and play dumb, which shouldn't be too hard for you, and that third man might make his slip."

"Then what?"

Jesse sneered like a hunting lobo wolf. "We'll have to teach that jasper a lesson he won't forget."

A man came out of the main building and looked at

the two of them. "Mister Hinch wants to see you two in the house, Jesse," he called out. "Pronto I"

"Which Mister Hinch, Shorty?" asked Jesse as he dismounted.

"The Big Man, Jesse."

Jesse shrugged. "Wonder what the hell is wrong now," he said in an aside to Burke.

"*Quién sabe?* I haven't got anything to hide."

Jesse's eyes went wide. "You haven't?" he asked in mock surprise. He turned and walked toward the big house.

Burke flipped away his cigarette and eyed the Kid as he followed him toward the house. Jesse was as sharp as a Barlow knife, under all his assumed nonchalance and carelessness. Burke was beginning to wonder just how much Jesse knew.

Ben Hinch had furnished his big house well, though nothing in it was ostentatious. Burke nodded as the two of them waited in the large living room. It was just such a way he himself would have furnished such a room, if he had the means. It was comfortable enough, but yet, to Burke, there was a haunting coldness about the place.

Ben Hinch walked into the room and sat down near the fireplace. He eyed the two of them. "Larry Newman said you did all right this morning, Jesse. That doesn't surprise me. I heard differently about your friend there."

"He doesn't know the rules, Mister Hinch," said Jesse.

"Well, Dane, what do you have to say for yourself?" asked the rancher.

"I don't know all the rules, Mister Hinch. But I do know you suffered no losses this morning, in cattle or men, and there are four rustlers buried up the canyon. Considering this is my first day of work for you, I can see no cause for complaint.'

"You talk like a shyster lawyer," growled Hinch. "One thing worse than an ignorant cowpoke is a smart one, or one who *thinks* he's smart. Which one are you?"

Burke smiled. "I've read a little law, Mister Hinch."

Hinch leaned back in his chair and lighted a cigar. "No matter about this morning. You did well enough, but next time don't be so squeamish. I've lost at least four men in the past few years, shot to death by rustlers. This is war in this country, Dane. I have the finest cattle in this entire area, and I mean to keep them, one way or another. That's why I keep the corrida I have. That is why I need men like you, and Jesse there. Don't worry about being brought to account for killing those human vermin. I take care of my men, legally or otherwise."

"Do you take care of their consciences too, Mister Hinch?" asked Burke quietly.

"Oh Lord," said Jesse. He rolled his eyes upward.

For a long moment Ben Hinch studied Burke. "The men I hire, Mister Dane, may have consciences, but those consciences are not active after such killings like those of this morning. There is a difference between justice and softness in this country."

"I almost forgot where I was," said Burke.

Hinch blew out a puff of smoke. "You'll learn. Now, let's get on to other matters. Two of my men were shot to death on the streets of Piñon early this morning. Harv Clayton and Curly Carter. The killers, and there are thought to be two of them, escaped. There were no witnesses. I've already sent my son Clete into Piñon to make an investigation. Matt Foxx, as deputy-sheriff of this county will deputize Clete to make it legal."

Very neat, thought Burke. The fact that Ben Hinch was pushing an investigation, outwardly legal, though manipulated by Hinch himself, might prove that the man thought someone outside the Hinch corrida had killed two of his men. He couldn't and wouldn't allow that. It was against his principles, and Ben Hinch, in order to keep the reins tight in the Rio Desperado country, would have to see that those killers were brought to justice. What would happen if he found out that Jesse Lester and

Burke Dane had killed those two men? What if the third man talked?

Hinch relighted his cigar. "I want Clete to learn the ways of the law," he said.

Like his Pappy, thought Burke.

Ben Hinch waved out the match flame. "A man has to know the law to keep in the saddle. The parts that protect him, and the loopholes, so that he doesn't get snarled himself." Hinch smiled. "You, as a student of law, Mister Dane, can hardly disagree with that theory."

"No, sir," said Burke.

Hinch stood up and walked to the fireplace. He flicked an ash from his cigar into the fireplace, then turned suddenly. "Just what do you two men know about those killings this morning?" he spat out.

Jesse smiled, like the innocent child he usually portrayed at such times. "Nothing, Mister Hinch. Why do you ask?"

Hinch thrust his cigar into his mouth and worked it back and forth from one side to the other. "From the circumstances, it looked as though Curly Carter, at least, was lying in wait for someone. Harv Clayton was found dead in the street. Although no witnesses actually saw the shooting, they heard voices calling out, the voices of two men other than Curly and Harv."

"How did they place the number at two?" asked Jesse easily.

"Because those two men spoke to each other *after* Curly and Harv were shot to death. A third man was evidently shot at and escaped from the killers by riding from Piñon." Hindi's cold eyes darted back and forth between the two men. "Both of you were in Piñon last night. Both of you left the Hinch Hotel Bar shortly before the shootings. From what I know about you, Jesse, and from Burke's shooting of Joe Moss in the Mecca yesterday morning, I would almost be willing to bet the pair of you could shoot your way out of most ambushes, and be able to cut a few new notches on the handles of your cutters after the shooting."

"Are you accusing us of killing those two men, Mister Hinch?" asked Burke.

"No. But *did* you?"

"No," lied Burke. "I heard the shooting as I entered my room in the Piñon Hotel. It was dark and it was raining. I could see very little from my window."

"And *you*, Jesse?" asked Hinch quickly.

Before the Kid could speak Burke broke in. "Jesse was pretty damned drunk last night, Mister Hinch. I had taken him home before I returned to my room."

"Very neat," said the rancher. "No witnesses either, eh?"

"My sister Belle," said Jesse. He smiled. "Belle always likes to tuck me in, Mister Hinch."

For a moment die man's face whitened in quick anger and then he smiled. "Fair enough! I won't press the matter. I happen to know Curly Carter was a good friend of Joe Moss'. Harv Clayton was Curly's sidekick. It would be like him to back Curly's play."

"That just leaves the man who escaped, as you tell the story, Mister Hinch," said Burke.

Ben Hinch threw his cigar into the fireplace. "Yes." He eyed Burke. "I can't bring those two men back to life. They weren't obeying any instructions of mine this morning. They paid the price for what they attempted." He walked to the table and selected another cigar. "Now get out of here. Take the rest of the day off. If I need you I'll send for you. In a few days I'll have a big job for you, and Dane, *this time you obey the rules. Comprende?*"

When they reached their horses Jesse blew out an explosive breath. "Chihuahua! The old vinegaroon stings, doesn't he?"

Burke rolled a cigarette and looked back toward the house. "He knows," he said quietly.

"What makes you think so, Burke?"

"It's his business to know everything that is going on around the Rio Desperado country. That's how he stays on top, isn't it?"

"It doesn't make sense to me, Burke."

Burke mounted and rode toward the bridge, followed by Jesse. Burke looked back at Jesse. "I wonder if he put Curly and Harv up to that ambush?"

"You're loco!"

Burke shrugged. "Did you ever get the thought through your thick head that maybe Ben Hinch doesn't exactly *want* you around? That he has used you and wants no more part of you?"

"What the hell are you talking about?" demanded the Kid angrily.

"Maybe he wants you out of the way, Kid. He could have used the death of Joe Moss to his advantage, by putting those men up to killing you."

"But you were there, too!"

"Exactly! Curly would have gotten the first one of us, and Harv and that third man the second of us, in less time than it takes to tell about it. Hinch didn't give a damn about Joe Moss."

"If he wants to get rid of me all he has to do is say so!"

Burke crossed the bridge and turned toward the road that led to Piñon. "You've forgotten one thing: Clete Hinch and Belle, Jesse. Clete isn't going to let his father get rid of you his usual way, not as long as Clete has his eyes on Belle."

Jesse rode up beside Burke and shot an uneasy glance at him. "But if I was shot down in the street by unknowns, it would sure serve the purpose wouldn't it?"

"You're getting the idea."

A slight shiver seemed to pass through the Kid. He turned in the saddle and looked back at the ranch. "I have one more thought on it, Burke."

"Yes?"

Jesse turned again. "Maybe Ben Hinch didn't know a

thing about the ambush, like he said. Maybe it was *Clete s* idea. I wouldn't put it past him."

"Whoever thought it up, it was a damned close thing."

Jesse eyed Burke. "And where do you fit in, Man of New Mexico? Seems to me, if I had wandered into this country like you did, and got belly deep in trouble the first twenty-four hours I was here, I'd been long gone."

"I got a job, Kid," said Burke.

"Yen, you got a job all right. You almost got measured for a nice new pine suit with brass handles on it, too."

Neither of them had much to say for the rest of the ride into Piñon, but every now and then Jesse would glance surreptitiously at the hawkface of the man riding beside him. As they entered the town Burke looked at the Kid. "What kind of trouble did Charley Mayo get into over here, Kid?" he asked.

Jesse's eyes narrowed. "Why do you ask?"

"Clete Hinch said he was a son-in-law to Print Campbell. I knew Print years ago. Print was a tough cob in the old days. I heard a story once that it was Ben Hinch who had Print blinded. Broke Print's spirit, from what I heard."

"You sure heard a helluva lot, didn't you?"

Burke swung down at the street corner and looked up at the Kid. "You mean to tell me the Hinches strung up Charley Mayo simply because he was son-in-law to Print?"

The Kid's face worked a little. "No."

"Was Mayo really a rustler, Kid?"

Jesse shoved back his hat. "I don't know. Mayo came over here to buy cattle from Ben Hinch. Ben has the best cattle to be had and his prices ain't *too* high, if a man wants them bad enough."

"So?"

Jesse shrugged. "Mayo was a good hand with the cards. Got into a big game at the Hinch Hotel. I started out in the game, but it got too rich for me. Mayo was taking pot after pot. Never seen anything like it. I swear he was ahead five thousand dollars by the time the game broke up."

Burke rolled a cigarette. He glanced down the street and saw Belle Lester standing at the gate of the little house, not far beyond the place where Curly Carter and Harv Clayton had died in a hurry early that very morning.

Jesse dismounted and took the makings from Burke's hand. He began to fashion a quirly. "Mayo said he had enough money to buy a helluva lot more cows from Ben Hinch. Never seen a man so excited. He was calm as an oyster during the tightest parts of the game, but when it was over, and he got to talking about buying them cattle, he reminded me of a kid eyeing his bulgin' Christmas stocking."

Burke lighted up and held the cupped match to light Jesse's cigarette. The Kid had known Charley all right. Charley was a cool man with the cards, damned near as good as Burke at his best. But when it came to cattle, Charley was actually like the kid Jesse had likened him to. It was almost an obsession with Charley. It was something Burke had not shared with him.

Jesse blew a perfect smoke ring. "Well, Charley headed out, all right. Hired a couple of boys to give him a hand when he got the cows. Needed hands to get them over Windy Pass and over to the Big Bonito country. You know the rest of the story." Jesse spat. "Charley Mayo was strung up for a sticky looper."

"Was he guilty?"

"*Quién sabe?*"

"With five thousand dollars in his hands, why would he steal cattle, especially when he knew the reputation of Ben Hinch for dealing with rustlers? It doesn't make sense."

Jesse took the cigarette from his mouth. "I didn't tell you who was the big loser in that poker game."

"Go on."

The Kid's eyes held Burke's. "It was Clete Hinch." A cold feeling crept over Burke. Pieces of the puzzle were slowly fitting into place. "Did Mayo get his cattle?" he asked quietly.

"Yes."

"Where are they?"

Jesse smiled. "He was hung for a rustler, wasn't he?" Burke's eyes narrowed. "So he loses his cattle, his winnings and his life."

"You're getting the idea, Burke." "Who were the men he hired to help him?" Jesse flipped away his cigarette. He took the reins of his horse. "Got to see Belle," he said. "See you later, Burke." He walked a few paces and then turned. "Don't ask so damned many questions around Piñon, amigo. 'Person might get suspicious. Ain't everyone around here like me, Burke. Keep that in mind. Adios!"

"Adios!" Burke watched the Kid walk toward his house, softly whistling, right past the place where he had killed Harv Clayton. Burke led his horse to the livery stable, then went to his room to clean up.

Jesse Lester's story about the last days of Charley Mayo had come as a shocking revelation to Burke. It was true that Ben Hinch was a hard and unscrupulous man, not averse to force and killings, but he was also a businessman. He had bred the finest cattle in that country for that purpose. Why would he have a man like Charley Mayo put to a degrading death when the New Mexico rancher had money and the wish to buy cattle from Hinch? It didn't make sense to Burke.

He dug out a bottle and poured a stiff drink. He paced back and forth in his room, smoking and trying to form a clearer picture of the tangled situation. His mission had gotten out of control. It seemed to take a way of its own, despite what he wanted to do. It had all started with his saving Jesse Lester in Windy Pass, and from then on he seemed to have become the tool of the fates, who were probably laughing toothlessly at the poor thing called man they had trapped in their ceshes.

Things that had been said to him drifted into his mind.

Clete is no wastrel and no weakling. His big trouble is he's already anxious to take over and the old man doesn't want to let go—yet anyways. Once in awhile the two of them go round and round, but the son ain't a big enough man to beat his old man's britches off, I tell you. He's biding his time...

He sipped his drink. "Charley didn't antagonize Ben Hindi," he said aloud. "It was Clete Hinch he antagonized. It was Clete who took the beating in that poker game. Why would Ben want to lynch a man like Charley? Sure, he'd lynch a real rustler and think nothing of it, but if a man came to him with five thousand dollars, wanting to buy cattle, Ben Hinch would become the legal businessman, not the avenging lyncher of a man who had never given him cause for stringing him up."

If it was Clete Hinch who had seen to it that Charley was lynched, he didn't do it alone, *and it was Jesse Lester's rope that did the job.* The rope that was taken from where Burke had hidden it. The thought made him put on his hat and coat, and leave the cheerless room. If Jesse Lester had been one of the lynchers, and he found out that his treasured rawhide rope had been found wrapped in the slicker of a man named Burke Dane, all the Kid's suspicions would come to a head, and Burke wasn't at all sure he could beat Jesse Lester to the draw.

Burke Dane now had three objectives in mind. He was quite sure it would be impossible to get all the men who had been party to the merciless lynching of Charley Mayo. Therefore, he would cut it down to the *one* man who had been responsible. The man who had given the order that had been the last words Charley Mayo had heard on this troubled earth. The second objective was to find out who had the five thousand dollars Charley had won in that poker game. That, at least, was the due of Marion Mayo and her two children.

The third and last objective was, for Burke Dane, after getting the man responsible for Charley's death and collecting the missing five thousand dollars, to get out of the Rio Desperado Valley with a whole skin. That, thought Burke, would likely be the toughest objective of the three. He remembered his last brave words to Print Campbell: "I'll ram my navel into the sand trying!" They echoed hollowly enough now.

CHAPTER EIGHT

It was dusk when Burke Dane convinced himself that finding his slicker and the incriminating rawhide rope that belonged to Jesse Lester was an impossible task. During his secretive search for both articles he studied Piñon and its people, knowing full well that the people of Piñon were also studying him. It's easy enough for a man to vanish, almost without trace in a big city, or out on the open plains, or in the mountain country, but no one can escape scrutiny, interest and downright suspicion in a small town such as Piñon; particularly when a man is stamped in the mold of Burke Dane.

An uneasy feeling had come to roost in Burke's mind. Every fiber in his body seemed to have an almost uncontrollable itch for Burke to fight a shuck out of Piñon and the Rio Desperado country and stand not upon the way of his going.

His association with Jesse Lester had started the ball rolling and his swift and efficient killing of Joe Moss had accelerated the speed of the ball. No one knew for sure, of course, that Burke Dane was one of the two men who peddled out sudden death to Harv Clayton and Curly Carter. To Burke, whose mind always seemed to work with amazing clarity in times of stress and danger, the danger signals were flying.

He did not delude himself into believing he was accepted as another gunslick of the feared and powerful Double Bar H corrida, and amongst their ranks he had already made dangerous enemies. Ben Hinch himself certainly had not as yet accepted Burke Dane at face value. Ben Hinch had not risen to wealth and power by being a snap judge of men.

There was a little pattering of rain upon the leaves of the trees as Burke stood on the bridge looking down into the dark waters of the river, at the eastern limits of Pifion, and it brought to mind the fact that he did not have a slicker. He rolled a cigarette and walked back up the main street until he saw a secondhand clothing store. He entered and looked about for a clerk.

A baldheaded man looked up from a sewing machine at the back of the dimly lighted shop. "Can I help you?" he asked.

"I need a slicker," said Burke.

The man nodded and stood up. "New or used?" he asked.

"New."

Again the man nodded. He eyed Burke's build and then took a slicker from a rack. "New goods," he said with a smile. Then he peered more closely at Burke and his face changed a little.

"Anything wrong?" asked Burke as he tried on the slicker.

"Not exactly, Mister Dane."

Burke eyed him quickly. "What do you mean?"

"You're buying this slicker because you lost your old one?"

"I wouldn't be buying a new slicker if I already had one, would I, mister?"

The man flushed. He looked toward the back of the shop. It was then that Burke noted the material the man had been working on at the sewing machine. It was yellow slicker material. Burke took off the new slicker and walked back to the machine. He turned back the collar of the slicker and saw his name neatly printed on it with India ink. "Where did you get this?" he asked over his shoulder.

"I deal in second hand goods, Mister Dane. A man brought that in. I bought it for a few dollars and was repairing it when I saw your name. I intended to let you know I had it, then charge you for the repair work."

Burke nodded. "Fair enough." He turned. "Who brought it in?"

The man hesitated. He glanced toward the front door.

"Come on," said Burke quietly. "I'm buying the new slicker anyway."

"Man by the name of Benny Peak. He's the town drunk, Mister Dane. You won't cause him any trouble, will you? Benny didn't mean any harm."

"I just want to talk with him," said Burke.

"Something missing?"

"In a way."

The man came closer to Burke. "Benny hangs out in Garvey's place when he has money." He smiled. "Probably drank up what I paid him for the slicker already."

"I'll reimburse you."

"Thanks." The man handed Burke the new slicker. "You want me to wrap up the old one?"

Burke nodded. He put on the new slicker, paid the man, and took the wrapped slicker.

The man glanced again at the front door. "Happens there was something else with the slicker, Mister Dane. A rawhide reata, Benny said. One of the best he had ever seen. He said he'd get enough for it to keep him going for two days. Lots of men around here would pay plenty for a rope like the one he found, he said. Was it yours, Mister Dane?"

Burke rolled a cigarette. "In a way."

The man's dark eyes studied him. "You don't have to worry about me," he said. "I hate the guts of the men who run this country. I got no use for any of them. Well, we got a good start this week. Three of them gone. Joe Moss, Harv Clayton and Curly Carter. Keep going, Mister Dane."

Burke was repelled by the hard look in the man's eyes, but he had to take a chance on the man. "Keep your mouth shut about me coining in here, you understand?"

"I don't know anything."

Burke walked to the door.

"Garvey's place, Mister Dane," called out the man. "He's probably there right now. Only got one eye. You can't miss him."

Dane turned up the collar of the new slicker as he stepped outside to face a chilly drizzle. It was an off-and-on rainy season in the high country this time of year. He walked up the street and into the livery stable where he kept his dun. He placed the old slicker in one of his saddlebags and then went on to Garveys saloon. He peered through the dirty, rain streaked window. There were several men in the place. From where he was it was impossible to see if a one-eyed man was one of them.

He walked in and nodded to Garvey. "Beer," he said.

"Wet night, Mister Dane."

Burke nodded. He glanced down the bar. None of the three men standing there were familiar to him. None of them were one-eyed. A drunk sat at a rear table, head back against the wall, mouth agape, snoring loudly. Burke sipped his beer, then walked toward the back of the place. There was a newspaper on the table next to where the drunk slept. Burke picked it up, then surreptitiously kicked the ankle of the man. He choked and snapped open his bleary eyes. "What the hell!" he said. Bleary as his eyes were, they were both there.

"Sorry," said Burke. He walked back to his beer. "Wrong paper," he said casually to Garvey.

"Only one we got."

Burke sipped at his beer. He was faced with the task of tracking down Benny Peak, probably through every saloon in Piñon. He had to get that reata. So far Jesse Lester didn't know about Burke's mission in the Rio Desperado country. If Benny got that rope back to him and told him where he had found it.

Burke finished his beer and waved a refusal for a refill. "Be back later," he said. He eyed Garvey. "I'm refitting out," he added. "Got me a new slicker. Now that I got a job with the Double Bar H, I can afford to get a new outfit. Need a few other things. New bridle and bit. Cartridges. Stetson. Yen, and a new rope."

"You won't have any trouble getting them in Piñon," said Garvey.

I usually fancy a rawhide rope," said Burke. "Hard to get a good one these days. Have to settle for a grass rope I guess."

One of the men at the bar turned. "Benny Peak was in here awhile back, packing a good-looking rawhide rope. Four stranded. *Bueno.*"

"Would he sell it?" asked Burke. "Maybe he needs it in his work though."

They all laughed. "Benny?" said the man. "Hell that rope ain't no use to him other than to sell it and get money for more forty-rod."

"Where can I find him?" asked Burke.

The man shrugged. "I heard him say he thought Jesse Lester might be interested in that rope. Mebbe he went over to the Lester place. Right up this next street, Mister. White painted cottage, picket fence, and window boxes."

"Thanks," said Burke quickly. "I know Jesse. I worked with him today. Maybe I can talk him out of it." He left the saloon and walked up the side street toward the place where he and Jesse had killed Harv and Curly. He looked back over his shoulder as he neared the fire ruined house in which Curly had placed himself in ambush. He saw that the Lester house was unlighted. Just as he passed the gaping window of the burned building he heard a hollow groan. His heart skipped a beat. He looked toward the window and saw a head bobbing up, exactly as he had seen the head of Curly Carter. Instinct triggered Burke. He jumped to one side, clawed beneath his unbuttoned slicker and had his Colt out and cocked before he had time to think.

The head sank out of sight and then reappeared and Burke could see the raddled face of a one-eyed drunk. He sheathed the six-gun and walked to the window. "What's wrong?" he asked.

The man hiccupped. "Come in here out'a the rain, he said. He shook his head. "Couldn't get out'a the damned window."

"You're Benny Peak, aren't you?"

"Yeah."

Burke looked up and down the street. "You had a rawhide reata for sale. What did you do with it?"

Benny hiccupped again. "Left it at Jesse Lester's place."

"Did you tell him where you found it?"

Benny tried to focus his eyes. "Eh?"

Burke handed him a five-dollar bill. "Where did you find it?"

"Wrapped in a dirty of slicker, stuck in a ramada over on Front Street. Sold the slicker to that skinflint Max Green. Figgered Jesse Lester might want to buy that rope." Benny eyed Burke more closely. "Who're you?"

"Never mind. Was Jesse home?"

"No. Front door was unlocked. Left the rope there with a note for Jesse."

Burke gave him a hand out of the window and watched him stagger up toward the main street. He was drunk enough to black out that night, but for a time he might mouth off that he had met Burke and that Burke was interested in that mysterious reata. Burke would have to chance it. He walked quickly up the street, walked to the barn and stepped inside of it to eye the darkened house. He'd have to chance going in there after that damned rope. He walked softly to the house and kept close to the side of it as he moved to the front. The place was deserted. He stepped up onto the porch and padded to the front door. He tried the knob and the door swung open easily. Burke stepped inside and closed the door behind him. He risked lighting a match to look for the rope.

There was no sign or it. He blew out the match. Had Benny been lying, or was he too drunk to remember where he had left the reata? Burke cursed under his breath. He worked all through the neat living room and there was no sign of the rope.

Burke opened the door that led into a hallway that ran the length of the house to the kitchen. Other doors opened onto it from each side. He opened the first door and stepped into a bedroom, obviously a man's room, and Jesse's of course. There were ropes in the room, one of them was braided rawhide, but was a six stranded rope, while the other rope was Manila.

He shook his head. Every minute he stayed in that silent house seemed like half an hour. He walked softly into the hallway and toward the kitchen and just as he passed a door it swung open and someone stood there. Once again Burke's instincts reacted and he swung short and hard with a right, catching the unknown on the side of the head. It was the subtle fragrance of perfume, mingled with the ripe odor of whisky reached his nostrils.

He looked down at the unconscious form of Belle Lester. Burke picked up the luscious body and carried it to the bed. He thanked God he had not marked her face. Quickly he scouted the remaining rooms of the tomes, to

find them deserted, and with no sign of the rope he
wanted so desperately.

Burke went back to the room. She lay as he had left
her. He filled a basin with water and reached for a cloth
with which to bathe her temples. He turned. She was
awake and watching him. Her slim right hand held a
double-barreled derringer. "Stay right where you are,
Mister Dane," she said quietly.

He eyed the little gun with the big bite. "I wasn't
thinking of moving," he said pleasantly.

"What are you looking for, Mister Dane?"

"What makes you think I was looking for something?" he asked.

"Why else would you be prowling about a darkened
house?"

Burke tilted his head to one side. "I knew Jesse wasn't
around," he said quietly.

"And?"

"I thought you might be home."

"So, when you *do* see me, you knock me out."

"You startled me, Miss Belle."

She shook her head a little. It was then that Burke
noticed the partly empty bottle on the night stand beside
the bed. Miss Belle had a bellyful. She was on a high lonesome in the darkened house. She just might be drunk
enough for him to play out his game of bluff. "I thought
for a minute it was Clete Hinch," she said a little thickly.

"Does he make a practice of visiting you like this?"

She shook her head again. "Jesse would kill him if he
found him in here with me, Mister Dane." She leaned her
head forward. "Just as he'd kill you if he walked in here
now."

"Protecting his sister's beauty and virtue."

She stared at him and then she laughed. "Virtue?
What virtue?"

"Can I put down this basin?" Go on.

She laughed again as he placed the basin on the

dresser and turned to look at her. "The mysterious Man from New Mexico gets trapped in a lady's boudoir like a kid stealing apples," she said.

Burke grinned a little. It was rather amusing. It might turn out to be far from amusing if Clete Hinch or Jesse Lester walked in.

"Pour me a drink," she said.

He didn't argue. She just might get drunk enough to pass out. He knew now he hadn't really hit her hard enough to knock her out. The whisky had helped the blow along. He poured her a drink. "Help yourself," she said.

He poured himself a drink and handed the other one to her. She took it in her left hand and downed it quickly. She shook her head as the hard stuff hit her stomach. Burke leaned against the wall. The window near him was partly open and he might have to leave in a hurry.

"You *were* looking for something, Mister Dane," she said in a low voice.

He sat down on the edge of the bed and her body moved toward him because of the slope of the mattress. She put down her gun hand to steady herself and a big hard hand closed on her wrist, pinning it to the spread. "Let go of it," he said. She tried to pull her hand free but the pressure of his grip numbed it. She released the derringer. Burke emptied it and placed it on the night stand.

"What are you going to do now?" she said. Her mouth was partly open and her breath came quickly.

"Get out of here," he said.

"No you won't, Mister Dane. You'll stay here as long as I want you to."

"Why?"

"Don't you know?"

He stared at her, half believing her implication, remembering the almost haughty look she had given him when she had first met him. She was quite different now from the well-dressed young woman he remembered. He likened her now to other women he had known in the plushier bordellos of the West.

"Jesse won't be back for hours," she said. "He's with Sally Depree."

"Figures."

She laughed softly. "So, he's with a shady lady, and his sister is playing the same game with a man he thinks is his friend. The man to whom he owes his life."

He stared at her again. She drew herself close to him. She kissed him and Burke pulled away from her. The temptation was almost overpowering but the situation was too dangerous, and the danger drove all thoughts of dalliance from his mind. "What's your game, Belle?" he asked.

She stared uncomprehendingly at him.

"Well?" he said.

Her open hand caught him stingingly across the mouth and drew blood. She clawed at his face with her long nailed fingers until he caught her slim wrists and gripped them tightly. He moved his face close to hers. "Listen, Belle," he said harshly. "I'm not fool enough to be playing games with Jesse Lester's beloved sister as long as he's walking around with two Colts hanging at his thighs, nor do I want Clete Hinch to find out I'm in his lady friend's bedroom in the dark. What's your game, Belle?"

She bowed her head a little. "Let me go, Burke," she said quietly.

He released her. He walked to the door and peered into the dark hallway.

"Always the cautious one, aren't you?" she said.

"It keeps me alive, Belle," he said dryly.

"It isn't a trap for you, Burke. If Jesse or Clete knew you were in here, they'd kill you without thinking twice about it."

"The rope you are looking for is under the bed," she said.

For a moment he was startled. He downed his drink.

"It's Jesse's rope all right. Benny Peak found it wrapped in your slicker, Burke."

"He said he left it here with a note."

"I told him to tell you that if you asked him."

"Why?"

"I wanted to talk to you."

Burke stared at her. "But why?"

"You didn't fool me, Burke. You came to the Rio Desperado country for a reason, and it wasn't to work for Ben Hinch. You're a gunfighter, but not of the same stamp as the men of the Double Bar H. You had me fooled for awhile. I know who and what you are, Burke Dane."

A cold feeling fled through his body. "Go on."

"You're Burke Dane, sure enough. But what no one else around here knows, but myself and one other person is that you're Charley Mayo's half-brother."

In the silence that followed Burke thought of how easy it would be to clamp those big, hard hands of his about that alabaster neck and squeeze the life out of the lovely young woman so close to him.

"Don't worry," she said at last. "I'm not going to talk."

"Who else knows?"

She laughed shortly. "You'd never know. I'll tell you though. It's Sally Depree. She saw you once or twice in Albuquerque a year or so ago."

Then Burke remembered his first meeting with Sally Depree. "Burke Dane," she had said. "I'm almost tempted to ask if that is your real name, Mister Dane. It sounds almost familiar."

"Seems as though Sally is mad about my brother. She might not act like it, but Jesse means everything to her.

She also knows I'd fight tooth and nail to keep Jesse from marrying her."

"Not in your social strata, is that it, Belle?" asked Burke dryly.

Belle flushed. "Well said, Mister Dane. My brother means a great deal to me. More than he does to Sally Depree, or anyone else. That was why I meant to marry Clete Hinch. It would only be a matter of time before Jesse would be killed by them. Clete hates his guts, but lets him alone because of me. Ben Hinch wouldn't let anything happen to his future daughter-in-law's beloved brother. When Ben is gone, I, as Clete's wife, could help make a future for Jesse."

"Beside Clete throughout eternity, Belle?" asked Burke softly.

She reached for the bottle and drank deeply. She took a deep breath. "I hate his guts," she said bitterly.

"You'd sacrifice your whole life and happiness to make sure Jesse had a future?"

"It wasn't until you came here looking for the men who had lynched your brother that I realized how wrong I was. But there is a solution, Burke."

"Go on," he said. His eyes narrowed.

She eyed him closely. "Jesse likes you. He'd do anything for you. He'd listen to you, Burke."

"Him?" Burke laughed harshly. "That lobo of a lad wouldn't listen to Jesus Christ himself!"

"You're wrong! I know."

"So what is the solution?"

She gripped his arm. "If I help you get back the money that was taken from your brother, will you take Jesse and me with you?"

He stared at her. "Just exactly what do you mean?"

She drew closer to him and held her face up to his.

"Take us with you, Burke! There's no way other than that where we can escape Clete Hinch. He'd kill both Jesse and me without a thought if we ran out on him. Up until the time you came here, I thought we were doomed, but now I know that if anyone can help us, it's you."

The rain suddenly beat a tattoo against the side of the house. Burke wet his lips and looked at the beauty so close to him. "You haven't told me everything," he said.

"Take us with you, Burke, after I help you get the money. When we are free from this damned place, marry me. Jesse will listen to you if I am your wife. I'll make a good wife to you, Burke. Please, Burke!"

He stood up. "There is such a thing as love, Belle," he said softly.

"For such a man as *you?* A born killer?" She laughed. "Tell me anything but that, Burke. When have you ever experienced love?"

He half closed his eyes and the lovely face of Marion Mayo came swiftly across the rain swept mountains to haunt him, as it had for so many years when loneliness was his constant riding companion.

"Burke?" she said questioningly.

He poured a drink and downed it, but alcohol seemed to have no effect on him that night.

"Burke?"

He turned. "All right," he said. "It's a deal."

She got up on her knees on the rumpled bed and held out her arms. He drew her close and kissed her, passing his hands up and down the back of her head and the small of her back. She drew back. "Stay with me a little while," she said pleadingly.

"No time, Belle," he said quickly. "That will come later, I assure you."

There was a hurt look on her flushed face. She reached' for the bottle, but he intercepted her. "Get dressed," he said. "I want you to show me where the money is."

"And Clete Hinch?" she said.

"Yes."

He stepped back as she got out of the bed. "Who killed my brother, Belle?" he asked.

"Clete led the party that followed him. He had Curly Carter, Joe Moss, Harv Clayton and Larry Newman with him."

"And Jesse?"

"No," she said quickly. "It was Clete that borrowed Jesse's rope."

"Don't lie to me, Belle!"

She came to him and kissed him. "I'm not lying, Burke," she said, and he knew in his heart that she was not. He walked to the door and closed it behind him to let her get dressed, and as he walked to the living room he drew his sleeve quickly across his mouth to wipe away the taste of her kisses.

CHAPTER NINE

The fine rain was slanting down upon Piñon and the dark skies were silver threaded now and then by the faint flashing of the lightning. The river was rising and the subdued roaring played an undertone to the sound of the rain and the sweeping wind that came down from Windy Pass. Burke Dane halted at the top of the covered outside stairs in the rear of the big rambling hotel. Belle Lester pressed up close behind him. "Clete's suite is just beyond the main staircase, Burke," she whispered.

Burke nodded. "Do you think he's there?"

"Yes."

"How do you know?"

"What time is it?"

He looked at her over his shoulder. "A little after nine o'clock. Why?"

She smiled faintly. "He's expecting me."

"That's why you insisted on dressing up?"

"You've got the general idea, Mister Dane."

Burke eased open the door and peered into the dimly lighted hallway. There was no sign of life. He peeled off his slicker and hung it over the railing. "You're sure the money is in his suite?" he asked.

"It was last time I was in it."

"You *do* get around, don't you, Belle?" Burke eased his Colt in its sheath. "Why doesn't he keep it in the bank?"

She laughed. "Because he was playing with money that belonged to his father. Ben Hinch allows his beloved son a free rein in almost anything, but he doesn't allow Clete to play with Hinch money. When Charley Mayo beat Clete at poker, he was signing his own death warrant. Clete asked Charley Mayo not to mention to Ben Hinch that he had won heavily from Clete. Mayo bought his cattle from Ben and started back to New Mexico with the cattle and the remainder of his winnings. He never got there, as you well know."

Burke turned to look at her. "Who rode with him, Belle?"

"I've already told you, Burke."

"When?" Burke eyed her closely. "You said Clete led the party that followed him. Clete, Curly Carter, Jos Moss, Harv Clayton and Larry Newman."

"It wasn't exactly like that, Burke. Mayo hired, or *thought* he had hired, Carter, Moss and Clayton. They rode with him from the valley, followed by Clete and Larry. I don't have to fill in any details now, do I?"

Burke closed his eyes, sickened by Clete's duplicity and murderous mind. Poor Charley had never had the suspicious mind that had saved Burke's life more than once.

"Clete is just waiting for a chance to get that money back where it belongs without his father finding out what had happened. God help Clete if his father ever does find out."

"God help Clete anyway," said Burke softly. He started forward, but she drew him back and shook her head. "What's wrong?" he asked.

"He's expecting me, Burke. Let me go ahead. I promise to keep his mind occupied until you get there."

"I hate hiding behind a woman's skirts, Belle."

She passed him, patted his cheek, then kissed him lightly. "Even mine, Burke?" She swished gracefully down the wide carpeted hallway.

Burke shook his head in admiration. There was a lot of Jesse in Belle, and maybe—in the long run—Belle was the more to be admired for certain qualities. He watched her tap on the door of Clete's suite, then enter, closing the door behind her. Burke gave her five minutes, then padded softly down the long hallway. Somewhere on the same floor was Sally Depree's room. Belle had insisted that they get Jesse when they were through with Clete. She had a lot more confidence in that thought than did Burke. Personally Burke was ready to leave after he had the money and the scalp of Clete Hinch.

He stepped into a linen closet just across the hall from Clete's room. He didn't like this business of being indoors, especially being on the second floor, but there was no helping it. Minutes ticked past and the tension grew until at last Burke knew he had to make his move.

He drew his Colt, walked quickly across the hallway, gripped the knob and turned it easily. The door swung open. He stepped into a brightly lighted room. Clete Hinch sat at the far side of a marble-topped table, with Belle, in all her glory, sat on a chaise lounge near the draped window. For a second Burke knew he should run, then he heard the door close just behind him. Something hard pressed into the small of his back.

"Stand easy, *Mister* Dane," said a familiar voice. It was that of Larry Newman.

Burke looked at Belle. She had betrayed him!

Clete slowly raised his right hand and rested it on the table. A nickel-plated Colt was aimed right at Burke's belly. Something moved at the right of the big room and a man stepped out from behind a drapery with a Winchester in his hands. Burke recognized him as the man named Shorty, from the Double Bar H. Then another man came into the sitting room from the bedroom, holding a cocked Colt in his hand.

"Drop that six-shooter, Mister Dane," said Clete easily.

The Colt thudded on the carpeted floor and Burke raised his hands level with his face.

Clete smiled thinly. "The 'Man from New Mexico,' eh? Who did you think you were dealing with, Dane? Rank amateurs? This is the Rio Desperado country! Not the backwoods of New Mexico!"

"You hold all the aces," said Burke quietly. "Stop the heroics, *Mister* Hinch. Get on with the killing."

"Who did you think you were fooling, Dane? We got a line on you within twenty-four hours after you arrived here."

Who had talked? The only person in Piñon who had even hinted at knowing Burke had been Sally Depree. It must have been her. Perhaps she had talked to Jesse Lester; perhaps Jesse, with his babyface and frankness only a thin disguise for his duplicity, had conspired with his sister to get Burke into the net with as little trouble as possible. If so, they did a neat job, and there would be but one answer to the question as far as Burke was concerned.

Print Campbell was sure that Burke Dane would never get back to the Valley of the Big Bonito. But he had to! Marion and her little ones depended on Burke. He'd have to cast the dice in a last wild throw—win or lose—take the stakes, or end up in a pine suit with brass handles for trimming, as Jesse Lester once suggested.

Clete smiled again. "Well, we've got plenty of rope here in the Valley, Mister Dane. A nice one for you, or anyone else who comes around here looking for trouble."

"How are you going to explain *this* murder to your old man?" asked Burke easily.

Clete's eyes narrowed. "What the hell do you mean?"

"It's a cinch he wasn't responsible for the death of my

brother, Hinch. So happens your *father* hired me. Is he letting you take over the Double Bar H right under his nose? That isn't like Ben Hinch, Clete."

"He's suspicious of you!" snapped Clete.

"Maybe," agreed Burke. He smiled. "Well, go ahead, Clete, string me up, then explain it to your father. Damned if I wouldn't crawl out of my grave to listen to you explaining it too!"

"He might be right, Mister Hinch," said Larry Newman.

"You crawling out of this, Larry?" sneered Clete.

"You know better than that. I got no use for this *hombre,* but I don't want to get into trouble with Ben Hinch."

"I'm running this show!" yelled Clete.

"Sure you are," soothed Burke. "You tell the boys that, Clete."

"Damn you!" Clete jumped to his feet, and as he did so, a silent message sped from Belle Lester's lovely eyes to Burke Dane. The young woman jumped to her feet and snatched a heavy cut-glass decanter from a side table. She swung it against the side of Clete's head and he went down heavily.

Belle grabbed Clete's gun from the table and fired at Shorty. The little man went down without a sound. Burke whirled, clamping a hand down on Newman's gun wrist. His Colt exploded, driving a slug into the floor. Burke's right fist smashed against Newman's jaw, driving him back against the door which flew open, letting Newman fall into the hallway. Burke whirled and drew his derringer, firing almost from floor level up at the man standing in the bedroom door. He grunted and staggered back and the second slug caught him full in the belly.

Belle darted across the room, raised a picture on the wall, and revealed a wall safe. "Keep guard!" she snapped at Burke. Burke picked up his Colt and then reloaded his derringer. Powder smoke was thick in the room. Burke picked up Shorty's Winchester from the man's stiffening hands. He walked to the door and kicked it open, Winchester at hip level, but there was no sign of Larry Newman in the hallway.

The safe clicked open. Belle took out a thick envelope and handed it to Burke. He flipped it open with a thumb, and saw the thick wad of bills in it. Belle picked up a Colt. "Let's get out of here," she said.

Burke looked at Clete. "I'm not done yet."

Her Colt prodded into his hard belly. "Forget him!" she snapped. "We're going to get Jesse and get out of this valley before dawn."

"I had two reasons for coming here," he said stubbornly.

"You kill Clete, and Ben Hinch will never stop hunting you down! Killing Clete won't bring back Charley Mayo, Burke! The money is yours. Now you keep your deal with me!" The Colt hammer clicked back under her thumb.

"All right," he said. She was using her head better than he was. He led the way along the hall, watching for a sudden movement. He remembered again Newman's threat, "I won't forget you, Dane. Ever."

Belle stopped at a door. She tried it and found it locked. She tapped on it. "Jesse? Sally?"

There was a soft rustling sound from within, then the door swung open. Sally Depree stood there, clad in a sheer negligee that did nothing to conceal, but instead accentuated her nakedness beneath it. The lamplight shone on her soft white skin, and on the little locket between her thrusting breasts. "Jesse ain't here," she said quickly. She paled at the look on Burke's face. He thrust her aside. Belle closed the door behind her. Jesse lay face downward on the bed, one slim hand resting on the floor, holding an empty whisky glass in it.

Burke walked to the Kid and pulled him up from the bed. He shook the lolling figure and slapped the flushed face. "No use, Belle," he said over his shoulder. "He can't walk."

"Carry him, then," she said sharply.

"Leave him be!" cried Sally.

Belle looked coldly at her. "We're getting Jesse out of this hellhole of a valley," she said thinly, "and no one is going to stop us, Sally."

The girl laughed. "You're not out of it yet. How many men have you killed tonight, Burke Dane? How many more will you kill before they kill you!"

There was only one thing to do. "Sally," said Burke. As she looked at him he struck her neatly on her smooth, small jaw. He caught her before she hit the floor. It was only a matter of minutes to bind her with her sheer silk stockings and thrust a gag into her pretty little red lipped mouth. The last thing Burke did was to take the locket from her neck, wipe it hurriedly on his shirt, then thrust it into a pocket.

Belle carried the Winchester and led the way as Burke carried the Kid along the deserted hallway to the rear stairs. She snatched up Burke's slicker and hung it over the Kid as Burke carried him down the stairs.

Burke splashed through the muddy water of the alley-way, thinking incongruously of Belle Lester's fine satin slippers as she waded along behind him, cursing softly under her breath. There was so little time. Larry Newman wasn't sitting on his duff at that moment. He was up to no good, and it was only a matter of time before Clete Hinch came back to the world of the living and made an attempt to peddle a little more death before that wet night was over.

They reached the livery stable in safety. The three houses were saddled before Burke and Belle went to the hotel and the liveryman, with twenty bucks in his jeans, had vanished for the night. Belle hurriedly stripped off her finery in the dark and dressed herself in trail clothing. Burke hoisted the Kid into a saddle and lashed him there.

They had need of his fast gun that night, but in his condition he could hardly see and think well enough to draw and shoot.

Burke led his horse and the Kid's out into the alley.

Belle slid the door shut behind her horse. Burke looked at her. She smiled. "So far so good," she said.

"Yen," he said dryly. He wished to God he was alone, but if it hadn't been for Belle Lester he'd be dead by now. A deal was a deal.

The rain slashed down as they reached the next street. Burke scouted ahead, then waved Belle on. She hurriedly crossed the street, and just as she did so, five horsemen splashed through the mud of the main street. Burke saw Larry Newman wave to them from the far side of the street.

Burke led the way along the alley until they reached the next side street. He motioned to Belle to stay there. He took his Winchester and padded up to the main street, stepping into a deep doorway where he could see the wet bulk of the Hinch Hotel. Horses stood in the side street, and even as he watched he saw Larry Newman come out of the side entrance, helping Clete Hinch to a horse.

Burke hurried back to Belle. "Newman's gotten some help. Clete just joined them. They have horses. They'll cover the roads out of town. We've got to get to the bridge before they do!"

They mounted and rode to the east toward the roaring river, then turned up the street that paralleled the river. "Take him across," said Burke. Belle led the Kid's horse across the bridge. A man shouted down the street.

Burke stepped out from behind the corner building and placed a shot in the leading horse. The man went down with a grunt into the cold mud. It wasn't either Hinch or Newman. Burke spurred the dun across the bridge. Water was already lapping over the upstream side. By dawn the bridge would either be swept away or feet deep in flood water. The icy thought came to him that they must again cross the river before hitting the road to Windy Pass. There was no other way as close as that to escape the Valley of the Bio Desperado. The bridge spanning the East Fork, miles to the east, was a structure long past its prime. If it was washed away before they crossed, they would be trapped.

On the far side of the river Burke turned and churned out half a dozen slugs down the center of the bridge, then he turned and galloped off after Belle and the Kid.

Time and time again in the next hours he waited as Belle went on through the wet darkness with Jesse, hoping their pursuers had given up. But twice more he had to fire back at them, and he knew then that Clete Hinch could never let Burke escape that damned valley with the money that rightfully belonged to Marion Mayo. If Burke didn't feel responsible for Belle and the Kid he would have been able to make it, he was quite sure of that.

Lightning crackled now and again across the streaming skies as they rode steadily toward the crossing of the East Fork. An hour before dawn Jesse Lester managed to get enough sense back into his drugged head to sit up in the saddle, and also enough sense to keep his mouth shut when he saw the taut faces of his sister and Burke Dane. Jesse knew well enough what would happen to all of them if Clete Hinch caught up with them.

They could hear the roaring of the East Fork long before they reached it, and when they did, a flood of sickness welled up within them, for the water was running inches deep across the floor of the bridge, and the structure was actually curved from the great pressure of the rising flood waters.

"The weight of a horse will cave in that damned thing," said Jesse thickly.

"We can't swim them across," said Burke.

"We can't go back" said Belle flatly.

Burke spat into the flood, then dismounted. He took the reins and started out on the sagging bridge, feeling the pull and tug of the flood. The water was at boot top level, and cold as ice. His heart was in his throat as he moved across foot by foot. It took him fifteen minutes to cross and even as he reached the safety of the ground something snapped in the middle of the bridge and it assumed a sharper curve.

The Kid was next. The mid-bridge water was rushing about his knees and even as he worked his way closer to the bank it rose above them. He led his horse up the bank. There was a sickly white look on his face. "She can't make it, Burke," he said. "Let her go back. They won't kill a woman. She's got Clete wrapped around her little finger."

"Not now," said Burke quietly. "That bastard won't ever forgive her for what she did."

The young woman led her mare to the end of the bridge and looked across at them. Burke's heart went out to her. He should have let her come across first, but if the bridge had failed them then, she would have been surely lost. Belle started across, with the water swirling about her thighs.

"Sheer guts," said Jesse. "That's my *sister*, Burke!"

"Shut up!" snapped Burke. He reached for his reata and coiled it in his left hand, letting the loop hang loosely at his side. "Get your rope, Kid."

She was twenty feet from the bank when the shot rang out from the west bank and the mare whinnied in pain, tearing loose the reins from Belle's hands. The mare floundered about and stepped from the side of the bridge. In an instant the surging waters carried her swiftly downstream and out of sight.

Burke threw his loop neatly about Belle's shoulders.

She had the presence of mind to thrust her arms through the loop and settle the reata under her armpits.

Burke began to pull her toward the bank, hand over hand.

Orange-red blossoms of gunfire dotted the darkness on the far bank. Hungry lead whined through the air. Slugs spurted the racing waters.

"Shoot, damn you!" yelled Burke to the Kid.

Jesse drew his Colts and began to pour hot lead across the river. Just as Belle reached the bank and Burke got his arms about her he felt her jerk. "Are you hit?" he asked.

"Just a skinning, Burke," she cried.

"Can we hold 'em here at the river?" said Jesse as he reloaded.

Burke looked closely at the young woman. She was holding her full lower lip between her white teeth. "Let's pull leather," he said. He hoisted Belle up into his saddle and led the dun along the muddy road. Jesse fired his guns dry, then followed them. Burke looked back at the bend in the road. Already one of them was halfway across the bridge and another of them had started across. Maybe the Kid had been right. Burke looked up at Belle. Her face was white and set. There was no time to examine her wound.

The sky was graying and the rain was slackening when they reached the foot of Windy Pass. An acute weariness flowed through Burke as he slogged on.

"Maybe we'd better make a stand, Burke?" said the Kid.

"Keep moving, damn you!" roared Burke.

Even as he spoke a gun cracked flatly, from *ahead* of them, and the Kid's horse went down thrashing. Burke jumped to one side and hauled on the reins of the dun. He led it into the thick wet brush and yanked his Winchester free from its scabbard. Then a rifle flashed behind them, followed by the reports of several others. A slug whipped through the top of Burke's soaked Stetson.

"Trapped, by God!" snarled the Kid. "We should'a held 'em at the bridge!"

Then it was quiet as the sky lightened and the powder-smoke drifted off on the freshening wind.

"How many of them?" asked the Kid softly.

"Six, counting Hinch and Newman."

"Great."

Burke checked the Winchester, then peeled off his slicker and tossed his hat to one side. "Stay here," he said. "I'll try a little bushwhacking."

"Let me go!"

Burke looked at him. "In *your* condition? You wouldn't have a chance, Kid." He vanished into the wet and clinging brush.

Jesse held his cocked Colts in each hand. He wet his dry lips. His head pounded like a tom-tom and the dregs of his liquor-drinking were playing hell with his guts. He shook his head. Belle opened her eyes. She winced a little as she moved. The Winchester was leaning against a log. She gripped it, steadied herself, then brought it down hard on her brother's head. Jesse sank to the soaked ground and lay still. A thin trickle of blood traced a zigzag course down the side of his white face.

CHAPTER TEN

T he icy water soaked through Burke's clothing as he bellied through the brush. He crawled across a ditch that was six inches deep in running water and lay flat against the ground, trying to skylight some of their pursuers. It beat him as to how some of them had gotten ahead of them on that road, but the fact that Burke was afoot and that Belle had been in greater pain than she had let on, had slowed them too much to reach the top of the pass before Hinch and his corrida did.

Burke cocked the Winchester. He saw a vague movement in the brush on the far side of the road. He picked up a rock and heaved it high overhead to land behind whoever was over there. A sudden movement betrayed the man. Burke got to his knees and fired twice and the lead found its mark. The man went down silently. Burke dropped flat and rolled over and over in the icy mud as bullets pocked the place from where he had fired. One down, five to go. Damn that drunken Kid anyway! He had left it all up to Burke, and the odds were far too high against one man.

Burke lay still, peering through the dripping brush as the fight grew steadily. Bagged dark clouds raced across the cold gray sky. The road was empty of life. It was too quiet to suit Burke. He bellied along the ditch, rounding a huge boulder and as he peered across the road he saw a man running across it. He fired three times and the man went spinning down the wet slope, screaming like a stuck pig.

Smoke rifted as the wind shifted a little. There were still four of them in those wet woods waiting for a shot at Burke. What the hell was the Kid doing? Burke lay flat and waited. There was nothing else he could do. They'd have to reveal themselves to him, for if they saw him, the odds were that at least one of them would get in a disabling or killing shot.

Burke moved a little. A gun snapped and the slug smashed into the rick inches from his face, stinging it with lead fragments. He winced in pain and raised his body. As he did so a gun cracked again and the slug smashed into his left boot heel, ripping it cleanly off and numbing his left foot. He scuttled for cover. As he did, he saw a movement in the brush. He snapped up the rifle and fired. The gun jerked in his hands. It didn't sound right. He peered along the wet barrel and saw a bulge on it, terminating in a split. He cursed under his breath. He had accidentally plugged the barrel with mud and the gas and slug of the cartridge he fired ruined the barrel.

He drew his Colt and checked it. He was at a distinct disadvantage now. One pistol man against four riflemen, and they were Double Bar H riflemen—three of them paid gunfighters. They wouldn't miss.

Suddenly there was an outburst of rifle firing from the place where Belle and the Kid lay hidden. A man yelled in savage pain. Another darted out of the brush, falling to his knees to claw at his shoulder. A slug drove him face flat into the mud and he lay still. Burke jumped to his feet and rounded the boulder. A gun cracked and the slug deeply skinned his left shoulder and the pain of it drove him staggering out into the open road before he could help it. He dropped his Colt and clawed for it

"Leave it be!" said the flat, cold voice.

Burke looked up into the set face of Larry Newman, Colt in hand. Burke came up at an angle, driving in hard at the gunfighter as the Colt exploded, ripping through Burke's jacket. Burke brought a knee up into Newman's groin and as the gunfighter grunted in agony, Burke tried to rip his gun away from him. The six-shooter slammed out a shot and the lead traced a burning course up Burke's left forearm to lodge in the hard muscle above the elbow joint. Before he fell he ripped out his derringer and fired it upward into Newman's chin two feet away, and the man's face seemed to explode as the soft-nosed slug drove home to his brain.

Sheer and excruciating pain flowed through Burke Diane and he knew he was through fighting. He fell flat on his face and managed to cock the derringer for the last cartridge in it. It was then he saw Clete Hinch running up the road toward him with Winchester in hand. There was a look of complete triumph on the man's face, mingled with the sheer lust of killing. He came on, passing the place where Belle and the Kid were hidden, and Burke Dane knew that death, in the shape of Clete Hinch, was on its swift and merciless way to him.

"Clete! Clete Hinch!" cried the voice.

The man turned. Belle Lester stepped out into the road, Winchester at hip level, face set and taut, with fines etched deeply on the beauty of it. Even as he stared she fired from the hip, reloaded and fired again. Hinch went down, and three more slugs rapped into his prone body. His hands dug into the cold mud then stiffened. A moment later Belle Lester fell beside him.

Burke forced himself to his feet. The woods were quiet again. He knew that none of them were left alive. He bound his wound with his scarf and walked to Belle. He turned her over and looked into her sightless eyes.

The Kid was sitting up, holding his battered head in his hands. "I never saw her buffalo me, Burke," he said.

Burke dropped on the log and passed out completely. When he came too, he found that the Kid had neatly bandaged his wound.

"The slug went clean through," said Jesse. "Damned lucky for you it didn't hit the bone."

They wrapped Belle's body in a blanket and placed it on one of the horses the Double Bar H men would never need again. The Kid found a mount and they led the horse carrying Belle's body up the long road toward the top of Windy Pass. They never looked back. After the slaughter of that morning, it was hardly likely Ben Hinch would attempt a pursuit. Besides, Ben Hinch knew better than to try his power beyond the Valley of the Rio Desperado.

At the top of the pass, Burke looked back, down on the swirling mists of the Valley of the Rio Desperado, as he did once before, not so long ago, wondering what was in store for him in that cold shroud of mist and rain. He did what he had set out to do, but at a terrible price. He knew now that his gunfighting days were over forever. The thought of Marion Mayo came to him from the eastern side of the windswept pass. If she'd have him, he'd settle down, but somehow he knew that a part of him was gone forever, and that it would be buried in the grave with the lovely body of Belle Lester.

"Come on, Kid," he said.

"Where to, Burke?"

"The Valley of the Big Bonito."

"What's there, *amigo?*"

Burke smiled evenly. "Your whole future life, Kid, if you want to make it that way. Once you descend the eastern side of Windy Pass, you can make your own decision."

As they started down toward the Valley of the Little

Bonito the sun appeared through a rift in the hurrying clouds and shone down on the two horsemen.

Jesse Lester rolled a cigarette and handed it to Burke, then rolled one for himself. He lighted both cigarettes, blew out a puff of smoke and said quietly, "I owe it to Belle, Burke. I've made up my mind."

To Burke it seemed as though somehow in the tangled way of life and death, his younger brother had been returned to him in the form of Jesse Lester. There was no use in looking back. The future beckoned. It was better that way. Somewhere in the woods below the pass a jay scolded. A doe bounded cleanly across the road. The clouds drifted off and the drying sun shined fully on the Valley of the Little Bonito. The storm was over.

TOP GUN

To My Brother George

CHAPTER ONE

T he Mogul puffed into life and pulled the rattling cars off into the darkness, trailing a cloud of smoke and sparks. Dade Averill stood beside the tracks and watched the cars swaying on the strap iron of the branch line as he lit a long cigar. He drew the smoke into his lungs and looked down the dusty main street of Estanque, dozing in the late afternoon sun. Five years before, Estanque had been nothing, but the decaying remains of an old New Mexican ranch. Now the street was lined with false-fronted wooden buildings intermingled with old adobes.

Dade picked up his heavy handbag and brushed the soot from it. The locomotive whistled dolefully in the hills to the north of town. Dade moved ahead and crossed Railroad Street.

A piano tinkled off-key as Dade passed the first saloon. He could see at least four other saloons along the main street. He was even with The Star of New Mexico when the batwings crashed open and a slim man staggered out, caught at a post, and then fell into the street. Dade stopped and took his cigar from his mouth. A bigger man loomed in the wide doorway of the saloon. He crossed the warped porch with plunging strides and reached down to grip the slim man by the collar. He dragged him to his feet and slashed at the bleeding face with a thick fist

Men stopped to watch. The young man, hardly more than a kid, was taking a deadly rawhiding. Droplets of blood flew from his slack mouth. The big man threw him to the ground and raised a boot, armed with a cruel Mexican spur. The kid rolled away and clawed for his six-gun.

The big man dropped both hands for a double draw.

The kid was almost out. Dade dropped his handbag and strode in between them.

"Get outa the way!" the big man yelled.

Dade looked into the broad face. "The kid hasn't got a chance," he said quietly.

The angry man glanced down at Dade's waist. The black frock coat was unbuttoned but there was no sign of a gun. Then the man looked up into the lean face, shaded by the white Stetson. The hard gray eyes held his.

Men had stopped to watch the byplay between the two. "That's Boone Burkitt, stranger," one of them said. "Fast as greased lightning and eleven claps of thunder with a six-gun."

Dade nodded. Burkitt's hands twitched. "You got brass balls cutting into this," he said in a low voice.

Dade smiled. "I happen to like fair play."

Burkitt looked about the crowd, desperately wanting to pare this tall stranger down to size, but not sure of his man. "Who're you?" he asked.

"Averill. Dade Averill."

Burkitt eased back. He spat to one side and hitched up his heavy buscadero belt. "All right," he said. "But get him outa my sight!" He strode back into the saloon.

Dade turned to the shaking kid. "You'd better have a doc look at that mouth," he said.

The blue eyes flashed. "I could have taken care of him."

Dade smiled. "Sure. Sure. But don't draw on a man from the ground, son unless he's got his cutter out."

The kid wiped his bleeding mouth and looked at the blood on his slim hand. "One of these days," he said, I'll..."

A short man leaning against a post glanced at Dade and then at the kid. "You'll do as the stranger says, Jimmy Harshaw," he said. "Get that mouth looked at. Burkitt would have killed you if this man hadn't stepped in between. Then there would have been hell to pay."

The kid thrust out his chin. "Yah? My dad would cut Burkitt down to size if he killed me."

"A lot of help to you that would be. Besides, your father wouldn't have a chance with Burkitt. You know it and he does, too."

"Shut up, Shorty!"

Shorty shrugged. He spat a stream of tobacco juice into the street. "It's your fight, Jimmy."

Dade picked up his bag. "Where can I find Miles Moilan?" he asked.

Jim Harshaw bent down for his hat and cuffed the dust from it. "I'll show you." He set off up the street. Dade glanced sideways at the kid. "What was the fight about?"

"Burkitt made a nasty remark about my sister." "Enough to make any man fight, eh?" Jim nodded. He grinned. "I guess I'm just too hot-tempered. I should have known better, but it got in my craw." He looked at Dade. "Why do you want to see Miles?"

"Business."

Jimmy jerked his head toward a frame building. That's Miles' place. The *Estanque Star.*"

"Newspaper?"

Jimmy nodded. Miles owns the newspaper, a saloon, a livery stable, and a feed warehouse. You might say he owns Estanque."

Dade stepped up on the boardwalk. "Keep away from that saloon, Jim. At least tonight"

The blue eyes held Dade's. "Thanks, I will. Say, I didn't see a gun on you. Where do you keep it?"

Dade smiled. "Where I can get at it the quickest"

Jimmy nodded. "I get it. I'll see you, Mister Averill!"

Dade watched the slim young man plod down the street. It had been a close thing.

Dade opened the door of the newspaper office. A bespectacled man wearing black sleeve guards looked up from a roll-top desk. He stood up and came to the counter littered with past issues of the paper. "Can I help you, sir?" he asked.

"I'd like to see Miles Moilan."

The pale eyes blinked behind the thick glasses. "You mean *Mister* Moilan?"

Dade nodded.

"I'll see if he'll see you. Mister Moilan is a busy man."

Dade pushed open the swinging gate and followed the man toward the back of the big office. The man turned. "You wait out there!" he Marked.

Dade grinned at the little bantam. "Look," he said, "I've ridden that damned train for the past eight hours to see Miles. At his request!"

"What's going on out there!" a bull voice roared from the inner office.

"Mister Moilan, there's a man out here who insists on seeing you," shrilled the little man.

"You tell him I'm busy."

The little man turned with a superior smile. "You see?"

Dade gripped the man by a thin arm and moved him aside. He opened the door of the office and coughed as the thick tobacco smoke flowed out around him. He said, "Do I have to fight my way in to see you?"

Miles Moilan was a big man, hewed from a solid block of hard flesh. His huge head was lowered as though he was thinking of charging Dade like a Ladino. The frosty blue eyes had a dangerous glint in them. Then Moilan raised his head. "Well, I'll be damned!" he roared. "Dade! Dade Averill, you old maverick!"

Dade grinned as he thrust out a hand and Moilan's paw gripped it. Moilan looked past Dade. "It's all right, Eskew," he said.

Eskew closed the door behind Dade, muttering to himself.

Dade dropped his bag and sat down in a battered chair. He shoved back his hat and rent his cigar. "You've put on weight, Miles," he said with a grin.

Moilan slammed a huge hand down on his littered desk. "I can still take you in a rough-and-tumble, Dade, 'and don't you ever forget it!'"

Dade waved a hand. "I can't."

Miles guffawed and leaned back in his chair, studying Dade. "It's good to see you," he said. "Tell me about yourself. Where have you been since we were together in Tucson?"

"I drifted south into Sonora. Bought an interest in a mine but the revolutionaries stopped that. I was in El Paso for a time. Later in the Panhandle. Spent some time in Hays City and Dodge."

"Still working as a lawman?"

"At times. A little gambling. Some speculation."

Miles nodded. He reached into a cabinet and brought out a bottle and glasses. He filled the glasses. "I suppose you're wondering why I wrote to you?"

"I didn't ride that two-bit train all the way here to ask about your health."

Miles grinned. "I've got a job for you if you're interested. How about it?"

"You're talking."

Miles sipped his liquor. "I came up this way four years ago. The old Estanque Ranch was for sale at a soft price. I bought it. I started a freighting business and made money. I built a saloon and made money. First thing I knew there was a town here. I was in the driver's seat. Why they even wanted to name the town after me. You know I couldn't see *that!*"

"You're too modest."

Moilan said dryly, "Anyway, I'm the kingpin in these parts. There ain't a thing goes on around here without me having a finger in it. I been running this town, and the county to boot, up until the last three months. A man by the name of Glenn Tagger buys the old Bascomb Ranch and calls it the Lazy T. First thing I know he gets the idea that he can run the county as well as me,"

"Impossible!"

"Shut up and listen! Well, Tagger gets riled at my sheriff. Gil Harshaw is a good man, but Tagger wants another man to wear the star."

"Did you say, Harshaw?"

Moilan looked quickly at Dade. "Yeh. Why?"

"I'll tell you about it later."

Moilan refilled the glasses. "The upshot of the whole thing is that Tagger has a *corrida* of hard cases out at his place. Come in here and raise hell and laugh at Harshaw. Harshaw is gutty, but he's getting too old to handle the job. Alex Ray, his deputy, is a good man but troublesome. The face is, Dade, that Tagger's men have Estanque almost treed."

"Go on."

Moilan suddenly looked a little tired. "I worked hard around here. I've got a lot invested here and in the county. If Tagger gets his man in for sheriff, it'll cost me plenty."

Dade leaned back in his chair and lit another cigar. "Has he got a man?"

"Yeh. Chris Guthrie."

"Who's he?"

Moilan leaned forward. "A man like you, Dade. Younger. But fast with a six-gun and not afraid to use it.

No nerves. Damned little conscience. He's working for Tagger now, biding his time until the election."

"Which you'll rig."

Moilan shrugged. "I'm not sure," he confessed. "Tagger has a lot of friends in the county. There's a chance Guthrie might get elected."

"Where do I come in?"

Moilan smiled. "You work for me. Like my right-hand man. I'll pay you three hundred a month and expenses."

Dade inspected his cigar. The same old deal. He had been offered many of them. Some of them he had taken. This gun for hire. A good gun, fast and accurate. Shooting down men who didn't agree with the boss.

"Well?"

Dade looked down.

"I'll make that four hundred!"

Dade drained his glass. Miles had once saved his life when Dade had been downed in a cantina brawl in Tucson. How could he tell him he was fed up being a hired gun slick? That he. wanted to settle down? He was thirty years old with nothing but his guns and clothes to show for it, plus a thousand eagles earned the hard, hard way in the toughest towns in the Southwest

Miles spat angrily into the cuspidor at his feet. The metal rang with the wet impact. "Dade," he growled, "you drive a hard bargain. All right! I'll give you a cut on my take. That plus four hundred a month!"

Dade looked up. "Give me time to think about it, Miles."

"Don't you play cozy with me, Dade!"

Dade grinned at the choleric old man. "Listen, I'll take the three hundred, *if* and *when* I decide to work with you."

Miles tilted his big head to one side. "You haven't lost your nerve?"

"You know Boone Burkitt?"

Miles sat up straight. "Do you?"

"He was whaling the devil out of Jim Harshaw outside a saloon when I was coming here. Harshaw was going to draw, and I figured Burkitt would kill him. I stepped in between them."

Moilan wet his lips. "And I thought you had lost your nerve!"

"Who is Burkitt?"

"Two-gun man. The town's hard case."

"Is he a Tagger man?"

"No. Neither is he a Moilan man. He looks out for Boone Burkitt."

Dade stood up. "I'm tired and mighty dirty."

"Try the Territorial House. Nice place."

Dade grinned. "Yours?"

"I own a half interest."

"I'll see you later, Miles." Dade smiled, picked up his bag, and left Moilan's office. Eskew looked up at him as he walked through the outer office and closed the front door behind him.

Miles Moilan came into the outer office. He bit the end from a short cigar. "Run a Personal, Eskew," he said.

Eskew picked up a pencil and looked expectantly at his boss.

Moilan paced back and forth. "Among the leading citizens of New Mexico now in our midst," he dictated, "is Dade Averill, Esquire. Mister Averill has served as a law officer in Arizona, Texas, and Kansas. He is here to visit his old friend and business associate of past years, Miles Moilan."

Eskew looked up, nibbling at the end of his pencil.

Moilan worked his cigar over to the far side of his mouth. "Mister Averill has survived many warm and tragic encounters with men who challenged his skill with the six-gun. It is safe to say that he is one of the fastest men in the West in the use of the six-gun. He has always used his skill and courage on the side of law and order."

Moilan looked through the dusty front window. "Italicize the last three words."

Eskew looked up. His face had paled. "He's really that good, Mister Moilan?"

"Good! Why he'd take Boone Burkitt and Chris Guthrie on and walk away leaving them dead before they got their cutters clear of leather!"

Eskew whistled. He ran a ringer around beneath his celluloid collar.

Moilan peered through the front window at the lamplit street. "Yes, sir! I've got a man here now who'll let people know that Miles Moilan hasn't lost his grip! Wait until this paper hits the street. Hawww!"

CHAPTER TWO

D ade's room was one of the best in the Territorial House. It overlooked the corner of Main and Ocotillo. He peeled off his frock coat and silk shirt and carefully washed the travel grime from his face and hands. He wet his comb and ran it through his thick brown hair. He eyed a touch of gray at the temple, and then grinned as he saw that it was a trace of soap from the comb. He leaned forward, studying the lean planes of his face. It had been a long, hard road since he had run away from home at the age of sixteen. It had been fourteen years since he had been in Missouri.

Dade dropped in a chair beside the bed and drew his silver-cased Colt.44 from the leather-lined hip pocket. He placed it on the bed after wiping the dust from it. From his bag, he took a stubby Colt.44 double-action. The front sight and hammer spur had been filed off and the front of the trigger guard cut away for easy access to the trigger. It was an ugly, deadly belly-gun. He added a Remington double-barreled derringer to the other guns and sat looking at them as he lit a cigar. They were the tools of his trade.

Dade leaned back in his chair and smoked slowly. He could have filed four notches on the Colt single-action, and one each on the belly-gun and the derringer. He could see the faces of the men he had killed. The unknown saddle tramp who had tried to take Dade's roan away from him near old Tascosa in August of 73. The Mexican in Tucson who had made the mistake of pulling a *cuchillo* on Dade in 75. The killer who had been trapped by Dade's posse in the Huachucas. The gambler who had drawn on Dade in Mobeetie in 77. The wild Texas trail-driver who had killed a hurdy-gurdy girl in Hays and then had gone berserk. That had been in 77 too. The hardcase in El Paso in 82 who had just been released from Hunts-ville Pen and had recognized Dade as the man who had put him there.

An old-time lawman in Benson had told him it was easy to loll another man once you had bloodied your guns, but it hadn't come true for Dade. He could remember all of them, and each of them sometimes came back through the haze of time to look at him with glazed eyes.

Dade got up and paced back and forth. It was his profession but how long could he last? Someday another man would come along a hair faster than Dade. Then Dade's killer would be sought after as the man who had killed Dade Averill. He, in turn, would wear the top badge until someone else finished him off. *Top gun.* It was a title hard to win and harder to keep.

He wondered what Chris Guthrie looked like. He was younger than Dade. Dade had more experience against the speed of youth. Burkitt was another possibility. A two-gun man. Dade grinned wryly. "If you can't kill with one gun, two won't make any difference," he said aloud. It was poor comfort to him.

Dade slid his single-action Colt into the leather-lined pocket, the belly-gun into his left coat pocket, the derringer into his right-hand coat pocket. He adjusted his string tie and placed his hat on his head. For a moment, he stood there before turning off the Argand lamp, and then he withdrew the belly-gun from its pocket and put it into his bag. The original action of arming himself with it had been automatic. But he wore no star now.

He left the hotel and stopped at the street corner. The light from a store window played across the board-walk in front of him. A cool, dry wind blew in off the range. He filled his lungs with it. It was a good country.

"Mister Averill!"

Dade turned quickly to see Jim Harshaw smiling at him. Beside the kid was a young woman. There was no doubt that it was Jim's sister. She had the same light-brown hair and clear blue eyes. Her face was oval, with the mouth just a little too wide to stamp her as a real beauty, but she was mighty pretty. Dade judged her to be about twenty-one or twenty-two.

Jim tilted his head toward the young woman. "This is my sister, Lucy," he said proudly. "This is Mister Dade Averill, Lucy. The man who helped me."

She extended a small hand. Dade held it for a moment. "Thank you, Mister Averill," she said. "Jimmy should have known better than to fight with Boone Burkitt."

"Burkitt started it!" said Jimmy angrily.

"You should have walked away from him."

"He was talking about you and Glenn Tagger!"

She flushed and looked away. "We must go home, Jim. There's been enough trouble for today."

Dade smiled. "Jim said he'd stay away from Burkitt!"

"It isn't easy to do in Estanque, Mister Averill." She eyed Dade. "Are you planning to stay long in town?"

"I don't know."

A *vaquero* walked past them, turned to look at Lucy and then Dade, and hurried off down the street, glancing back over his shoulder.

Jim placed a hand on his Colt. "That was Lefty Corse," he said. "One of the Lazy T *corrida*."

Dade looked at the hurrying puncher. "So?"

"Hell run and tell Glenn he saw Lucy talking with a strange man."

Lucy flushed. "We'd best go home, Jim."

Dade raised his hat. "Good night, Miss Harshaw!"

He watched them walk down the dark street and then looked after Corse. The *vaquero* was spurring his horse out of town. Dade shrugged and crossed the street to The Star of New Mexico. The rack was lined with hipshot ponies. One of them, he noticed, bore the Lazy T brand.

He pushed through the batwings and walked to the end of the long bar. The place was filled for so early in the evening. Some of the men looked up at him. Boone Burkitt was bucking the tiger, his black hat hanging at the back of his neck from the *barbiquejo,* chin strap. A fat man leaned over and spoke to Burkitt. The two-gun man turned and looked at Dade coldly, then concentrated on his game.

Dade ordered rye. The bartender was a little man with a crop of red hair. "Stranger in town?" he asked.

"Yes."

"You're Dade Averill?"

Dade nodded.

The bartender nodded his red head. "I thought so. I seen you down in El Paso a coupla years ago. You was deputy-sheriff then. You up, here on business?"

"Yes."

"Law business?"

Dade sipped his rye. "Take care of your bar, Red."

The bartender bobbed his head. "No offense, Mister Averill."

A lean puncher was beside Dade. He watched Red hurry down to the end of the bar. "Red don't mean no harm, mister."

"I didn't think so."

"He's nosy, is all. Knows more about town news than the *Estanque Star.*"

"Have a drink."

"Don't mind if I do. I'm broke and was thinking of heading back to the ranch." The puncher filled his glass. "I'm Slim Boyd. Wrangler on the Lazy T."

"Glenn Tagger's spread?"

"Yes." Boyd sipped his liquor. "I was figgerin' on goin' on a high lonesome tonight, but I lost my *dinero* bucking the tiger."

Dade grinned. "Can I stake you?"

Boyd raised his shaggy eyebrows. "Now that's right handsome of you. Me bein' a stranger and all." He scratched his bristly chin. "I shouldn't ought to take it."

"How much?"

"Twenty-five will do. Ten, if twenty-five will strap you."

Dade took out two tens and a five and placed them on the bar. "I'm staying at the Territorial House."

"Ok, I'll get it back to you."

Boyd folded the bills and thrust them into a shirt pocket. He drew out the makings and rolled a smoke. "You plannin' to work here?"

Dade eyed the wrangler.

Boyd flushed. "Hell. I'm as bad as Red." He drained his glass. "I'm hungerin' to get goin'"

Dade nodded. He watched Slim walk to the table where Burkitt was playing.

"There's a lady at the door, Red!" called out a man at the end of the bar.

Red hurried around the end of the bar. Dade turned. A tall woman was standing just beyond the batwings. Her face was shadowed by her stylish hat. She spoke to Red. Red shook his head and went back behind the bar.

"Who was the lady?" asked a grinning cowpoke.

Red flushed. "None of your business, Danny."

"It was Mae, wasn't it?

"Yeh."

"Lookin' for Chris Guthrie, I'll bet."

"You win," said Red.

"You think she'd get tired of asking for him."

"Mae Delano wouldn't have to come looking for *me!*" put in another man.

Dade looked quickly at the last speaker. *Mae Delano!* He hadn't seen Mae for two years. The last time had been in Amarillo. He downed his drink and threw some money on the bar. He walked out into the darkness. A block away he saw her, crossing the street. There was no doubt in his mind that it was Mae. There was no mistaking her hourglass figure and smooth walk.

Dade crossed the street and saw her go into a trim frame house set back from the row of buildings. He walked to it and stopped at the low picket fence. Mae might have changed her ways in the last two years.

Dade stepped over the low gate and walked up on the neat porch. He tapped at the door. It swung open. She stood there in the light of a big Rochester lamp. Her thick russet hair was piled high on her shapely head. The hazel eyes, big and heavy-lashed, studied him. "Dade Averill!"

"May I come in, Mae?"

She glanced past him. "All right," she said hurriedly.

Dade closed the door behind him, wanting to take her in his arms and taste those full lips he had so often kissed. She was a woman of rich color, from the thick hair to the creamy skin, smooth and unblemished.

She sat down in a chair and eyed him. "What are you doing here?"

"Miles Moilan wanted to see me."

She raised her shapely head. "Miles? Then there will be trouble here."

"What makes you say so?"

She smiled coldly. "I know Miles Moilan and I know you. Is your gun still for hire, Dade?"

"Perhaps." He paused to light a cigar. "Nice place you've got here, Mae. How's business?"

She sat down. "I don't know what you mean."

He leaned back in his chair and eyed her. Man, but she was a woman! They had had a fine time in Amarillo until Dade had gone broke paying for her expensive tastes. His offer of marriage had been laughed at. Mae liked men, and their money, too much to have one man slip a spade bit into her pretty mouth.

"There's brandy in that decanter," she said.

Dade poured two drinks and placed one on the marble-topped table beside her. He let his hand rest on her bare shoulder. She took it away. Dade shrugged and sat down. "Odd that we should meet here," he said.

"You followed me?"

Dade shook his head. "When you turned me down, I swore I'd never think of you again."

"And have you?"

Dade looked at her. "Yes, many times."

She looked away. "I...I managed to get some money. I came here to start a place of my own. Miles Moilan wanted fifty percent of it."

"*He* would."

"Yes. I met a man here I love, Dade. I'm respectable now."

Dade raised his glass. "Congratulations."

She bit a ripe lip. "I don't know why you had to show up."

"I won't bother you, Mae... But what about Miles?"

"He hasn't talked."

Dade sipped the brandy. "Chris Guthrie is the man?"

"Yes. Do you know him?"

"Haven't had the pleasure."

She rested her head on the back of her chair. "You will. Heaven help all of us if you do."

"What do you mean?"

"Chris is Glenn Tagger's top gun. I know Miles sent for you to back his play. I don't like it, Dade."

"I'm not working for Miles yet"

"You will."

Dade shrugged.

"Your gun has been for hire for years, Dade. How long can you go on like that?"

Dade looked down at his strong brown hands. "Just how good is Chris Guthrie?"

"I wouldn't copper a bet on either one of you winning."

"He's that good?"

"Yes."

Dade stood up. "Don't worry, Mae. Your past is safe with me."

Her eyes were troubled as she looked at him. "Yes. But is my future safe with you?"

"I told you I hadn't agreed to work for Miles."

"It isn't that. If Chris hears about you, he'll want to try you. It's his way."

Dade smiled grimly. "They're all like that. Every fast man wants to be top gun."

"Why don't you leave town, Dade?"

He gripped the doorknob. "I might! Good night, Mae."

Dade walked slowly up the street. Mae Delano was the only woman he had ever met that had really excited him. There had been others. Too many, in fact... But Mae had been the only one that counted. He walked toward the nearest saloon. Somehow he seemed to see the oval face of Lucy Harshaw in the reflection of a lamp in a store window:

CHAPTER THREE

It was nine o'clock by the saloon clock when the thud of hoofs on the hard street came clearly to the men in the Bull's Head. An idler sitting by *the* door got up and peered through the dusty window. "The Lazy T bunch," he said.

The bartender paled. A man standing beside Dade downed his drink in a hurry. He wiped his mouth on a sleeve. "You'd better get the big mirror down, Harry," he said. "Me, I'm going home!"

Harry looked at the flyspecked mirror. "To hell with it," he said. "Last month I took the other mirror down and put it against the back wall. Damned if one of the Lazy T boys don't fall against it and smash it"

Dade emptied his glass and refilled it. The saloon was quiet except for the soft slap of cards and the shuffling of feet on the gritty floor.

The door banged open, and three *vaqueros* stamped in. The hanging lamps swung slightly in the strong draft from the door. Dade eyed the three men through the lifting cloud of tobacco smoke. Two of them were ordinary leather pounders. One of them was the little man Jim Harshaw had called Lefty Corse. The man next to him was tall and skinny, wearing a gaudy cowhide vest. It was the third man who stood out. He was shorter than Dade but fuller through the shoulders. His clothing was of better quality, from the figured boots to the loose gray coat. The hat was black, and of excellent quality. His six-gun was sheathed in a Missouri holster, worked in an intricate basket-weave carving.

The three Lazy T men lined up at the bar. Dade looked up into the big mirror. His eyes met those of the third man. They were hard and cold.

"That's Chris Guthrie," said a man softly to Dade. "Foreman for Glenn Tagger's Lazy T spread."

Dade looked down at his glass and refilled it. When he looked up again, he could see Lefty Corse talking out of the side of his mouth to Guthrie. Guthrie downed his drink swiftly. The old familiar look came into his eyes. The testing look.

"Have you seen Slim Boyd, Harry?" asked Guthrie.

The bartender shook his head.

"Tagger wants to see him."

"I heard he was in town, Chris."

Dade leaned his left elbow on the bar. "He's over at The Star of New Mexico," he said. "Leastways he was a while ago."

Guthrie looked at Dade. "Thanks. I'm obliged. You know Slim, stranger?"

"The name is Averill. Dade Averill."

There was a curious look in Guthrie's eyes. He glanced at Dade's waist. "Well, thanks, Averill."

Dade waved a hand.

Guthrie turned. "Let's go," he said. "You've cut the dust."

"Hellsfire," said the slim man, "I haven't had but one drink, Chris."

"That's enough."

"I'll have another."

Guthrie raised his head. "You heard what I said, Lanky."

Lanky was older than Guthrie by a decade, but he shrugged. Guthrie walked toward the door. "It's him," said Lefty excitedly. "The *hombre* that was talkin' to Lucy Harshaw!"

"Lucy's Tagger's filly, not mine. Let him worry about it," said Guthrie.

The door slammed behind them. Harry breathed a deep sigh. "I sure got off easy. I pity The Star of New Mexico, though." "Why?" asked Dade.

"I can see you're a stranger all right. The Lazy T *corrida's* been treeing Estanque for weeks."

Dade grinned. "Just good spirits."

"Yeh," said Harry dryly. *"Rye* spirits."

"How does the town take it?"

Harry refilled Dade's glass. "Well. Gil Harshaw don't like it, but Gil's getting too old to control em. You know how it is? A man wears the star for years, and then suddenly realizes he's lost his speed and guts, but he's too proud to quit the job. You get it?"

Dade nodded. "I follow you."

Harry leaned against the bar. Seems as though there's more to it than a few cowpokes feelin' their likker. Harshaw is a Moilan man. Tagger wants, to see Guthrie get the star. So Guthrie and his boys have been makin' it rough on old Gil."

"From what I've seen, you either have to be a Moilan man or a Tagger man in this county."

"That's about the size of it"

"How do you stand?"

Harry held out his hands, palms upward. "I run a nice place, Averill. Most of the small stockmen come in here.' I don't get the business The Star of New Mexico does, but I ain't sure I want it. Moilan is a good man. Tagger is a good man. By and large, I lean toward Moilan because I'm a town man. But a bartender has to be neutral, and I'm as neutral as all hell!"

Dade downed his drink. "I'll be rolling," he said.

Harry nodded. "Come in again." He watched Dade walk out of the saloon.

"Who's he?" asked a man at the end of the bar.

Harry shrugged. "The name is Averill. That's all I know."

Dade stopped to light a cigar. All of the saloons were brightly lighted and noisy. Hipshot ponies lined the racks. He suddenly realized it was Saturday night.

Dade paced slowly down to the weathered depot and sat down on a bench, watching the moon rise over the humped hills. The wind was warm and dry, bringing with it the fresh odor of sagebrush. He liked the country. He had been looking for a place like Estanque. A man could start a small business, say, a livery stable or a gun shop, and make a nice living. He took off his hat and let the wind dry the sweat. He had thought of a ranch, but he was a town man. If he stayed, he would have to side with Miles Moilan. Maybe Miles could stake him and make the way easy for him, but Miles would expect a price. A price Dade could pay but didn't want to.

Dade felt the hardness of his six-gun in its leather-lined pocket. That was the price Miles would want, Dade's skill with a gun and his ability to wear a star to put the fear of God into the Tagger outfit.

A buckboard rolled past the depot. The driver was hunched on the seat. Beside him was a bonneted woman. Two towheads showed up in the back of the vehicle, among sacks and boxes. They stared at Dade with wide eyes, shifting their jawbreakers as they rolled past the lights of the depot. There was almost a feeling of envy in Dade. Maybe he should be rolling home in the shank of the evening with a few slugs of rye in his gut and a satisfied woman next to him thinking of the new dress material she had bought to make a dress for the next square dance. Rolling along through moonlit hills to a snug ranch.

Dade put on his hat and strolled up the tracks. The

rails shone in the moonlight. Beyond the tracks he could see a low hill, the top encircled by a weathered picket fence, the crosses and headstones casting sharp shadows on the dry earth. Boot Hill. He wondered how many of the occupants had died with their boots off.

A shot split the quiet behind him, its echo slamming back and forth between the false fronts and then dying away in the hills.

Dade whirled and strode toward the street, then slowed down. A tall man was standing in the middle of the lamplit street. As Dade watched, the man fired again. The slug smashed into a store front. The man was Lanky, one of the Lazy T *vaqueros.*

"Yiiii! Yippee!" Lanky howled at the moon like a coyote. His Colt spit fire again and glass tinkled to the street from a smashed window.

"Watch this, Lanky!" a man yelled from the shadows. A six-gun spat flame three times. A tin can bounced along the street as the big slugs smashed it. It was Lefty Corse.

Dade stepped into the shadows and threw away his cigar. The few people on the street scuttled for cover. Lights went out in the windows. A man swung up on a horse and gave it the steel, cutting down a dark side street.

Corse weaved a little as he walked toward Lanky. "You drunken idiot!" he roared. "You scared the man!"

They fired together. A water bucket jumped from a hook and clattered on the ground. Another window was shattered.

A broad-shouldered man stepped out from behind a building. The moon shone on a star pinned to his shirt. He eyed the two men, wiped his dragoon mustache both ways, and then stepped into a doorway. The two cowpokes fired.

"Let's get that tin can down there, Lanky," said Corse.

Lanky grinned as he fumbled for cartridges. Corse drew out the makings and clumsily rolled a smoke.

The lawman stepped out of the shadows. A sawed-off scattergun rested across his left arm. As he passed Dade, a lamp lit up his face. It was hard and set. His hat was shoved back revealing his iron-gray hair. Dade knew it must be Sheriff Gil Harshaw.

The lawman stopped twenty feet behind the two men. "Calf rope!" he said loudly. "Grab your ears!"

Lanky dropped a cartridge. Corse turned slowly, still holding his cigarette. "It's Harshaw."

"Who did you expect?" asked Lanky with a grin. "Wyatt Earp?"

Harshaw moved forward. "Drop those cutters," he said.

Lanky laughed. Corse threw away his smoke.

Harshaw glanced nervously up and down the street. Looking for help.

"He's lookin' for Alex Ray," said Corse.

Lanky guffawed. "Alex is down at Dolly's Place."

Harshaw wet his lips. "I've got Blue Whistlers in this scattergun," he said thinly, "with split wads. Drop those guns!" Lefty shrugged. He dropped his Colt. Lanky spat and then dropped his cutter.

Harshaw moved forward. "Walk to the *calabozo,*" he said.

The trio moved slowly toward the big adobe jail. Dade felt for a cigar. Harshaw had played it right. Wait until the guns were empty, pick up a scattergun, and move in. He knew his business. Technically he had managed it. Spiritually he had been going on the drive of fear rather than the cold courage necessary to wear the star.

Dade walked toward The Star of New Mexico. Slim Boyd was leaning against his pony watching his two mates.

"What will happen now?" asked Dade.

Slim turned quickly. "Oh, it's you." He spat, "Glenn will come in the morning and pay the fines."

"Just like that."

Slim looked at him curiously. "Yeh. Just like that"

"How often does this happen?"

"Every weekend."

Dade puffed at his cigar. "Harshaw handled it well."

Slim nodded. "Gil is a good man. Damned if I don't think he's running on nerve nowadays."

The jail door closed behind the trio. Slim looked at Dade. "I got to get out to the ranch," he said. "I lost that twenty-five."

"Pay me when you get around to it."

"That's right handsome of you."

"Chris Guthrie was with those two hellions. Where is he now?"

Slim grinned. "Down at Mae Delano's. I'll tell him on my way out. *Adios, amigo!*"

"*Vaya con Dios,* Slim."

Dade watched the wrangler ride down the street. He walked to his hotel and went upstairs. He stood there for a long time looking out of the window.

The moonlight shone dully on the empty cartridge cases lying in the dusty street.

CHAPTER FOUR

A Sunday-morning calm hung over Estanque, but there was an air of tension mingled with it. The bell of the Baptist Church rang out and then the echoes died away in the nearby hills. Dade walked out of the beanery and felt for a cigar. He had had a good night's rest and had slept later than usual. In the clear morning light, the false-fronted buildings looked shabby.

A swamper shambled out of The Star of New Mexico and dumped a bucket of sour-smelling water into the street. A drunk was sprawled on one of the benches in front of the Bull's Head. A latecomer for church touched up his team as his buckboard rounded a corner dripping dust from its red-painted wheels. The woman beside the driver eyed Dade appraisingly and then looked down as her man spoke out of the side of his mouth.

A mule bawled from a corral down the street. Dade strolled toward the corral. He planned on buying a horse.

A man sat in a tilted back chair in front of Mason's Livery Stable. He nodded at Dade. "Fine mornin'"

"It is. I'm looking for a horse."

"Lost?"

"No. I'm thinking of buying one."

The man shifted his chew of spit-or-drown and spat

expertly at a tin can in the street. It jumped with the impact. "You new in town?"

"Just got in last evening."

"I got a nice roan. Five years old. Had a saddle gall but I cured it."

Dade squatted in the warm sunlight. "Is this the livery stable Miles Moilan has an interest in?"

The man grinned. "He owns it if that's what you mean."

"I'm a friend of his."

"Sho! Why didn't you say so? I got a fine bayo coyote. Three years old. That's him in the corral."

Dade looked at the horse.

The liveryman thrust out a lean hand. "I'm Joe Fettis. I run the stable for Miles. A good boss."

Dade gripped the liveryman's hand. Three horsemen jogged toward the town, raising a lazy plume of saffron dust behind them.

"Glenn Tagger," Fettis said. "Come to get his two bad boys."

"Which one is Tagger?"

"The tall good-looking *hombre* on the sorrel. The other two are Dan Wilcox and Fred King."

Dade leaned back against the sun-warmed wall. Tagger was dressed in sober black, wearing a gray hat. His blond mustache was neatly trimmed and waxed. The two hands were hard cases, both big men.

The trio drew even with Dade and Tagger looked him over. "Hello Joe," he said. He nodded at Dade.

As they passed, Joe Fettis looked at Dade. "Tagger is quite a gentleman," he said. "Some folks say he's English. Me, I think he's a Yankee from Boston or thereabouts. Loaded with *dinero*."

"I think I'll watch the show," Dade said.

Joe grinned. "There won't be any. Gil Harshaw will accept the fines and let the two boys go. It happens all the time."

Dade, strolled along the plank walk and crossed the street. The three Lazy T horses were tethered to the rack. Fred Xing leaned against the adobe wall, rolling a smoke. He looked at Dade with curiosity.

The jail door opened and Lefty Corse and Lanky shuffled out. Tagger followed them. "Where's Chris he asked.

"Damned if I know," said Lefty. He pressed a hand to his forehead. "That rotgut was terrible."

King spat. "You're gettin' old, Lefty."

"Go to hell!"

King grinned.

Tagger looked at Lefty and Lanky. "Get back to the ranch," he said.

The two cowpokes shambled to their horses. Lefty glanced at Dade and turned back to Tagger. He spoke in a low voice. Looking over Lefty's shoulder at Dade, Tagger nodded.

Lefty and his shaky pal rode out of town.

As Tagger walked toward The Star of New Mexico with his two men, Dade saw a young woman coming up Ocotillo Street. He threw away his cigar, adjusted his string tie, and walked toward Lucy Harshaw. He raised his hat. "Good morning, Miss Harshaw," he said.

She smiled. "You're up and about early," she said.

"I usually am."

"I missed church," she said. "I don't like going in late."

Dade smiled down at her. "Because all the men in the congregation would look at you and lose all interest in the sermon?"

She flushed. "There are lots of pretty girls *in* Estanque."

"You're the only one I've seen so far."

"You're forward, Mister Averill."

He bowed slightly. "Can I escort you anywhere?"

"I'm going to the jail."

"Then I'll go along."

She walked toward the adobe *calabozo*. "Dad likes his morning coffee. I usually watch the place until he gets back."

Dan Wilcox came out of The Star of New Mexico, eyed them, and went back into the saloon.

Dade opened the jail door and followed her inside. Gil Harshaw looked up from his desk. "Good morning, Lucy," he said. He looked curiously at Dade.

"Dad, this is Mister Dade Averill."

Gil Harshaw thrust out a big hand. "How are you, Averill? I've heard about you from Miles Moilan." He looked at Lucy. "Glenn is in town. He just paid the fines for Lefty Corse and Lanky Jones."

She paled a little. "Have they been making trouble?"

Harshaw stood up. "The usual thing. Shooting in the street. One of these days they'll hit somebody. I'd like to see Tagger pay their way out of that!" He picked up his hat. "I'll get my coffee," he said. "Coming, Averill? "

"I'll stay and keep Miss Lucy company."

Harshaw's eyes hardened. "You come with me. I want to talk with you."

Lucy looked from her father to Dade, then sat down and began to arrange the disorderly desk.

Harshaw opened the door.

Dade looked at Lucy. "I'll see you later," he said.

She did not look up. "Yes," she said quietly. "Later."

Harshaw walked toward the restaurant. "Averill," he said, "I know all about you."

"That so?"

"Yes. Miles expects trouble. That's why he sent for you. What do you intend to do?"

"That's my business, isn't it?"

Harshaw stopped and looked at Dade. "Yes. But Lucy is *my* business." Harshaw raised' his head. "I'm. getting too old for the star. I don't know if you know what that means." He paused. "Glenn Tagger likes Lucy. Glenn has money. He'll make her a good husband. You seem interested in Lucy. Do her a favor. Keep away from her."

"Are you speaking for Tagger?"

Harshaw's eyes went cold. "Tagger can speak for himself... and he *will* when the time comes. Frankly, I wouldn't want a man like you sparking Lucy, even without Tagger being interested in her."

Dade eyed the officer. "Supposing I tell you to go to hell?"

Harshaw flushed. "I can hold up my own end. I've handled many a man like you before."

That so? "

"Don't doubt it."

Dade grinned. "I saw you arrest Jones and Corse last night. You know your business."

Harshaw's eyes half-closed. "Yes."

Dade inspected the street. "I understand Tagger is running Guthrie against you in the election that's coming up.

"Yes."

"Curious. You're a Moilan man. Yet you give Tagger a clear track with Lucy."

Harshaw made big fists.

"What do you mean?"

"You figure it out."

"Listen to me! You keep away from Lucy. That's all you have to know."

Dade shrugged. "All right."

Harshaw stepped back. "Thanks for helping Jimmy out last night."

"It was nothing," said Dade.

Harshaw nodded. "Jimmy is wild. I'm thinking of sending him away for a time."

"You'd better. Burkitt's plenty tough."

"I can handle him!"

"Sure. But can Jim?"

Harshaw showed his fear in his eyes. The man was

worried sick, with a cancer of fear forming in him. "Remember what I said, Averill."

"I will." Dade watched the lawman walk toward the restaurant, then he turned back toward the livery stable. Suddenly he wanted to take that bayo coyote out on the open road.

The liveryman was gone when Dade entered the stable. He led the bayo coyote into the building and picked a saddle from a rack. He had just tightened the girth when he felt someone behind him. He turned. Two men were standing in the sunlit doorway eyeing him. Dan Wilcox and Fred King.

Wilcox took a cigarette stub from his thick lips and threw it away. "Where you goin' with that hoss?" he asked Dade.

Dade looked from one to the other of them. "If it was any of your business, I'd tell you."

Wilcox grinned. "Listen to *him*, Freddie. Tough *hombre*."

Fred King nodded. "I wonder if he's as tough as he talks."

Wilcox raised his thick eyebrows. "Yeh. Maybe we oughta find out." He spat

King moved to one side until there was ten feet between him and his partner. Suddenly Wilcox moved forward. Dade jumped back. Wilcox snatched up a bucket and threw it at Dade. He fended it with his left arm, wincing as the rim smashed against the bone. King whipped out his Colt. "Raise em," he said quietly.

Dade raised his arms. He could feel blood running down his numb left arm. Wilcox felt Dade's body. He whistled as he drew out the engraved Colt. "Fancy," he said. He tossed the six-shooter on top of a straw bale. He removed the derringer from Dade's pocket and placed it beside the Colt. Then he stepped back. "All right, Fred. He's clean."

King sheathed his Colt and unbuckled his gun belt He hung it on a hook. "Me first, Dan?"

"He's your pigeon."

King spat on his hands and balled big fists. Suddenly he rushed Dade. Dade stepped aside, ducking a wild blow, measuring the big man. King drove in with smashing blows. Dade blocked them and circled easily out of reach.

"Stand still, damn you!" grunted King.

He rushed. Dade jabbed out a left, felt it meet flesh, and followed through with a hard right that drove King back against a post. A bucket clattered to the floor from a hook.

"Get going, Fred!" scoffed Wilcox.

"Shut up!"

Then Dade knew they had been sent to mark him up. Beat him to a bloody pulp and dump him into the street. King rushed. Dade moved sideways, felt a fist graze his chin, hooked King in the ribs, and sledded a blow behind the puncher's ear. King wobbled. Dade hooked to the belly and followed with a sharp uppercut that drove King back against the wall. King bounced back and clipped Dade, with a meaty right.

Dade shuddered with the powerful blow. Blood filled his mouth in a salty flow. He circled about, waiting for the lights to stop dancing in front of him. King grinned, lanced in a stinging left, and followed with a right that shook Dan down to the heels.

"Get after him," jeered Wilcox.

"He's no soft touch," growled King.

You're the soft touch looks like, Freddie."

King turned to speak over his shoulder. "I'll take *you* any day!"

Dade closed in swiftly as King's head was turned. His right smashed against the thick jaw. King gagged and turned with clouded eyes. A left snapped his head back. The big man went down.

Dade stepped back, wiping the blood from his abraded hands, his breath harsh in his throat

Wilcox looked down at his unconscious *amigo*. "Well, I'll be dipped," he said with a grin. "I guess it's up to Mrs. Wilcox's little boy, Averill." He unbuckled his gun belt.

Dade spat blood. King was tough, but Wilcox looked like the big casino.

Wilcox shuffled his big feet. He tucked his granite jaw behind his left shoulder and extended a thick arm. He moved in. The blows came thick and fast, driven with terrible strength. Dade was on the ground, spitting blood and feeling a cracked tooth with his tongue before he really knew what had happened.

Wilcox grinned.

Dade got up. Wilcox skinned Dade's forehead with a left and sank home a pile-driver right that sent Dade back against the wall with a crash. The big man got eager. He sent out a hard right. Dade tilted his head. The wall shook with the impact of the fist. Wilcox roared with rage.

Dade ducked, jumped over the prostrate King, and raised his fists to meet Wilcox's bull-like rush. Dade speared him with a left and danced back. The pace was too fast, but he knew he'd have to stay on his feet or get roweled into a bloody hash.

The Lazy T man shuffled to the right as Dade circled. Dade reversed. Wilcox responded slowly. Dade blocked a right and closed in, hanging onto Wilcox. Wilcox threw him back, but Dade hit him with a hard left that shook the big man. Again Dade moved to the right. Wilcox turned. Dade landed a blow to the gut and then moved to the right. Wilcox turned clumsily, met a left jab and a right that staggered him.

Wilcox's breath rasped in his throat. He shook his head to clear it. Dade drove a fist into his rib cage. Wilcox grunted and threw his arms out wide. Dade brought up a left uppercut and snapped the big man's head back.

The head came down and met Dade's hard-rising knee. Dade felt the nose mash as it hit the knee bone. Wilcox went down on hands and knees. Dade kicked him behind the ear, and he lunged onto his face.

Dade staggered back, fighting for breath. King groaned and raised his head. Dade kicked out viciously, and King's head bounced on the ground.

Dade picked up a water bucket and slopped some of the water on his swollen face. Then he leaned against a post and felt his hands. No bones were broken.

Hoofs rang on the hard earth of the street in front of the stable. Glenn Tagger sat his fine sorrel, a puzzled look on his face as he saw Dade.

Dade jerked, his head. "Your two killers are in there."

Tagger looked past Dade. His jaw dropped. Dade felt for his gun and realized that both weapons were on the straw bale. Tagger's Colt came up and leveled. "Stand easy," he said.

Dade felt cold sweat work down his sides. Tagger lowered the Colt. "Where are your guns?" he asked. "In there."

Tagger holstered his six-gun and rested gloved hands on his saddle horn.

Dade looked up at the ranch owner, cold fury in his eyes. "The next time you want me marked up, Tagger," he said, "why don't you have the guts to try it yourself?"

A muscle twitched in Tagger's jaw. "You talk big, Averill," he said.

Joe Fettis came down the street. He stared at Dade's battered face. Dade spoke over his shoulder. "There's some manure littering your clean floor, Joe. You'd better clean it up."

Joe peered inside the livery stable. "Hellsfire," he said. "Fred King and Dan Wilcox! You do it alone?"

Tagger kneed his sorrel away from Dade. "Those two

boys will get back at you. The next time they'll kill you. You won't help Miles Moilan that way."

Dade spat blood. "I'm staying in Estanque as long as I damned well please."

Tagger shrugged. "I warned you." Dade moved forward. "Get off that cayuse," he said. Tagger rested his hand on his Colt. "Moilan is through here. Hiring a gunslick like you won't help him any. You can be cut down to size, Averill." "Get down from that cayuse and try it!" Tagger kneed his horse away from the cold-faced man. "Some other time." He spurred the sorrel toward the road, looking back over his shoulder.

Dade went inside, got his guns, and looked down at the unconscious men.

Joe slopped water on the two men. He looked at Dade. "Big casino," he said.

"Shut up!" said Dade. He wiped his mouth with his handkerchief and walked out into the bright sunlight He was sick of Estanque.

CHAPTER FIVE

The church bells were ringing for the evening service when a hard fist hammered at Dade's door. He got up off the bed and removed the wet cloth from his battered face. He picked up his Colt and stood to one side of the door. "Who is it?"

"Miles Moilan!"

Dade opened the door. The big man stamped in, shot an angry glance at Dade, and then dropped into an armchair. "Hellsfire, Dade! What are you trying to do?"

Dade filled two glasses. "Tagger's men tried to mark me. They did."

Moilan accepted his glass.

Dade sat down on the bed and gingerly touched his gashed forearm.

Moilan leaned forward. "What started it?"

"Tagger saw me talking with Lucy Harshaw. Or one of his boys did. Tagger decided to cut me out."

Moilan's frosty eyes half-closed. "Lucy Harshaw? A nice girl."

"Too nice for a gunslick?"

"I didn't say that."

"Harshaw did. Harshaw thinks Tagger is a good choice for his daughter."

"I'll agree to that. Glenn has money. Education. Breeding."

Dade downed his drink. He felt mean. "Odd that a Moilan man should want his daughter to tie in with Tagger."

Miles savagely bit the end from a short cigar and lit up. "Harshaw has been slipping. I've decided to take the sheriff's job from him."

"How about the voters?"

"Dammit! What about them?"

Dade refilled Moilan's glass. "If you kick him out, who will you replace him with?"

"You."

"I'd be shot in the back inside twenty-four hours."

Moilan eyed Dade from beneath shaggy eyebrows. "I've got Alex Ray, but I don't trust him. Ray bull-crapped Harshaw into appointing him deputy."

"Run *him*, then."

"I told you I don't trust him!"

Dade shrugged. "It's your problem, Miles."

"I might just as well have not written to you. You come here to work for me and get yourself in one helluva mess."

Dade grinned. "Oh, what a tangled web we weave when first we practice to deceive."

"Good grief! Poetry!" Miles leaned back in his chair and threw out his hand. A dollop of rye sloshed from his glass. "I can get the town votes. They know you'll keep the Lazy T *corrida* buffaloed. I still hold a lot of votes with the nesters and farmers. Tagger has the ranchers. I think we can win."

Dade walked to the window and looked out across the drab roofs of the town toward the dim hills. "I'm tired of law work, Miles. I can tell *you* that. What have I got for the years of wearing the star? Some clothes. Good guns. A thousand eagles." He turned. "You think that's all I want out of life?"

"What *do* you want?"

"A job. Maybe a business."

"Hawww! You? In a business? You make me sick."

Dade leaned against the wall watching some of the townspeople heading for the churches. "This is a nice town, Miles. A nice country. I like it."

"What changed you? Lucy Harshaw?" Dade looked at the angry man. "Supposing I am interested in her?"

Miles seemed to soften. "Look. If you take the sheriff's job, I'll cut you in on some of my profits. I've got a nice five-room house you can have. Court Lucy. Marry her. Settle down. That's fair enough."

"You conniving, low-down!"

Miles stood up and balled huge, hairy fists. "Listen! I taught you all you know about rough-and-tumble. Now I'll beat some sense into your thick head!"

Dade spoke coldly. "Don't start after me, Miles. That was years ago. I've got twenty-five years on you."

"I can still take you."

"Get out," Dade said. "I'm sick of you."

Miles chewed at his cigar. He walked to the door. He turned. "Don't buck *me*, Dade."

They looked at each other. Miles bit his lip. "I'm sorry, Dade."

Dade did not answer. The door opened and closed, and he heard the slow footsteps down the carpeted hall. It was the first time he had ever heard Miles Moilan apologize for anything.

Dade placed the belly-gun beneath his waistband in the leather pocket he had sewed inside the trousers. He buckled on the wrist clip for his derringer and snapped the little gun beneath the spring clasp, pulling his shirt and coat sleeve down over it.

Dade walked down into the lobby. The desk clerk looked up from the paper he was reading. "Good evening, Mister Averill. I see your Personal in the paper."

"What do you mean?"

The clerk turned the paper. He placed a finger on the Personal and looked at Dade as he read it aloud. "Among the leading citizens of New Mexico now in our midst is Dade Averill, Esquire. Mister Averill has served as a law officer in Arizona, Texas, and Kansas. He is here to visit his old friend and business associate of past years, Miles Moilan. Mister Averill has survived many warm and tragic encounters with men who challenged his skill with the six-gun. It is safe to say that he is one of the fastest men in the West in the use of the six-gun. He has always used his skill and courage on the side of *law and order.*"

The clerk eyed Dade. "Nice, Mister Averill."

"Who put it in?"

The clerk looked surprised. "Didn't you?"

It was the day of the paid Personal in the West. It had been Miles' way of letting his enemies know who he had drafted to help him in his political wars. Subtle as a Nueces Ladino crashing through the *tornillo* brush.

Dade walked outside. Gil Harshaw passed on the far side of the street, making his rounds. He did not look at Dade. Harshaw was Moilan's man all right. Street patrolling was a function of the city law forces: the marshal or policeman. Yet here was the top law officer of the county acting like a watchman.

Dade walked to the Bull's Head. The place was empty except for Harry the bartender and a tall man who leaned against the end of the bar with a bottle before him. He looked at Dade with hard green eyes. His hair and mustache were reddish. A bad combination thought Dade, green eyes, and red hair. Then Dade saw the star pinned to his vest.

Harry placed a bottle in front of Dade.

"I didn't expect to see you walking around after a fight like that," he said.

The man at the end of the bar looked up. "You're Averill, aren't you?"

Dade nodded. "I'm Alex Ray, deputy-sheriff." Ray walked to Dade's side. "Have a drink on me."

"Thanks."

Ray's tied-down Colt was nickel-plated with an ivory handle, fitting in with the rest of his flashy attire. He leaned on the bar. "You planning to work for Miles?"

"No."

"That ain't what the town is saying."

Dade turned his head to look at the man, slowly.

Ray smiled easily. "Don't get riled."

"I'm not."

Harry wet his lips, looked from one to the other of them, and moved away.

Ray lit a cigarette and shoved the sack of Sitting Bull toward Dade. "Smoke?"

Dade rolled a cigarette. Ray lit it for him and glanced at Harry, who was industriously polishing glasses at the far end of the bar. "The talk is that Miles is thinking of running another man instead of Harshaw for the sheriff's job."

"That so?" asked Dade politely.

"Harshaw is slipping. Figuring that you don't run for the job, I got a good chance."

"More power to you."

Ray seemed relieved. He refilled Dade's glass. Thanks. I didn't want to put you out of a job."

I'll bet you don't, thought Dade.

Ray expanded his chest. "I've got friends in town and in the county. They like me."

How can they help it? thought Dade.

Ray sucked at his smoke. "Yes, sir! The county will be in good hands if I get the job."

"You've" still got the Tagger crowd to buck. Maybe Guthrie will get the star."

Ray's eyes narrowed. "Well, I'll handle Tagger, and Guthrie as well." He tapped a finger on his Colt. "I'll show them who's boss."

"I'll bet you will."

Ray smiled with a self-satisfied smirk.

The door banged open and Boone Burkitt came in. Harry glanced at him, at Dade, and then at his treasured mirror. Boone stopped as he saw Dade. Ray turned. "Have a drink, Boone."

Burkitt swaggered to the bar and helped himself. "I been lookin' all over town for you, Alex."

"You've found me."

Burkitt downed a drink and then another.

Take it easy," said Ray.

"I can take care of myself." Burkitt glanced down at Dade's waist.

Still looking for the gun, thought Dade.

"Miles wants to see you, Alex," said Burkitt.

"Ok. See you later, Averill."

Dade nodded.

When the door closed behind the two men, Harry came down the bar. "I'm glad that's over."

"What do you mean?"

Harry shook his head. "Alex always looks for trouble and Burkitt is worse."

"They're friends?"

"In a way. Alex usually swears Boone in as special deputy when he goes after a man. Three times they went out last year. Three times they come back with the outlaw's hoss and saddle."

"So?"

Harry spat. "One of the men they killed was innocent. Miles raised hell about that, I'll tell you. Him and Bay had a helluva argument about it. They ain't been the same toward each other since. Another time they killed a man. Poor fella didn't do nothing but steal a hoss. Friend of mine told me he give up his guns. He saw it. Next thing we know, here's Bay and Burkitt comin' into town with his hoss, saddle, and guns. Sold them for what *they* called *expenses.*"

"Nice *hombres*."

"Yeh. I'd as soon bed down with a sidewinder as either one of them."

Dade glanced up at the mirror. "Why don't you sell that mirror, Harry?"

"Why?"

Dade grinned. "Every time you think there's a chance of a hassle you keep looking at it."

Harry grinned. "Yeh. Had three busted last year."

"Why don't you get rid of it?"

Harry looked at his pride and joy. "Why, man, it gives the place *tone!*"

"It sure does." Dade dropped his smoke and stepped on it. "See you later, Harry."

He walked out into the street. Only the saloons showed light.

Sunday evening. A quiet, dark night in Estanque.

CHAPTER SIX

There was no horse in front of Mae's neat frame house. Dade tapped on the door. She opened it. "You," she said quickly. "Did anyone see you come here?"

Dade closed the door behind him. "No."

"What do you want?"

"I was lonely, Mae."

"Dolly's Place is two blocks east."

Dade sat down and placed his hat on the table. "How you talk." He grinned.

"Everything is over between us, Dade. Why don't you let me alone?"

Dade leaned back. "A nice way to talk to an old sweetheart, Mae."

She filled glasses. "I'm sorry, Dade, but that's the way it is."

She brought his glass and looked down at him. "You stay here in town, and you'll get killed."

"By who?"

"Chris. For bothering me. Wilcox and King for your beating them up. There are others."

She sat down. The yellow lamplight brought out her

creamy coloring. She could act the part of a lady if she wanted to, yet there was a subtle harshness about her.

"Chris is my man, Dade."

"Has he asked you to marry him?"

"Yes."

"Don't lie; Mae."

"All right. He hasn't."

"You're making a fool of yourself, Mae."

She looked away. "You don't know what it is to want to be respectable."

"I offered you all that."

"I know."

"You loved me then."

She drained her glass and refilled it. She was slightly drunk. "I waited for him all day. I wanted to go to church."

Dade sipped the brandy. "Trails seem to cross when you least expect them," he mused. "I had no idea you were here."

"You'd better leave before he gets back." She drank again. "What do you want, anyway?"

"Just a sociable visit."

Her face was flushed. "Get out," she said.

Dade picked up his hat and walked to the door. She came to him, unsteady on her feet. "He *knows* I'm waiting for him!"

Dade turned and leaned back against the door. "Why wait? You're a good-looking filly, Mae."

She looked up at him. Her face worked. "I told you I wanted a husband."

"There are men who would do anything for you. I ought to know."

Suddenly she pressed her face against his chest. "Can we go back?" she asked.

"You know it's too late."

She slid her smooth arms about his neck and drew him close. Her lips met his, slightly parted.

Dade kissed her throat and felt her quiver. Then she drew back and looked at him. "I'll change into something else." She touched his face with warm soft hands. "I won't be long, Dade."

Hoofs clattered down the hard street. Mae paused, fear in her face.

The front gate squeaked open. She said, "It's Chris!"

Dade felt immensely relieved. He crossed the room with quick strides and went through the kitchen. He eased the door open as he heard hard knuckles on the front door.

The moon was faint in the sky. Dade crossed the backyard and went through the sagging rear gate.

He picked his way down the littered alleyway and came out on Mesquite Street. It was a street of sagging adobes, dwelled in by the Mexicans who had once populated the old Estanque ranch.

Dade stopped beneath a ramada. The dry wind cooled his overheated body. The door of a cantina opened, and a thick-bodied man came out holding a scrawny Mex by the nape of the neck. "You crazy Mex," said Harshaw. "I've told you before, Jesus, not to pull a *cuchillo* and start trouble!"

"But, Señor Sheriff! Bartolome insulted my father and my mother. That *canalla!* That *bazofar!*"

Harshaw kicked the door shut. "I'll lock you up tonight, Jesus. Tomorrow you get on your burro and head outa town!"

Dade grinned. Jesus swayed in Harshaw's tight grasp. *"Sí Sí! Mañana"* he promised eagerly.

Harshaw shoved the cringing Mex toward the alleyway.

Something moved in the shadows. Dade raised his head. The faint moonlight shone dully on the twin barrels of a scattergun. He opened his mouth to yell. The scattergun roared out with both barrels, splitting the night. Harshaw staggered with the impact of the shot went down and lay still. Jesus screamed and sprinted down the alleyway.

Dade whipped back his coat and drew his Colt. Boots smashed against the hard *caliche*. A shadowy figure threw down the shotgun and swung up over an adobe wall. Dade snapped a shot. The man grunted and rolled over the wall. Dade ran after him, tripped over a box, and hit the ground hard, skidding along on his palms. The Colt clattered against the wall.

Dade grunted in pain as he got up. His left knee was slashed open. He limped to his gun and then to the wall. He pulled himself up. Hoofs clattered against the hard earth like beans in a gourd. The man was gone. Dade walked toward Harshaw, through the hanging acrid smoke. The cantina door was open. Three Mexicans looked out at the sheriff, then saw Dade and slammed the door shut.

Dade heard boots hitting the hard earth of the street. He knelt beside Harshaw and touched the back of his head. It was completely shattered, a messy jam of bone, flesh, and blood. He felt sick as he stood up. A man stopped behind him. "What the hell is this?"

"Sheriff Harshaw has been killed," said Dade. The man looked at him. Another man hurried up the street. It was Alex Ray. He looked down at Harshaw and then at Dade. The moonlight flashed on his nickel-plated pistol as he drew it "You're under arrest, Averill," he said.

Dade spat. "Look at his head," he said. "He was killed with a shotgun. I snapped a shot at the killer. I think I winged him."

The other man knelt beside Harshaw. "He's right," he said. "No six-gun did this."

Ray holstered his Colt. "Get a stretcher, Casey," he ordered. "Who did it, Averill?"

"I don't know. Harshaw never had a chance." Ray rubbed his jaw. "He had enemies," he said. Dade looked up to see Jimmy Harshaw running toward them. The kid stopped short. "Who killed my father!" he yelled.

No one answered. Jimmy gripped Dade by the sleeve. "You did it! You got mad at Pa because he told you to keep away from Lucy."

"Shut up," said Casey. "He didn't do it."

"Then who did? *Who killed my father, Averill?*" he screamed.

Dade slapped the kid's face, hard. "Shut up! You'll do no good yelling like that!"

Jimmy placed a hand against the place where Dade had struck him. His blue eyes were wide in his white face.

Casey picked up the shotgun and looked at Dade. "Both barrels," he said.

Ray took the warm gun from Casey's hands. He lit a match and peered at the breech. "Property of the Wells-Fargo Company," he read. He looked at Casey. "The initials C.R.G. are on it, too."

"That's Chris Guthrie's scattergun!" said Casey. "He used to ride shotgun for Wells-Fargo! Took it with him when he left."

Ray grounded the heavy weapon. "Then it was Guthrie," he said thinly.

Dade was about to open his mouth. He knew Guthrie was at Mae Delano's. "You're sure?" he asked quietly.

Ray nodded. "Harshaw buffaloed Chris some weeks back. Chris said he'd get him."

Casey bobbed his head.

Dade gripped Jimmy by the arm. "Come on," he said. The man he had shot at was shorter than Guthrie by half a head and thirty to forty pounds heavier.

Jim walked slowly to Main Street with Dade. "I'll kill Guthrie," he said.

Dade shook his head. "He didn't do it, Jimmy."

"How do you know?"

Dade stopped. "I'm sure he didn't do it. Keep your mouth shut. You hear?"

The kid looked up at him. "What's going on, Dade?"

Dade looked back at the dead man. "I don't know. But you won't find out by chasing Guthrie."

"What can we do?"

"Go home and tell your sister. Stay there until I come."

The kid walked up the street.

Dade hurried toward Mae Delano's house. He untied Guthrie's roan and led it into the alleyway. He ground-reined it and walked back to Main Street. Men were hurrying toward the scene of the killing. One of them was Slim Boyd. Dade grabbed him by the arm. I want to talk to you."

"I ain't got the money I owe you, Averill."

"Forget the money! Harshaw has been murdered. Alex Ray thinks Guthrie did it. I know he didn't. Guthrie is with Mae Delano. I put his horse in the alley. Warn Guthrie to get out of town."

Slim nodded. "You want me to tell him that you sent me?"

"No. Just get him out of here."

"Ok." The wrangler walked swiftly toward Mae Delano's house.

Dade picked gravel from his ripped palms. He had no love for Chris Guthrie, but he knew the foreman hadn't killed Harshaw. Dade had marked the killer with a slug. He listened to the loud voices from the street, where Gil Harshaw lay in his blood. Ray would track Guthrie down. Things had smoothed out for the green-eyed deputy. The two men who were in his way for sheriff had been neatly taken care of, Harshaw supposedly murdered by Guthrie. Dade thought of Burkitt coming to see Alex Ray in the Bull's Head. Burkitt had said Miles Moilan had wanted to see Alex Ray. There was something insidious about the whole thing. Murder wasn't Moilan's way. Yet the big man was being driven against the wall by his enemies.

Dade walked up the street toward Miles Moilan's office. The time had come for them to talk business.

———

MILES MOILAN WAS in his own saloon, the Bee Hive when Dade walked in. The big man was standing at the end of the long bar, holding a glass in one hand and a bottle in the other. He looked up as Dade approached him. "Who did it, Dade?" he asked.

"I thought you might know."

Moilan turned slowly. "Dade, you don't think..."

Dade glanced at the bartender, who was looking out the front window at the people hurrying by in the street to the scene of the killing. Dade lowered his voice.

"No," he said. "It isn't your way, Miles. At least it *wasn't.*"

Moilan looked down at his big hands and then at Dade. "You know my way. Besides, why should *I* have Harshaw killed?"

"Ray is sure Chris Guthrie did it."

"I find that hard to believe. Guthrie has a mean streak, but if he wanted to kill Harshaw, he would have done it in the open. Guthrie is too proud of his leather-slapping ability to miss a chance like that." Moilan looked up at Dade. The usual spark and fire was missing from the older man. "I never figured on a thing like this. I figured I'd pull Harshaw out of the nomination for sheriff and try to run another man. Frankly, Dade, that's why I sent for you."

"Alex Ray wants the job."

Moilan downed a drink. "A good sheriff would have held Ray down. He had Harshaw buffaloed. Gil let Alex take over more and more of his job until Gil was nothing but a" constable. Harshaw had no business patrolling these streets at night, a prime target for anyone with a grudge against him." Moilan felt for a cigar. "What makes you think Guthrie didn't kill him?"

"I didn't say that. *You* did."

The older man glanced up at Dade and then looked away. "So I did."

"Here comes Alex Ray!" called the bartender.

The flashy deputy came in, followed by half a dozen men. "I'm forming a posse, Miles," he announced loudly. "We'll root Guthrie out of the Lazy T."

"You sure he did it?" asked Miles quietly.

Ray turned and took the murder weapon from the hands of another man. "He left this, Miles. It's Guthrie's scattergun. It's got his initials on it."

"Did you see him use it?"

"No. But Averill did!"

Dade leaned against the bar. "I didn't say I saw Guthrie use the gun."

Ray's jaw tightened. "You got in a shot at him!"

"I got in a shot at *some* man. I don't know who it was. I think I winged him."

"You sure?" asked a scowling man behind Alex Ray.

Dade shook his head. "I'm not sure of anything. I fired a shot. He grunted like he was hit. He may have hurt himself going over the wall. He was well enough to ride in any case."

Ray slapped a hand on the bar. "Drinks for the boys, Kelly," he said. "They all agreed to ride posse with me. How about you, Averill?"

Dade shook his head.

Ray spat. "You don't have to be worried," he said. "I can handle the Lazy T bunch."

Moilan spoke out of the corner of his mouth. "Maybe you'd better go, Dade. This will start a shooting if I know Alex."

"He's your man. You stop him."

Moilan glanced along the crowded bar. I'm not so sure about that."

Ray swaggered along the bar slapping men on their backs. "Drink up," he said. "I'll issue Winchesters and shotguns at the jail if you haven't got a long gun with you." He stopped beside Miles.

Miles shifted his cigar. "Don't go out there tonight, Alex."

"Why not?"

"You ride onto Lazy T land, and you'll find out"

"I'm not worried."

"Whether Guthrie did this or not, you won't bluff Glenn Tagger. Slow down. Go out there in the morning, maybe with one man. Act real nice. Maybe you'll be able to talk with Tagger, instead of getting run off with bullets helping you along."

Ray said to Dade, "Listen to *him*

"He's right," said Dade.

Alex filled a glass. "I suppose you'd handle this differently, with all your experience?"

"I would."

"How?"

"I'd look for witnesses.

"You're the only one we got."

"Did you *look* for any others?"

Ray flushed. "You didn't say anything about any others!"

"There might have been."

"Who?"

Dade was about to mention; the drunken Jesus who had been hauled from the cantina. "It isn't my job."

Ray refilled his glass.

"Go easy on the liquor," said Moilan.

"You telling me to lay off?"

Moilan's eyes flashed. "Yes!"

Ray flicked his star with the fingers of his right hand. "You see that star?"

"You keep it polished enough for a blind man to see it," said Moilan dryly.

"Well, I'm the legal law officer now in this county. Gil Harshaw was killed in the performance of his duty. I'm goin' to get the man who did it. Politics don't enter into this, Miles."

Moilan straightened himself up. "What do you mean by that?"

Ray stepped back a little. "I'm the law here. Don't you interfere with *me*, Moilan?"

In the silence that followed, the big clock chimed eleven o'clock. The men looked at Miles Moilan. This was a test of the old man's strength in Estanque, and in the county as well. Miles took his cigar from his mouth. "All right, Ray," he said. "You go ahead. But I warn you. If you go out there and start a shooting war, there'll be all hell to pay."

"I can handle myself."

Moilan looked down at the flashy Colt. "Yeh! But you've got a posse of bums from the town. They run into those Lazy T *buscaderos* and you'll all come back here with your tails between your legs."

Ray laughed. "You're getting old, Miles."

"You figure maybe you can take my place here?"

Dade shifted a little. He knew that soft warning in Miles Moilan's voice.

Ray glanced at Dade and then at' Moilan. "I fight alone, Moilan," he said.

"Meaning?"

"We all know why you brought Averill in here. Trouble is, Averill, ain't goin to play your game."

"How do you know, Ray?" asked Moilan.

"He told me so himself."

Moilan looked at Dade for a moment and then he looked away. "Go ahead then, Deputy-Sheriff Ray. Go ahead."

Ray walked away. Some of the possemen hastily slopped down an extra drink, then streamed out of the saloon after their swaggering leader.

Kelly began to gather up the glasses.

Miles relit his cigar. He looked down at his empty glass. "He tell the truth there, Dade?"

"Yes."

Miles grunted. "Seems as though I raised a traitor in the ranks," he said.

Dade flushed. "Meaning me?"

Moilan shook his grizzled head. "I know better than that. I should have known better than to have you come in here to back my play. You never went in much for politics, son. I meant Ray."

"You can get rid of him."

"Not tonight. If it had been Harshaw, I would have *ordered* him to take it easy. Seems as though I've not only got to contend with Tagger but also with Ray." Moilan shook his head.

Dade lit a cigar. "Did Ray and Burkitt come to see you about seven-thirty tonight?"

"No. Why?"

"Burkitt came into the Bull's Head and told Ray you wanted to see him."

"That's not true."

Dade nodded. He filled his glass.

Moilan eyed Dade. "Why did you ask me that?"

"No reason."

"You're lying." Moilan worked his cigar over to the far side of his mouth. "You're not planning to work against me, Dade?"

Dade stepped back from the bar. "I'm not working against anyone, Miles. But I do aim to find the man who murdered Gil Harshaw."

"All for nothing?"

"All for nothing."

Moilan nodded. "Good hunting, Dade."

Thanks, Miles."

Dade walked to the door. Miles Moilan watched him

leave. Kelly leaned against the bar. "What's bothering him, Boss?"

"His conscience."

———

DADE WALKED down the street toward the *calabozo*. It was well lighted. Horses were tethered at the hitching rack. Through the open door, Dade could see Ray swearing in his posse. Boone Burkitt was behind him, taking Winchesters from the gun rack, passing them out to the men.

Dade walked on to his hotel.

CHAPTER SEVEN

The thud of hoofs awakened Dade. He got out of bed and walked to the window. It was shortly after dawn. Coming up the broad street in the graying light, he saw Alex Ray and Boone Burkitt with two other men. A cold feeling came over Dade. Ray had sworn in at least ten men.

Dade dressed swiftly and hurried downstairs. The dusty horses were tethered in front of the jail. Dade walked toward the big adobe. Miles Moilan was coming up the street. He nodded at Dade and walked into the jail office. Dade followed him and stood just inside the door, leaning against the wall. Alex Ray was seated at Harshaw's desk. Burkitt leaned against a back wall. The other two men were gone. "Well?" Moilan asked.

Ray spat. "We got to the ranch. They was formed up for us. Some of the boys got nervous and took off like yellow-striped Ladinos. I figured I'd better come back for more help. Then we find that the Lazy T boys are behind us, in the brush and trees along the creek."

"So?" asked Moilan coldly.

"What could I do? If we made one move for a gun, we would'a been cut down. We had to leave without Guthrie."

"I could have told you that."

"We didn't see you along," said Burkitt. "Shut up!" said Miles.

Alex Ray smashed a fist down on the desk. "I'm formin' a bigger posse. With tough men. Not them drunks I took along last night."

"You think it will make any difference?" asked Moilan.

"I'll get forty good men."

"Where? You know damned well nobody will buck up against the Lazy T with them forted up."

"So what would you do?"

Miles grinned. He looked at the brightly polished star. "Remember what you said last night? 'I'm the law here. Don't you interfere with *me,* Moilan!'"

"Throw the old windbag out," said Burkitt.

Miles grinned coldly. "Take off that gun belt, Burkitt! You try to' throw me out!"

Burkitt looked past the old man at Dade. "Shut up," he said. "You talk too much."

Miles started forward and Dade gripped him by the shoulder. "Ray," he said, "go out there yourself. *Alone.* Warn Tagger that he must give Guthrie up."

"And get killed?"

"Leave your guns behind. Tagger won't shoot at an unarmed man."

Ray fiddled with the papers on his desk.

"It's your job," said Dade quietly. "Either go or send someone else."

"Who?"

"Deputize me. I'll go."

Miles Moilan eyed Dade. Then he looked at Ray. "Well?" he asked.

The deputy-sheriff glanced at Burkitt. Burkitt shrugged. "Let him go. We'll have a nice funeral service for him."

Ray stood up. "All right," he said.

Dade was duly sworn in. He pinned on the star Ray handed him. "Write out a warrant," he said.

Ray took the warrant from his shirt pocket and handed it to Dade. Dade slid it into his coat pocket, and Miles Moilan followed him into the street.

Ray looked at Burkitt. "Why did you back him?"

Burkitt grinned. "Let him go. Maybe Guthrie will get him. Maybe he'll get Guthrie. Either way, we win."

"Supposing he brings him back?"

Burkitt spat. "We've got ropes in this town. Harshaw was a popular man. I'll round up the boys. Fill 'em with likker. By the time Averill brings Guthrie back here, providin' he *does,* we'll have a nice necktie party arranged for Guthrie."

Alex Ray grinned. "Sometimes, Boone, I think you've actually got a brain."

———

MILES MOILAN WALKED beside Dade to the livery stable. "What's your game, Dade?" he asked.

"Joe has a nice bayo coyote. I want to borrow it."

"It's yours."

Joe Fettis was brewing jamoke as they entered the livery stable. He silently filled granite cups and then went to saddle the horse.

Miles took a Winchester from its rest on the wall. "Take this," he said.

Dade shook his head. "I won't need it"

"You want me to go along?"

"No."

Fettis led the horse to the front of the stable.

Dade finished his coffee, walked outside, and swung up on the bayo coyote. "I'll see you, Miles," he said and touched the bayo coyote with his heels.

Joe came to the door holding his coffee cup. "He going after Guthrie?" he asked.

Miles nodded.

"He's either got no nerves or he's loco."

"Yeh."

"You know something, Miles?"

"What, Joe?"

"I think he'll bring him back."

————

THE LAZY T ranch buildings crowned a low rise a mile from the road. The creek flowed past the ranch buildings and along the tree-bordered road which led down to the main road. It was a nice spread. The early-morning sun flashed from the blades of a big Eclipse windmill. It also flashed from something in the trees along the creek. Dade eyed the trees as he turned into the ranch road and got down to open the gate.

A man came out of a building, eyed him, and then ran back into the building. A tall man came out and leaned against a tree, rolling a smoke as Dade walked the bayo coyote toward him. It was Glenn Tagger.

Dade reined in fifty feet from the rancher. "'Morning, Tagger," he said.

Tagger nodded. "Nice day for a ride, Averill."

A man moved behind a shed. The sun glinted from a rifle barrel. Someone was watching Dade from a window in the ranch house.

Dade rested his hands on the pommel. Tagger eyed the star on his black coat. "So you've finally thrown in your hand with Moilan?"

Dade shook his head. "I've come to get Guthrie," he said.

Tagger lit his smoke. "What makes you think you can do it alone?"

Dade shifted a little, watching the riflemen.

"You're safe as long as you keep your hands away from your coat," Tagger said.

"I'd like a smoke."

Tagger flipped open his coat and took out the makings. He walked to Dade and handed them up to him. Dade rolled a smoke and lit up. Tagger stepped back. "Why do you want Guthrie?" he asked. "He didn't kill Gil."

"I know that."

Tagger eyed Dade from beneath his hat. "I won't let him go into that town. He'd be strung up in ten minutes."

Dade nodded. "I don't intend to let that happen. I think I can clear Guthrie. But as long as you protect him, there will be trouble. One way or another, Ray will get at him. You know Ray's reputation. It seems as though he doesn't believe in having the county stand any expenses feeding a prisoner."

Tagger tilted his handsome head to one side. "I can't figure you out."

"It's easy. I know Guthrie is innocent."

"That so?"

"That's so."

The windmill banged as the fresh wind shifted. Tagger flipped away his cigarette. "Turn that horse around and ride back to town. I'll see that you're not bothered."

"I came for Guthrie."

Tagger spat. "What makes you think you can take him? He's protected by me now. *Alone* he'd give you a battle, Averill."

"Let me talk with him."

Tagger shrugged. "You're armed, of course?"

Dade nodded and dismounted: "I'll leave my gun here."

"Fair enough."

Dade had left his derringer and belly-gun in his room. He drew his Colt and handed it to Tagger. Tagger looked at the fine weapon. "You're clean now?"

"You can search me."

"No. Stay here. I'll get Guthrie."

Dade leaned against the bayo coyote. Tagger walked into the big house. The rifleman behind the shed moved a little. It was Fred King.

Tagger came out of the house with Chris Guthrie. The foreman's Missouri holster was empty. He scowled as he saw Dade. "I don't like this, Glenn," he said over his shoulder.

"All he wants to do is talk with you."

Guthrie's cold eyes glanced down at Dade's waist. He walked up to Dade. "Well?"

"Guthrie, I know you didn't kill Harshaw."

"So?"

"I want you to come back to town with me, under my protection."

"You've got your gall thinking *you* can protect me against Alex Ray and Burkitt." Guthrie laughed. "Ray is sure I killed Harshaw. He won't stop a mob from stringing me up."

"There are a lot of people in Estanque who'll see that he doesn't."

"Who?"

"Miles Moilan for one."

Guthrie felt for the makings. "I doubt that."

"Moilan didn't want Ray to come out here. It was Ray's idea."

Guthrie rolled a smoke. "The old bull is losing his grip"

"Ray wants to be sheriff."

Tagger looked at Guthrie.

Guthrie said, "Keep talking, Averill."

"I know you didn't kill Harshaw. I saw the man who did it, but he got away before I could identify him. He was shorter and heavier than you." Dade shook his head. "Who warned you to get out of town?"

"Slim Boyd. Why?"

"Did he tell you who told him to warn you?"

"No."

Dade looked at Tagger. "Get Boyd."

The ranch owner walked toward the corrals.

Guthrie eyed Dade. "What's your game?"

"I'm only interested in getting the killer, Guthrie."

Boyd and Tagger came toward them. The wrangler nodded. Dade raised his head. "Who told you to warn Guthrie to get out of town?"

"You did."

Guthrie spat. "Well, I'll be danged!"

Boyd shoved back his hat. "That's the way I feel."

Tagger looked at Boyd coldly. "Averill a friend of yours, Slim?"

Slim flushed. "He staked me to a faro game."

Guthrie scratched his jaw. "So you think I ought to go in with you?"

Dade nodded.

"I'd feel like a sitting duck."

"You keep your guns. Do you think Burkitt or Ray will buck up against the two of us?"

Slim grinned. "I'd like to see them do it."

Guthrie looked uncertainly at Tagger. "Well?"

"Go in if you want to, Chris. Clear yourself. Averill seems to know a lot more about this than he lets on."

"What I can't figure out," said Guthrie, "is how the dry-gulcher got my scattergun."

"When did you last see it before the murder?"

Chris flushed. "I left it with Mae Delano for her protection."

"Seems as though someone else got it," said Tagger dryly.

"Yeh. *But who?*"

Dade straightened beside his horse. "That's what I aim to find out. One man saw the shooting. A Mex by the name of Jesus. He was drunk in that cantina and Harshaw had arrested him. When the shooting started, Jesus took off. Maybe he saw the killer."

Tagger laughed. "You think a Mex would talk? Ray has them scared to death. Look, Averill, Ray wants Guthrie. I'm not sure why, but he'll do his damnedest to loop a noose around Guthrie's neck."

Dade looked at Guthrie. He said quietly, "There's been a helluva lot of friction between the Lazy T and the people of Estanque. This thing might bring it to a shooting head. If I can clear you, maybe it will calm things down."

"Maybe," said Tagger dryly. "I'll have my boys in town until Chris is cleared."

"No," said Dade. "You'll only start trouble."

Tagger hooked his thumbs under his belt. "Moilan has bucked me ever since I tried to upset his political apple-cart, Averill. He knows Guthrie has a good chance of being sheriff."

"I'll agree that a Moilan sheriff will back Moilan's play. But a Tagger sheriff will back the ranchers. Let me take Guthrie in. I'll clear him. Then you can have your honest election."

"Fair enough," said Slim.

"Shut up," said Tagger.

Guthrie smashed a big fist into his other palm. "Averill is right, Glenn."

"It's your neck, Chris."

"I'll chance it."

"Go on, then. Slim, you follow them. If trouble starts, you raise the dust back here."

"Ok, Boss."

Guthrie turned. "I'll get my horse," he said.

Tagger came close to Dade. "If anything happens to him while in your care, I'll come looking for you, Averill. *Alone.*"

Dade grinned. "I'll take my six-gun now."

Tagger withdrew it from his belt and handed it to Dade. "Any man that can take Fred King and Dan Wilcox on and beat them, in turn, has a lot of guts."

Dade sheathed his Colt. "One of these days maybe you'll come yourself and try me."

Tagger flushed. "I'm no rough-and-tumble man, Averill."

Guthrie led up his horse and mounted. His Colt was sheathed in its holster. "Let's go," he said.

They rode down to the main road. Tagger watched them. Slim spat. "I don't like this," he said, "but Averill did warn me to get Guthrie out of Estanque."

Tagger stroked his blond mustache both ways. "I wonder how he knew where Chris was?"

Slim raised his eyebrows. "Yeh. I wondered about that myself."

"Get Wilcox and King, and ride into town. Leave the two boys outside of town. If they go after Guthrie, I want you to come back and get the *corrida*. If Estanque thinks the Lazy T has treed them before, they've got a *real* treeing coming!"

CHAPTER EIGHT

Men were out in the streets when Dade and Chris reached the edge of town. Joe Fettis met them in front of the livery stable. "Boone Burkitt has been talking war," he said.

Dade nodded. "Where's Alex Ray?"

Joe shrugged. "He left town right after you did, riding north."

The two horsemen rode up the broad sunlit street. Here and there a man eyed them and then went about his business, making sure it took him off Main Street. But there was a group in front of The Star of New Mexico that made no move.

Boone Burkitt came out of the saloon and spoke in a low voice. A dozen men stepped off the boardwalk and walked toward the adobe jail.

Guthrie looked at Dade. "You'd better play your hand well," he said quietly.

Dade drew rein in front of the *calabozo*. Burkitt halted fifty feet away. He rested his hands on his twin Colts. "There's the dry-gulcher," he said.

Dade touched the warrant in his pocket. "I have a warrant for this man's arrest," he said. "He came into town on good faith. He claims he didn't kill Harshaw."

Burkitt looked down the sunlit street as though expecting to see the Lazy T *corrida* materialize!

A man wiped his loose mouth. "Guthrie killed old Gil with his shotgun."

"There's no proof of that. A man is innocent until he's proven guilty," said Dade.

"Hawww! Listen to *him!* Guthrie said he'd get Harshaw for buffaloing him. It all figures."

Burkitt lowered his bullet head. "Get off that hoss, Guthrie," he said.

Guthrie moved a little. The sun shone on the butt of his pistol. Dade rested his hand on his own belt. Burkitt eyed Guthrie's six-gun, then his little eyes looked at Dade. "He's got a gun."

Dade grinned. "Why... so he has."

Two men eased out of the mob and stepped up on the boardwalk. The two horsemen sat there quietly, holding the crowd with their eyes.

Burkitt shifted. "There's only two of 'em," he growled.

"Yell," said a short man. "But we never figgered on this Boone."

"Two against a dozen."

Dade slid his coat back. Burkitt looked nervously at Guthrie. Down the street, Miles Moilan appeared with three men. Shopkeepers. One of them carried a Winchester. Another had a sawed-off shotgun. They stopped fifty feet behind the nervous mob. Burkitt shot a glance toward them.

"Get out of the way," warned Dade.

Two more men drifted off. Burkitt eyed his shrinking mob. "All right," he said. "Alex will take care of this. Until he gets back here, there ain't no law in Estanque other than lynch law."

Dade smiled and touched the star on his coat. "You're wrong. I'm deputized. And I'll stay deputized until Ray gets back."

"We'll see what happens then," said Burkitt.

The mob drifted back, and Dade swung down from his horse. Guthrie followed suit. They went into the jail.

Dade looked at Guthrie. "Nervous?"

Guthrie rolled a smoke. "You carried it off."

"Keep that six-gun with you."

"Thanks." Guthrie lit his cigarette. His hard eyes studied Dade through the smoke. "What's your angle, Averill?"

"I believe you are innocent. I aim to clear you."

"Where's my cell?"

Dade jerked his head toward the cell row. "Take your choice."

Guthrie walked into the end cell, nearest the back door.

Miles Moilan stamped in. He wiped the sweat from his broad face. "You're loco," he said. "Plumb loco."

Dade lit a cigar. "Thanks," he said.

"For what?"

"Backing my play."

Moilan sat down. "Now what?"

"Where's Ray?"

"*Quién sabe?*"

Dade puffed at his smoke. "If anyone tries to take Guthrie from here, there will be hell to pay."

"I suppose Tagger is on his way to town?"

"Not unless trouble starts. Then this town *will* have some property damage."

Moilan stood up. "I'll round up some boys."

"No. Tell them to keep their guns handy. You'll know when to call them out."

"You've got ice water for blood." Dade, grinned. "Oh, I don't know." The big man stamped out of the jail. Dade leaned back in his chair. Maybe Moilan was right about the ice water blood, he thought. His shirt was pasted to his body with cold sweat.

Evening veiled the town in shadows. From Guthrie's

cell came the steady slap of cards as the foreman played
solitaire. Dade had had their meals brought in from the
restaurant. The waiter had told Dade that Burkitt was
still in The Star of New Mexico with his mob, drinking
steadily. The coroner's report lay on the desk in front of
Dade. It said that Sheriff Gil Harshaw had been shot in
the back of the head at close range by a person unknown.
No more; no less. The death weapon also lay on Dade's
desk, tagged, with a notation to the effect that it had
been identified as belonging to one Christopher R.
Guthrie, foreman of the Lazy T.

It was eight o'clock by the jail clock when Dade heard
the noise up the street. He stood up and walked to the
door. Shadowy figures moved about in front of The Star
of New Mexico. Dade took a Greener from the rack and
broke the breech. The brass bottoms of the shells shone
in the lamplight. He felt the weight of his belly-gun in his
coat/pocket. Joe Fettis had brought it and the derringer
from the hotel.

Dade picked up' another shotgun and walked back to
the end cell. He opened the unlocked door and placed
the scattergun on the bunk. Guthrie looked up. "Burkitt
has stirred the drunks up," said Dade. Guthrie nodded.
He placed a hand on the shotgun. "You've got a broad
back, Averill," he said.

Dade grinned. "I'll keep it turned toward you. No
shooting unless you're cornered."

"Ok."

The back door is locked, but the key is in it. Your
horse is tethered out there."

Guthrie nodded.

Dade walked back to the office. Burkitt was walking
toward the jail with at least fifteen men. Some of them
staggered a little as they walked. One of them had a
noosed coil of rope in his hands.

Dade placed the shotgun just inside the doorway and

stepped out in front of the jail. The mob halted in the street.

Dade leaned against the doorway and folded his arms.

"He can't stop us!" yelled a drunk at the back of the mob.

The front men edged forward until they stood at the edge of the warped boardwalk.

"Rush him!" yelled a man.

The mob moved closer. Dade reached a hand inside the doorway and swiftly slid, the scattergun across his left forearm. He placed his fingers inside the twin triggers. The barrels steadied on Boone Burkitt. The two-gun man shifted a little, eyeing the deadly muzzles. He looked sideways.

"Let's get him, Burkitt!"

"It's only one man!"

"Who the hell does Averill think he is?"

"Cut down on him, Boone! You can take him!"

Burkitt was pressed forward. He stepped up on the walk, ten feet from the lethal muzzles. He looked both ways. If he drew, he'd get a load of buck and ball in his body, and the blast couldn't miss at that range. If he broke, either way, the shot would reach out and tear him down.

"Well?" asked Dade.

Down the street Miles Moilan appeared, carrying a Winchester. A grocer showed up beside him, still in his white apron, a shotgun cradled in his arms. Three other men stopped beneath a ramada directly across the street from the jail. They were all armed... and sober.

Dade smiled. There's eighteen buckshot in this Greener and the wads are split. You move an inch closer, Burkitt, and you'll get it, as well as a few on each side of you."

The men at the rear of the mob pressed forward. The men at the front began to sober up under those deadly muzzles. They wanted Chris Guthrie, but they didn't want to pay a blood price for him.

The men at each side of the mob began to slink away. Moilan came closer, eyeing Dade over the mob. He had turned pale under his reddish skin. Burkitt was afraid to move. Seconds ticked past, an eternity to Dade. Burkitt opened his mouth and closed it. He wet his lips, looked away. "Well get him some other time," he said.

The man with the rope eased away. He dropped the deadly coil into the dust and vanished into the Bull's Head. Burkitt walked back into the crowd. They gave way before him. Then suddenly the whole drunken lot was drifting back toward the saloons.

Dade lowered the Greener. His hands were greasy with cold sweat. Moilan came up to him. "How long can you keep it up?" he said.

"As long as Burkitt doesn't want to die to see Guthrie strung up."

Moilan nodded. "Get out of here for a while. I'll stay here."

Dade handed him the shotgun. "Lock the front door. Don't try to face them down."

"*You* did it!"

They looked at each other. Moilan gripped Dade by the shoulder. He said, "You've been nothing but trouble since you got here, but I'm damned glad you *did* come."

Dade grinned. "Partners again, Miles?"

"Yeh. Why I don't know."

Dade slanted his hat over his eyes and stepped out into the street. "See you later, Miles."

"Yeh," said Miles.

CHAPTER NINE

Dade tapped on the front door of the Harshaw house. He wondered if it was the same house Miles had offered to him if he would take Harshaw's job and settle down with Lucy.

Lucy came to the door. Her eyes were shadowed. She glanced at the star on his coat. "Come in," she said.

Jim Harshaw was standing in the kitchen doorway. "I heard about you getting Guthrie," he said. "I never thought you'd keep that mob from getting him."

Lucy sat down. "Who killed our father, Dade?" she asked.

Dade shook his head. "It wasn't Guthrie."

"It was his gun."

Dade sat down. "The man who killed your father was shorter and heavier than Guthrie."

"Like Burkitt?" asked Jimmy, and Dade nodded.

Jimmy reached for his hat.

"Where are you going?" asked Lucy.

"To brace Burkitt."

Dade stood up. "Look, Jimmy. You walk out in those streets looking for Burkitt and you'll find him. He'll kill you before you clear leather. I said the man was like Burkitt. I didn't say it *was* him!"

Jimmy threw his hat onto the table.

Dade sat down. "There's a dozen men in this town who are the same build as the man I saw. I want you to work with me."

Jimmy bit his lip. "All right, all right What do you want me to do?"

"Your father arrested a man by the name of Jesus. I want you to help me find him."

"There are twenty Mexicans living around here by that name."

"Well find him. Another thing. Keep your eyes open for a man who limps or has a sore arm."

"Why?"

"I hit the man who killed your father. If he's around town, he's wearing a bandage. Look for him. And keep your mouth shut about this."

Jimmy picked up his hat. "I'll see you," he said. He left the house.

Lucy looked at Dade. "Why are you doing this?"

"Guthrie is innocent."

"You're sure?"

"Do you think I would have gone after him and brought him in if I didn't think so?"

"You had no reason to like my father. He certainly didn't like you."

"Because of you?"

She flushed. "Yes." Her blue eyes held his. "Why are you doing this? To help Miles Moilan?"

"Miles offered me a job. I turned it down. I want no part of this townspeople-rancher feud."

"It seems to me you're right in the middle of it."

Dade looked down at his temporary star. "Estanque is a nice town. The ranchers are nice people. Throw politics out of this county and it will be a fine place to live."

"Glenn Tagger might take Miles Moilan's place."

"Tagger is a lucky man."

"Why do you say that?"

"Your father said he had money, education, and breeding. He seemed to think Glenn would be a good match for you."

She flushed for the second time. "Glenn and I have no agreement."

Dade touched his bruised face. "He seems to think so."

"Glenn and I are no more than friends."

Dade stood up. "I'm glad to hear that."

"You're a strange man."

"I have been called so."

She walked to the door with him. "Be careful."

"I always am."

She looked up at him. "Jimmy admires you."

He smiled. "I wish you did."

She looked away. "They say you're a dangerous man. A man who has killed and will kill again."

"It was my job."

She shook her head. "That's what I mean. How can killing men ever be legal?"

Dade flushed. "Good night, Miss Lucy."

She closed the door behind him. Dade walked to the street and looked back. Somehow he wanted her good opinion. More than anyone else's in the world.

———

HE WALKED along First Street to its intersection with Mesquite. Here and there, dull lamplight showed in the dirty windows of the adobes. A mongrel looked up from a pile of garbage and then slunk away through the darkness. Dade stopped at Bartolome's Cantina. The mingled odors of sweat, greasy cooking, raw spirits, and tobacco smoke flowed about him as he walked in. A fat man stood behind the zinc-topped bar. He paled a little as he saw Dade.

Dade looked about the smoky, empty room. "Good

evening," he said in Spanish.

"Good evening, *Señor* Sheriff."

Dade leaned against the bar and lit a cigar. "Mezcal," he said.

Bartolome brightened. He took a bottle from the shelf. "Baconora mezcal," he said. "The very best!"

Dade tasted the potent liquor. It *was* good. "Where's Jesus?" he asked quietly.

Bartolome opened his greasy hands and spread them wide. "Jesus? *Which* Jesus? Jesus Diaz? Jesus Chavez? Jesus Madera? Jesus Bernardo?"

Dade held the cantina owner with hard eyes. "The man who was arrested by Sheriff Harshaw just before he was killed."

Bartolome shrugged. "I do not know such a man."

"That so?"

"That is so!"

Dade studied his cigar. "There's a man in the *calabozo* who has been accused of this crime." "May he roast in hell!"

"He didn't do it, Bartolome." Bartolome looked surprised.

Dade placed his hands flat on the bar. "Now tell me who this Jesus is."

"Before God, I do not know!"

Dade's left hand shot up, gripping the fat Mexican by his greasy shirt front. His right-hand whipped down and cleared his Colt from its pocket. He cocked the six-gun and held the muzzle inches from Bartolome's nose. "Talk," he said quietly.

Bartolome swallowed. "It is Jesus Madera." Dade smiled. "Where can I find him?"

"*Quién sabe?* He is a muleteer. There are times he is gone for weeks."

"Where is he?"

"*Por favor, señor,* please to take the gun away from my nose."

Dade lowered the Colt.

Bartolome wiped the sweat from his face. "He lives a mile from town. In a jacal beside the creek. He is your man."

"*Gracias,* Bartolome."

"It is nothing. Please to have another drink." Dade nodded. Bartolome poured, the neck of the bottle jiggling on the rim of the glass. "You will not tell him where you learned about him?"

"No."

"With the knife, he is dangerous. You will not tell?"

"I give you my word."

Bartolome gripped the edge of the bar. "A terrible thing, *señor,* a terrible thing."

Dade left the cantina, passed through the alleyway, and tapped on Mae Delano's back door. She opened it. "Come in, Dade," she said.

She sat down at the kitchen table. Her hair was dressed carelessly. Her hands shook as she reached for a bottle. Dade clamped a hand on her wrist. "Lay off that stuff," he said. "I want to talk to you."

He sat down in a chair and rested his elbows on the littered table. Mae was in a bad way. Her eyes were red-rimmed and shadowed. Her hands shook so that she was forced to clasp them together in her lap. "What will they do with Chris?" she asked.

"Nothing."

She looked up at him. "Who did it, Dade?"

"I'm trying to find out."

"Why? If you still want me, it would be an easy way to get rid of him."

Dade shook his head. "You know me better than that."

She nodded. "What do you want to know?"

"When did Guthrie's shotgun get out of your hands?"

"I'm not sure." She bit her full lip. "It was here two weeks ago."

"Where did you keep it?"

"Behind a chair in the living room."

"You sure you don't know who got it?"

"No."

"Who could have taken it?"

"I have a Mexican cleaning woman. I know she wouldn't take it."

"Who else has been around here?"

"None of your business!"

Dade eyed her. "Look, Mae," he said. "Chris is in a spot. I know he didn't kill Harshaw. But it looks like I'm the only one who believes in him. *Now, who could have taken that shotgun from here?*"

"I don't know."

The waggle-tail clock sounded loudly in the stillness. Mae reached for the bottle. Dade did not stop her this time. She had a bad case of the shakes. "Well?" he asked.

She downed the hooker. "There have been other men here," she said.

Seeing the expression on his face, she protested quickly, "You ought to know how men are. A woman living alone in the town. They just come here."

"Who?"

Suddenly she seemed older than she really was. She looked at Dade. "Alex Ray. Boone Burkitt. Yes, and your friend, Miles Moilan."

"Miles Moilan!"

"He just wanted to talk business."

Dade leaned back in his chair. "You think any of them took the shotgun?"

"I don't know. Who else could it have been?" "You've got something there."

She rested her head on her slim hands. "I want no trouble," she said brokenly. "I just want Chris. I want to get out of here."

Dade felt embarrassed. "Look, Mae," he said. "I've got a chance to clear Chris, but you've got to help me.

"How?"

"Work on Moilan, Burkitt and Ray. Get them drunk. *Find out who got that shotgun!*"

She raised a flushed face. "You know what you're asking, don't you?"

He stood up. "Think of Chris Guthrie. If I can find the man who took that shotgun, I'll put a noose around the *real* killer's neck."

She nodded and looked away. "All right, Dade." Dade closed the back door behind him and crossed the uttered backyard. He did not see the shadowy figure behind the outbuilding, nor the shotgun in his hands. The man looked at Mae's house and then down at the shotgun. "I won't need you tonight," he said with a grin. "I've got a better weapon." He faded into the darkness toward Mesquite Street.

CHAPTER TEN

D ade finished dressing in the back room of Krepp's Barber Shop. He shrugged into his coat and left the steamy room. Bob Krepps looked up from his newspaper. "Everything all right, Averill?" he asked.

Dade nodded and paid the barber. Krepps pulled down the front shades. "When do they hang Guthrie?" he asked.

"What makes you think they will?"

"He's guilty, isn't he?"

"I don't think so."

"You're one of the few in town that doesn't."

"Maybe."

Krepps shook his head. "I don't know why you braced that mob today. I was worried for a time there."

"I wasn't exactly enjoying it."

"Where was Alex Ray?"

"I'd like to know, myself."

"Trust Alex to keep out of the way during a situation like that. Some of the Lazy T boys have been seen in town. You think they might try to break Guthrie out?"

"No."

Krepps took off his apron and put on his coat. "I

came out here from Chicago for my health. Picked this town because it was so quiet. Now I think I should have ignored Miles Moilan and gone on somewhere else. But Miles said they needed a good barber."

"You a Moilan man?"

I've got no love for Tagger and his boys."

Dade left the barbershop, enjoying the cool night wind which swept up the street. It was the same all over town. Most of them thought Guthrie was guilty.

Miles Moilan looked up from the desk as Dade came into the jail office. "Certainly took your time coming back," he growled.

"Business."

Moilan stood up. "Everything's quiet. I put Guthrie's gun in the rack."

Dade looked up at the big man.

Moilan flushed. "Danged if I want him sitting in that cell with a loaded.44 in his hands."

Dade sat down. "You'd better get busy around town," he said quietly.

"How so?"

"People are talking about Guthrie. They think he killed Harshaw. Next time a mob comes, it might consist of the whole town."

"So?"

Dade looked up. "You're too good a man to let a mob lynch an innocent man, Miles."

"I'm still not sure he's innocent."

"I'm saying he is."

Miles shrugged. "I'll see what I can do."

Dade put on a pot of coffee and smoked while it brewed. He filled a cup and walked back to the end cell. Guthrie was seated on his bunk. "jamoke," said Dade.

Guthrie made no effort to take the cup. His eyes held Dade's. "You sneaking double-crosser!" he said.

Dade eyed the foreman. "What's rilin' you?"

Guthrie stood up. "Where have you been since you left here?"

"Why?"

"Tell me!"

Dade shoved back his hat. "I was over at Gil Harshaw's. Then at Bartolome's Cantina." He stopped suddenly.

Guthrie gripped the bars. "Go on," he said.

Dade placed the cup on a chair in the corridor. "What's biting you, Guthrie?"

"After you left Bartolome's, where did you go?"

Then Dade knew.

Guthrie eyed Dade coldly. "You went in to see Mae Delano, didn't you?"

"Yes."

"It all figures. A neat way of getting me out of the way."

Dade shook his head. "I wanted to find out about that shotgun you left there."

Guthrie spat. "A likely story. I've been suspecting her of seeing other men."

"You're a fool, Guthrie!"

Chris Guthrie turned away. "I was a fool to fall for your line, Averill."

"I saved you from that mob, Guthrie."

"Yeh, you good-for-nothing! A play to make yourself a big casino around here. Well, it's working out. But let me tell *you* something, Lawman! I'll get out of this *calabozo,* and when I do, I'll come looking for you and that conniving woman."

"Guthrie, you're crazy. I don't want Mae Delano. Nor does she want me."

"Get out of my sight."

Dade gripped the bars. "How did you find out I saw Mae?"

"I've got friends."

"Who told you?"

"Never mind, Lawman," sneered Guthrie. Dade studied him for a moment, then walked back into the office. There was no use to talk to the foreman in his present mood. It had been a neat trick. Playing off Guthrie's jealousy against Dade. Dade rolled a smoke. He was sure no one had been around when he had gone into Mae Delano's. A cold feeling came over him. Someone had seen him coming out. It couldn't have been Miles Moilan. He had been guarding Guthrie. Alex Ray was out of town or was supposed to be.

Dade checked the rear door. Guthrie followed him with smoldering eyes as he went back to the front office and locked the door there. Dade placed his Greener against the wall and made up the bunk in the first cell.

The town was quiet. Now and then a thud of hoofs penetrated the thick walls of the jail. A door banged somewhere up the street. Dade peeled off his coat and hung it up. The lamplight shone dully on the polished star on the coat

He wondered what would happen if Guthrie, or anyone else in Estanque, found out that he had known Mae Delano years ago.

A temptation came over him to leave the jail, get his horse and ride out in the windy night, heading anywhere.

———

THE BANGING on the front door awakened Dade. He looked at the clock. It was a little after seven in the morning. He rolled out of his bunk and walked to the door.

"Who is it?"

"Alex Ray."

Dade opened the door and the deputy walked in. "Guthrie here?"

Dade nodded.

"Any trouble?"

Dade sat on the edge of the desk and yawned. "Some. I expected you here when I returned."

Ray flushed. "I had a job to do."

"That so?"

"What's riling you this morning?"

Dade stood up. "You! I took this star long enough to get Guthrie. I didn't expect to face a drunken mob led by that skunk Burkitt."

Ray rolled a smoke. "Nervous?"

Dade shrugged into his coat. "I don't like facing men like Burkitt backed by a mob."

"It's part of the job."

Dade whirled. "Then why didn't *you* face them?"

Ray studied him. "Maybe I oughta take that star away from you."

Dade took the star from his coat and threw it on the desk. "There it is!"

Ray grinned. "I'll have a check made out to you."

Dade tied his tie. "One thing. You keep that man safe in there."

"I can handle this town."

"See that you do."

Ray came closer to Dade. "I don't like your attitude."

"You stink!"

Ray's hand whipped down for his Colt. Dade stepped in close, slapping his left hand down on the gun wrist. He hooked a hard right to Ray's jaw. Ray's head snapped back. Dade plucked the Colt from its holster and threw it across the room. Alex Ray started for the shotgun leaning against the wall, but Dade caught him by the collar of his coat and whirled him around. He belted a left below the belt and smashed a right to the jaw. Ray lashed out at Dade clumsily. Dade blocked the blows and rammed a right cross to the jaw. Ray hit the wall and slid to the floor.

Dade wiped the sweat from his eyes. "Once more,

Ray. You take care of that man in there, or I'll work you over into a bloody hash."

Ray wobbled his head and touched his smashed face. "I'll get you," he mumbled. "One way or another, I'll get you."

Dade looked down the line of cells. Guthrie was looking through the bars. "Big casino," he sneered.

Dade walked outside. All the accumulated hate of facing the mob had flowed out of him to smash the loud-mouthed deputy. He had made a bitter enemy, one more to add to the list.

When he passed the Star of Mexico, he saw Dan Wilcox and Fred King leaning against the hitching rack. They watched him with cold eyes as he walked toward his hotel.

Jim Harshaw was waiting in Dade's room. He glanced curiously at Dade's lacerated hands.

"What did you find out, kid?" asked Dade as he washed his hands.

"Nothing about a wounded man."

"The man we want for a witness is Jesus Madera. A muleteer. He lives just outside of town. He's not at home now, though. He left for a job in the hills."

"What' do we do?"

Dade dried his hands. "Play our cards close and pray for a break."

"Just that?"

Dade nodded. "Just that."

"Alex Ray came back to town this morning."

"I know."

"Even if Guthrie *is* innocent, as *you* say, I don't think he's very safe with Ray watching him."

"If anything happens to Guthrie, Ray will answer to me."

As Dade began changing his shirt, Jimmy eyed the man before him. "Yeh. Yeh," he said. "Alex Ray won't brace *you,* Dade."

"How about a little breakfast?"

Jimmy grinned. "Fine."

They walked downstairs. Jimmy looked at Dade. "You know something? I think Lucy likes you."

Dade tilted his head to one side. "That's a change."

Jimmy nodded. "Seems as though sometimes a woman puts on a big act of hating a man she really likes." Dade held open the door. "Only sometimes, kid. Only sometimes."

CHAPTER ELEVEN

V aqueros of the Lazy T began to show up in town early in the afternoon. Fred King and Dan Wilcox had been there all morning. They were joined by Lefty Corse and Lanky Jones. Slim Boyd rode in later on in the afternoon. He found Dade in the Bull's Head. "Tagger is getting riled," he said. "Word got to him that you turned in your star." Dade nodded.

"Tagger says you gave your word nothing would happen to Guthrie."

"Nothing has."

Slim poured a drink. "No. But Tagger thinks you let him down. He doesn't like you, Averill, but he thinks you meant it when you said you'd see that nothing happened to Chris."

Dade lit a cigarette. "Puts me in a spot," he said quietly. "I got so riled at Ray that I walked out on him."

"Maybe that's what he wanted you to do." Dade looked at his skinned knuckles. Alex Ray hadn't been seen outside of the *calabozo* all day; probably nursing his battered face. "Is that why the Lazy T boys are in town?" he asked.

"You guessed it. Tagger is on his way in, too. He ain't about to let anybody lynch Chris."

Dade filled his glass. "I've been wondering who works on the Lazy T, Slim."

"I don't get it."

"Seems as though a good many of the Lazy T *corrida* spend their time here in town looking for trouble rather than punching cows."

Slim rolled a smoke. "Glenn has twenty good men out there. He sent a man down south to hire five more. He said he wasn't worried about how good they was with cows, just how good they was with guns."

"Sounds like war."

"It will be if anything happens to Chris. Mebbe you'd better do something about it."

"What, for instance?"

"Get back that star."

"I don't want the damned thing, Slim."

Slim picked a piece of tobacco from his lip. "I don't blame you, Averill. But I do know this: If another mob comes after Guthrie, Ray sure won't stop them."

Dade slammed a fist down on the bar. "Seems as though I'm damned if I do and damned if I don't."

"It's too late to worry about that."

"What do you mean?"

Slim shrugged. "You should have figured that out before you got mixed up in this silly feud between the town and the ranchers."

Dade emptied his glass. "You've got a cool head, Slim. Somehow I think I can rely on you."

Slim grinned. "Long's I owe you twenty-five eagles, I guess you have to."

"Keep an eye on that stinking Burkitt. If he starts working up a mob, I want you to tip me off."

"Me and the Lazy T boys will back you."

"*Gracias,* but I don't want that. Not unless they storm the *calabozo.* Keep the Lazy T boys quiet and watch Burkitt. Understood?"

"Ok."

Dade walked out of the saloon and down to the newspaper office. Eskew looked up at him and jerked a thumb toward the rear office. "Glenn Tagger is in there," he said quietly.

Dade tapped on the rear door.

"I'm busy, Eskew!" roared Moilan.

Dade opened the door. "It's me, Miles."

"Come in. Take a drink."

Tagger was seated near the wall. He looked up at Dade. "Chris all right?" he asked coldly.

"Yes."

"How long *will* he be safe?"

Dade sat down and poured a drink. "That depends on Boone Burkitt and Alex Ray."

"Meaning?"

"If Burkitt riles up another mob, he'll make sure he works it right this time. Alex Ray won't stop him. He won't even try."

Tagger looked at Miles. "That's exactly what I was saying to Moilan here."

Miles chewed at his short cigar. "What can I do?"

Tagger leaned forward. "I'll tell you! One hair on Guthrie's head gets hurt and I'll come in here and go through this town like a dose of salts."

Moilan spat. "We'll see!"

Tagger turned to Dade. "You gave me your word that he'd be safe."

"I was temporarily deputized to get Guthrie. I did. The job is done."

Tagger stood up. "So that's the game between you and Moilan?"

Miles slammed a big hand flat on the desk. "It was Averill's idea, not mine."

Dade shoved back his hat. "Can you get me deputized again, Miles?"

Moilan snorted. "I run the town, don't I?" He looked quickly at Tagger.

"I had a little run in with Ray this morning," said Dade. "I had to swallow fork his ears."

Miles said, "What's happened now?"

"I felt he should have been here when I brought back Guthrie. He wasn't. Hiding out of town somewhere when Burkitt led his mob to the *calabozo*. I braced him on it. He tried to draw. We settled it out of court. I warned him to take care of Guthrie."

Miles half-closed his frosty eyes. "You don't look marked to me."

"Ray is," said Dade dryly. "That's why you'd better use your influence to get that star on my coat again, although heaven knows I don't want it."

Miles stood up. "I'll talk to him," he said and stamped out of the office.

Tagger eyed Dade. "You carry your guts in your fists," he said.

"I get by."

Tagger gripped the door handle. "One thing. Watch Ray. That tinhorn will carry a grudge. He's got more brains than Burkitt, but a lot less guts. Watch your back."

Dade nodded. "By the way," he said, "Guthrie thinks I'm trying to cut him out with Mae Delano. He isn't exactly friendly toward me."

Tagger turned. "*Are* you trying to cut him out?"

"No."

"Where did he get the idea?"

"I went to see Mae. Somebody shot off his mouth."

"Man, you live on the thin edge. Chris doesn't stand for anyone being near Mae."

Dade shrugged.

Tagger opened the door. "It seems that, in addition to your other skills, you're quite a hand with the ladies."

Dade stood up. "What do you mean, Tagger?"

"Lucy Harshaw."

"So?"

"I was courting her, Averill."

"Not the way I heard it."

Tagger wet his lips. "I'm telling you now." His eyes were hard as agate. "Right now, I'll overlook your associating with Lucy. When this mess is over, maybe we'll settle it. Out of court, as you put it."

"I'll be available."

Dade poured another drink after Tagger left. The ranch owner had meant what he said. There was a strong strain of honor in Tagger. He had warned Dade about watching Ray and had also made it plain that he would brook no interference with Lucy. Harshaw. What was it Harshaw had said about him? He had education, breeding, and money. A gentleman. Dade had met his type before, mostly Southerners; and they could be as dangerous as an ignorant Brasadero who had neither money, education nor breeding.

"The polished rattlesnake," said Dade.

Eskew poked his head through the doorway. "You say something, Mister Averill?"

"I was talking to myself, Eskew."

"A bad habit."

Dade grinned. "It seems I have a lot of bad habits." He walked to the outer door. "Eskew," he said, "would it hurt Moilan very much if he lost his power here?"

Eskew looked up. "Yes. A great deal."

"Would it hurt Tagger if Miles stayed in power?"

Eskew shrugged. "I'm not sure. Mister Tagger has a great deal of money."

"I wonder why he's bucking Miles?"-

Eskew peered through his thick glasses. "Perhaps for power. Wealthy men seem to like power. They have money, so there is no need for them to grub like the rest of us. They seek something. Prestige. Power. Sometimes I think they do it to prove to the world that they *can* make their mark, even if they *were* born with a silver spoon in their mouths."

Dade nodded.

Eskew leaned against the counter. "We all have our dreams. I wanted to be a crusading editor. I went broke. Moilan came along and bought up my whole newspaper... and me. Now I'm just a mouthpiece."

"I wonder what Miles is striving for?"

"Moilan came up from the very bottom. He has told me he knew neither his father nor his mother. Everything he's earned, so he tells me, he earned the hard way."

"I wonder what *his* dream is?"

Eskew shrugged. "Who knows? But a man without a dream is dead. You have a dream, Mister Averill?"

"Yes. Not very promising, though."

"May I ask what it is?"

Dade looked at the serious little man. "To do a job well. To have honor... and possibly prestige."

CHAPTER TWELVE

Dusk had settled over the town by the time Miles Moilan sent for Dade. Dade left the restaurant and walked to the jail. Moilan was seated in a chair tilted back against the wall. Alex Ray was sitting at his desk. His face was still swollen from the beating he had taken. He did not look at Dade as he came in. Miles dropped his chair to the floor. "There's your star, Dade," he said.

Dade looked down at the bit of metal, a small help to him in the feud that was filling the town with tension. "What's the deal, Miles?" "What do you mean?"

"I want to know where I stand in this mare's nest you've built."

Ray looked at Dade and mumbled something under his breath.

Miles lit a cigar. "Alex has agreed to forget about the beating you handed him."

"I'll bet."

Ray thumped a clenched fist on the desk. Moilan lit a cigar and puffed out a thick cloud of smoke. "Alex will act as temporary sheriff until the election. You will be his deputy." "Very cozy," said Dade dryly. "Shut up!" barked Miles. "Tell him the rest, Miles," said Ray. Dade said politely, "I'm all ears." Moilan spat. "You'll take orders from Ray, providing they're in the line of duty."

Moilan got up and paced back and forth. "In return, I'll back Alex here for the sheriff's job in the next election."

Guthrie laughed from his cell. "The plot thickens," he called out.

Ray stood up. "I'll gag that jailbird," he said. "Try it, you tinhorn!" yelled Guthrie. Ray started for the cell row. *"Sit down!"* yelled Moilan.

Dade grinned. "When's the election, Miles?" he asked. "Week after next."

Dade' leaned against the wall. "There's a job of work to do then."

"What?"

"Find the man that killed Harshaw. Clear Guthrie. Very simple."

Alex Ray sat down. "I still' think Guthrie did it."

"It's not your job to think a man is *guilty*," said Dade dryly.

"You tellin' me my job?"

Moilan cursed. "Now listen here! Dade, you're so sure Guthrie didn't kill Harshaw, supposin' you come up with some evidence instead of talking about it?"

Ray grunted. "I couldn't have put it any better."

"Shut up!" said Moilan. He eyed Dade. "Well?"

Dade nodded. He walked to the gun rack and took a Winchester from it. He took a fresh box of .44/40 cartridges from a drawer and slipped them into his pocket.

"Where you goin?" asked Ray.

Dade grounded the rifle. "To get evidence."

"Where?"

"I want an open warrant."

"For who?"

Dade leaned across the desk. "I'm not sure. If I find the man I want, I want a warrant for him."

"If you know who the man is," persisted Ray, "I can fill his name in right now."

Moilan spat. "Give him the warrant, Alex! I'm sick of you two fighting cocks clashing your spurs and kicking up dirt."

Ray took out a warrant and threw it across the desk. "Just be careful," he said. "Don't run in a man with a good alibi. We've had trouble like that before."

Dade folded the warrant and slipped it into his inner pocket. "Like the man you and Burkitt arrested? The one who was innocent and you two killed? Or the horse thief who gave up his guns and was shot down?"

Ray turned deathly pale beneath his tan. He dropped his hands into his lap. Dade raised the Winchester until the muzzle was close to the lawman. Then he turned his back and walked outside.

Miles Moilan followed Dade. He took off his hat and mopped his face. "What's got into you, Dade?"

Dade shrugged.

"Don't underestimate Alex Ray, Dade. You've pushed him to the killing point twice today."

Dade looked at the older man. "You were the one that taught me never to underestimate a man. I don't. Remember that, Miles. It includes *you*, too." Dade walked toward the livery stable to get his bayo coyote.

Miles Moilan wet his lips. "I built a mare's nest all right," he said to himself.

Dade got his horse and borrowed a gun sheath from Joe Fettis. He headed the bayo coyote out on the road that ran past Jesus Madera's jacal.

There was a dim light in the pole-and-mud shack as Dade reined in the horse and slid from the saddle. He checked the magazine of the repeater and filled it with three more cartridges. He eased his Colt in its leather-lined pocket and then walked through the gateway of the sagging fence. He went to the rear of the jacal. A burro was in a shed. A pair of heavy *aparejos* hung from a hook.

Two more burros were in the corral, already laden with
aparejos. Jesus Madera was a muleteer. He would have
needed his mules if he had gone to work.

Dade walked to the front of the jacal and tapped on
the weather-beaten door.

"Quién es?" a woman called.

"A friend."

"What is it you wish, *señor?"*

"Jesus Madera."

Feet scuffled on the floor. A moment passed. Then
the door creaked open, and a woman looked at him. "He
is not here, *señor."*

"Where is he?"

"At work in the hills."

"Without his burros?"

The woman bit her lip.

Dade pushed past her. A pot of chili was on the table,
lifting a thin veil of steam. Fresh tortillas were on a plat-
ter. A bottle of wine had been uncorked. Two bowls were
on the table. Dade turned. "I am sorry," he said. "I did
not mean to disturb your meal."

She smiled. "It is nothing. Perhaps the *señor* would
like some chili. A glass of wine, perhaps? *Por favor?"*

Dade shook his head. "It is late. I wanted to see my
amigo, Jesus. Some other time perhaps."

"Yes. Go with God, *señor."*

"Gracias."

Dade walked to the road and swung up on his horse.
He turned it toward town and rode a quarter of a mile.
Then he kneed the bayo coyote into the shelter of the
trees, rode behind a low ridge, and headed north behind
its shelter, paralleling the road. Two miles from the jacal
he slid from the saddle and ground-reined the horse. He
padded through the brush, topped the ridge, and looked
south. There was a dark shadow on the road, moving
swiftly.

Dade sank down into the brush. The clop-clop of

hoofs came closer, then he saw the moonlit face of the Mexican. Jesus had a thick fold of tortilla in his hand. He munched at it as he belabored his burro with a thick stick. Dade waited until he was within twenty feet and then he stepped out into the road, levering home a round into the rifle. "Good evening, Jesus Madera," he said.

The burro stopped. Jesus slowly took the tortilla from his mouth. A trickle of rich brown juice ran down his thin jaws. "For the love of God, *señor bandido,*" he quavered. "I have no money."

Dade shook his head. "Get off that burro. I want to talk with you."

Jesus slid from the pad that served as a saddle.

"Raise your arms," said Dade.

"I have no gun."

The knife then."

Jesus plucked a knife from his waistband and threw it into the road. "What is it you want?"

Dade leaned on his rifle. "You were arrested by Sheriff Harshaw the night he was killed, for creating trouble in Bartolome's Cantina."

"Me? Before God, *señor,* I was in the hills."

"Don't lie."

Jesus wet his lips. "It was not me."

Dade spat. "It *was* you. You were running away when Harshaw was shot down."

Jesus spat. "Bartolome! That *canalla!* That *bazofa!* He told you this? He hates me!"

Dade came closer. "Who was the man who killed Harshaw?"

"I do not know."

"You looked right at him."

"A he! Who told you this?"

"I saw it. I was the man who shot at the killer."

In the silence that followed the burro brayed.

Jesus turned. "Tomas is nervous."

The Mexican went to the shaggy beast and pulled at

his long ears. Then the muleteer whirled. The moonlight glinted on a thin-bladed *cuchillo*. Dade threw up his Winchester. The blade skidded down the barrel and slashed his fingers. He dropped the rifle with a curse. Jesus flicked out the knife and it drew blood from Dade's left forearm. Dade clawed for his Colt as Jesus moved in.

Dade lashed out his left hand and gripped Jesus' right wrist, forcing it upward. He stepped in close, snaked his right arm under Jesus' right arm, forcing it up and backward.

Jesus grunted. His breath was thick with the mingled odors of chili and wine. He struggled. Dade's superior height was too much. Jesus bent backward, still struggling. Then the thin bones snapped in his wrist and the knife clattered to the hard earth. Dade threw the little man back and whipped out his Colt. The double click of the cocking sounded loudly in the stillness.

"Get on the burro," said Dade.

Greasy sweat ran down the greenish face of the muleteer. "Where do you take me?"

"To the *calabozo*."

Jesus whirled. "He will kill me! Before God, *he will kill me!*"

Dade wet his lips. *"Who* will kill you, Jesus?"

Jesus cradled his broken wrist. "I do not know," he said sullenly.

Dade came closer. "Have, you ever seen a man's face after a slug from a pistol hits it at two feet?"

"No, no, *señor!* Not that!"

Dade spat. "Then who are you so afraid of?"

"I do not know."

Dade raised the pistol.

Tears ran down the greasy face. "You will tell my wife?" he asked pitifully.

Dade nodded. "Lead the burro up that draw. My horse is up there."

They reached the bayo coyote. Dade mounted and

followed the little man back to the road. There were times when being a lawman sickened him. But then he thought of Gil Harshaw lying in the dusty street with the back of his head smashed like an egg. "Move that burro!" he said. *"Vamonos! Pronto!"*

———

DADE SAT on the little front porch of Doc Safford's house, watching the people walk by, passing in and out of the lighted areas from the windows. Jesus was inside, moaning like a bull calf looking for its mother's milk. "Dammit!" yelled Doc. "Sit still, Jesus!"

Dade felt tired. He had been getting wearier every day. He looked at the moon-bathed hills beyond the town. Maybe after this mess was over he could take a trip up into the mountains, make a camp, and get in some fishing. He was thinking of a mess of brook trout when he saw Boone Burkitt walk by on the far side of the street.

Burkitt did not look across at Dade. He was looking ahead, toward Mae's well-lit frame house. Dade watched Burkitt look up and down the street, and then duck alongside the house. The two-gun man vanished. A few minutes later, Dade saw the front shades pulled down.

Doc Safford shoved Jesus out on the front porch. "He'll live," he said.

Dade stood up. "Send your bill to the jail," he said.

Safford leaned against the side of the doorway. "What'd he do?" he asked, jerking his head at Jesus.

"Ran away," said Dade.

"A knifing?"

Dade looked down at his lacerated fingers. "Yeh. A knifing."

"Let me take a look at that."

They went back into the house. Safford worked swiftly. "No stitches." Dade winced as he cleansed the wounds. Safford bandaged the hand quickly. "Good thing it wasn't your right hand," he said.

"Why?"

Safford looked up through his glasses. "I hear you're a good man with a gun."

"I haven't done any shooting here."

"No. But your reputation is spreading. Must be quite a thing to have a reputation like that. How many notches?" asked the medic.

Dade shifted his feet. "How many men have died on your operating table?"

"Doctors don't talk about things like that"

"Neither do I."

Safford looked quickly at Dade. "No offense. I understand. Professional interest is all, Averill."

Dade nodded. "If anyone asks you about Jesus, just say he fell and broke his wrist. Beyond that, you know nothing."

Safford washed his hands in the pinkish water of a basin. "Jesus have anything to do with Gil Harshaw's death?"

"No."

"A witness?"

"It's none of your business."

Safford slipped into his coat. "I think it is. Gil Harshaw was my best friend. I'm interested in learning who killed him."

"I'm sorry, Doc!"

"Forget it."

"There's one thing you can do for me," said Dade.

"Go on."

"Have you treated any bullet wounds lately?"

Safford scratched his wispy goatee. "No. I did treat a nester two weeks ago. He dropped his shotgun and got some of the shot in his leg."

"That won't do me any good."

Safford lowered the Argand lamp. "There was one

curious case in here a short time ago. A man came in here one morning with a gouge across his left bicep; Claimed he ripped it on a protruding nail."

"Who?"

Safford picked up his hat. "I cleansed the wound. Took lead flakes out of it. Besides, that wound wasn't made by any nail. I could have sworn he had been creased by a bullet."

Dade felt tight all over. "Who was the man?"

Safford jerked his head toward Jesus. "I don't want to talk in front of him."

"Write the name, then."

Safford took a prescription pad and wrote in a typical doctor's scrawl. Dade looked at it. *Boone Burkitt.* "Any help?" asked Safford.

Dade took the slip and lit it. He let the burning fragments fall into the cuspidor. There was a strange look in his gray eyes. "Yes," he said. "You said Harshaw was your best friend. Keep this to yourself until I call on you again."

Safford nodded. "Gil and I often talked about what we'd do when we both retired. Gil liked fishing. We got away once in a while. A *long* while. Sheriffs and doctors are busy men in this country. Gil's best days were over. He knew it; I knew it. But there was a stubborn pride in the man. He could have resigned, but he wouldn't."

"Why?"

Safford filled his big pipe. "For one thing, he didn't want to see Alex Ray get the job. He wanted to finish his term and then quit forever, but he just couldn't stand seeing Ray get the job."

"Maybe Chris Guthrie would have made it."

"Guthrie is a good man with a gun. Gutty, with a cold killer's courage. It wouldn't be long before he shot one or two. Gil always said it took more than gun skill to wear the star. It isn't easy."

Dade nodded.

"Years of wearing the star takes something from a man unless he's just a machine. With Gil it was different. He started figuring the chances. The odds get longer as your speed diminishes. Gil started working at jobs that weren't his, just to earn his pay. Like what happened the night he was killed.

"Patrolling the streets. Arresting drunks. That wasn't a *sheriff's* job. I remember what he said to me one night in this very room. We had split a bottle between us. He asked me if I knew what a sheriff was supposed to do. I couldn't answer."

Jesus moaned a little.

Safford looked at Dade. "Gil said this: 'A sheriff is an officer who represents the administrative power of a state within one of its counties; an officer who executes the mandates of the courts of record within a county; the chief ministerial officer in a county.'"

A buckboard rolled by in the street. Safford looked at the floor. "Miles Moilan made a fool of Gil In this town, and in the county, too. Gil was nothing but a tool in his hands."

Dade took Jesus by the good arm. "Come on, *amigo,*" he said.

The three of them walked out into the dark street Safford snapped open the lid of his hunting-case watch. "I'm due at Mrs. Cafferty's. She's having a baby. Her seventh."

"Thanks, Doc," said Dade.

The old man waved a hand. He plodded down the street and then he turned, a lonely figure in the darkness. "Do you like to fish, Averill?" he asked.

"Very much."

"Maybe we can go together sometimes. When we're not so busy."

"Yes. When we're not so busy."

Safford plodded off into the shadows, and Dade led Jesus across the street toward the jail.

CHAPTER THIRTEEN

Alex Ray got up off the bunk in the first cell when Dade appeared with the muleteer. "What's he doing here?" he asked.

Dade threw the warrant down on the desk. "Fill in the name of Jesus Madera."

"Why?"

"Madera was under arrest by Gil when Gil was killed. Madera saw the killer."

Ray eyed the muleteer. "Who was it. Madera?" he asked.

"I don't know. I must be in the hills to work. This man took me under arrest."

"Who was the man?"

"I do not know!"

Ray looked at Dade. "He'll be a lot of help," he said sarcastically.

Dade gripped Jesus by his good arm and led him down the line of cells to Guthrie's cell. The foreman looked up from the book he was reading. There was no friendliness in his eyes. Ray came along behind Dade. "Is this the man?" asked Dade.

"I don't know," said Jesus.

"Stand up, Guthrie," said Dade.

"Go to hell!"

"This man may clear you. Stand up!"

Guthrie got slowly to his feet. Jesus looked at him. "I am not sure," he said.

"You'd better be sure," said Guthrie.

Jesus cradled his broken wrist and moaned a little. "I am not sure, *señor,*" he said to Dade.

Ray leaned against the wall. "I don't believe he even saw the man," he said.

Dade led the Mexican to the first cell and pushed him in.

"Wait a minute," said Alex. "How can we hold him?"

"As a material witness."

"He claims he doesn't know."

"Then hold him for resisting arrest."

"A *false* arrest?"

Dade bit the end from a long cigar. "Harshaw arrested him for creating a disturbance in Bartolome's Cantina. He fled when Harshaw was killed. We'll hold him on that."

Alex Ray sat down. "All right. One thing you'd better learn around here. There are a lot of Mexicans in and around Estanque. They won't like this."

Dade grinned. "There are a lot *of* people around here that don't seem to like *anything.* Book him."

Ray shrugged and booked the Mexican. Dade locked the cell door. "You want me to stay here tonight?"

"No. I'll take the night shift." Dade walked out into the street. He knew Jesus couldn't identify Guthrie. The next thing he wanted to do was show Burkitt to Jesus.

He walked to the Harshaw house and knocked at the door. Lucy opened it. She silently showed him in. Dade took off his hat. "I've rounded up Jesus Madera, Lucy. I think he knows the man who killed your father."

She looked at his bandaged hand. "You're hurt?"

"A scratch. Jesus is locked up."

"He'll be afraid to talk. Jesus has always been a troublemaker in Estanque. Dad used to run him in about once a month. He's a terrible coward, Dade."

"Where's Jimmy?"

"I don't know. He has been around town this evening. I'm afraid for him, Dade. Dad was his idol. It's just like Jimmy to face any man whom he thinks might have had anything to do with murdering his father. I'm afraid."

Dade nodded. "I'll round him up."

She came close to him. "I want to thank you for helping us. You've made many enemies here in town. Why are you doing it?"

Dade looked down at her. Suddenly he drew the lonely girl close. She raised her face and Dade kissed her. She rested her head against his chest. "Be careful," she said. "I don't want anything to happen to you too."

"I'll be all right." Dade kissed her again.

She stepped back. "Come back with Jimmy," she said.

"I will."

Dade left the house and walked up to Main Street. He looked in at the Bull's Head and the Bee Hive. Jimmy wasn't in either of the saloons. He crossed the street to The Star of New Mexico. The kid was at the end of the bar, leaning against it, holding an empty glass in his slim hand.

Dade pushed through the batwings. Glenn Tagger was at a poker table with Fred King and Dan Wilcox. Slim Boyd and Lefty Corse were bucking the faro game. Lanky Jones leaned on the bar a few feet from Jimmy. He eyed Dade. "Here comes the law," he said loudly.

Dade stopped beside Jimmy. "Your sister wants you to come home," he said.

"The kid's nurse is here," said Lanky.

Dade eyed the cowpoke.

Tagger and his men looked up from their games.

Slim caught Dade's eye and shook his head. He made a motion as though drinking and pointed at Lanky. The pantomime was unnecessary. Lanky's bilge was full, and he was primed for bear.

Lanky spat. "Damned kid thinks he's a lawman too, asking questions."

"Shut up, Lanky," said Red, the bartender.

Red looked at Tagger. Tagger leaned back in his chair watching Dade. His men did not move.

Dade placed a hand on the kid's shoulder. "Come on," he said quietly.

"I'll have another drink!"

"I'm cutting you off," said Red.

Lanky grinned. "Yuh got sarsaparilla, ain'tcha?"

Jimmy threw Dade's hand from his shoulder and clawed for his Colt. Lanky moved swiftly for all his drinking. He stepped back from the bar and went into a crouch. Dade shoved the kid back against the wall so hard that a bottle fell from the back of the bar and smashed on the duckboards. Lanky's Colt came up. Dade closed the gap between them. He thrust an arm up under Lanky's and drove it up. The Colt boomed. Smoke swirled about the two tall men. Dade slammed Lanky in the gut with his left fist. He freed his own Colt and swung it in a short, Chopping arc. The long barrel slashed Lanky just over the left ear. The tall *vaquero* went down like a falling pine.

Dade stepped back and looked at Tagger. "Why didn't you stop him?" he asked coldly. "Do you *want* a killing?"

Lefty Corse shifted a little. Dade lowered his hand, sweeping back his coat. "Sit tight, Lefty," he said.

Tagger stood up. "The kid was looking for trouble, Averill. Red tried to get him to leave."

Dade stepped back, watching the cold-eyed Lazy T men. "Lanky is one of your *corrida*. Maybe you should have made him leave."

Red looked at Dade. "The kid was getting pretty bad," he said. "Asking questions. He thinks one of the boys here mighta done his father in."

Dade looked back at the pale-faced kid. "Get out," he said.

Jimmy weaved his way to the door and left the saloon.

Dade backed to the door.

"Big casino," said Lefty.

Tagger cut his hand sideways. "Shut up, Lefty! Let him go. He's swinging a big loop now. Let him play."

"The loop might get bigger," said Dade. "Tagger, keep these boys in line, or I'll run the lot of you in."

Lefty laughed, "Take the kid home," he said. "Maybe Lucy will give you a kiss for the night's work."

Tagger whirled. His hand shot out, cracking like a pistol shot against Lefty's face. "Get out of here," he said thinly. "Go back to the ranch and take your drunken partner with you."

Lefty touched his reddened face and walked over to Lanky. He did not look at Tagger, but there was feral hate in his eyes.

Dade walked out onto the porch. Jimmy was leaning against a post. "Come on," said Dade.

"I'm going to the Bee Hive."

"You're going home."

Jimmy walked out into the street. "Who the hell do you think you are?"

Dade came up beside him. "You've got Lucy worried."

At the corner, Jimmy stopped. He looked up at Dade. "I heard about you," he said. "Playing up to me to get in with Lucy, you damned tinhorn."

Dade gripped the kid by his shirt and turned him around. "Don't ever say that again," he said quietly.

"Let go of me. I'm gonna get another drink."

Dade slapped the flushed face hard. He shoved the kid back and Jimmy hit the ground. He cursed as Dade stood over him. "I told you never to shoot from the ground," he said, "unless the other man's gun is in his hand."

Jimmy spat! The moon shone on his pale face. Then

he clawed for his Colt. Dade stepped in close and smashed a foot on the gun wrist. He gripped Jimmy by the collar and yanked him to his feet. The kid tried to raise his Colt as Dade gripped the gun wrist. He slipped the derringer free from its clasp and shoved it into Jimmy's belly. "Now what?" he challenged softly.

Jimmy's face turned fish-belly white. "You win."

"Go home and clean up," Dave said.

Jimmy holstered his Colt. He swayed as he walked. Suddenly he began to run clumsily, clasping a hand over his mouth. Then the sour flood poured out. The kid retched,' staggering about the dusty street. Dade watched him. He'd learn if he wasn't killed first.

Dade turned and walked down Main. A shadowy figure bulked in the darkness next to a building. Dade eased into a dark doorway. Boone Burkitt stopped in the street and lit a cigar, swearing. Then he said, "All that talk and likker and no go." He staggered a little as he headed for The Star of New Mexico.

Dade walked down to Mae Delano's and tapped on the door. She opened it. "Come on in," she said quickly. "Burkitt was here."

Dade stepped in and took off his hat. A bottle was on the marble-topped table. Another was on the mantel of the fireplace. Dade looked at Mae. "Well?"

"He was drunk, Dade."

"You seem sober."

She nodded at the bottle on the mantelpiece. "Cold tea," she said.

Dade grinned. "You're learning."

Her face was set. "I want Chris freed."

"He will be."

"How?"

Dade lit a cigar. "I picked up the man who saw the killer. Jesus Madera, a muleteer." Dade's even white teeth clamped on his cigar. "What did you learn?"

"Nothing about the missing shotgun."

Dade bit his lip.

Mae poured a drink and downed it swiftly, "*tip* hinted that Chris hadn't done the job."

"Is that all?"

She slammed her glass down on the marble-topped table. It shattered, cutting her hand. "What did you expect me to do? Cross-examine him?"

Dade poured a drink and handed her his handkerchief. "Chris is riled at me. Someone told him I had been here."

"That's just dandy. Oh, you've done a fine job, you have!"

Dade sat down. "If you could only remember when that shotgun went missing."

"Well, I can't! Why don't you let me alone?"

"You *will* be alone if they string up Chris."

She wrapped the handkerchief about her hand. "I pumped him a little about Chris. At first, he said Chris was guilty. Then later, he hinted that Chris hadn't done the killing."

"So?"

Her troubled eyes held his. "He's coming back later tonight. I'll get it out of him, Dade."

He downed his drink and stood up. "I'm sorry, Mae."

She shrugged.

Dade opened the door, then turned back to the woman. "I'd go easy on the bottle, Mae," he said dryly. "You'll need all your senses tonight."

He closed the door and walked toward the hotel. He was fed up with the whole dirty business.

CHAPTER FOURTEEN

Boone Burkitt was drunk. Strange thoughts drifted through his simple mind as he watched Dade Averill leave Mae Delano's house and walk toward his hotel. Boone had little imagination, but there was an animal cunning in him, coupled with a viciousness that made him dangerous.

Burkitt leaned against a post and watched Dade enter the Territorial House. Then he crossed to the jail and walked in. Alex Ray was sound asleep in a small room that opened off the outer office, the Rochester lamp turned low. Boone padded down to Chris Guthrie's cell. The foreman was fast asleep. Boone rested a hand on his Colt. It would be so easy, but then Boone would have a hell of a time getting out of that mess.

He padded back up the hallway. Something moved in the first cell. Burkitt placed his broad face close to the bars and looked in. A scrawny man lay on the bunk, looking up at the ceiling. He turned to look at Boone.

Boone stared at the little man.

"What is it you wish *señor?*" politely inquired the frightened muleteer.

"Who're you?"

"Jesus Madera."

"Oh! Drunk again, Madera?"

"No. *Señor* Averill arrested me."

"Why?"

"It has something to do with the killing of *Señor* Harshaw."

Burkitt stared.

Jesus got up. "You can help me?" he asked. He walked to the front of the cell and peered through the thick bars. *"Sacre Dios!"* he said. "It is you!"

Burkitt shifted his big hands on the bars. *"What do you mean, Jesus?"*

Jesus paled. His eyes widened.

Burkitt shot a hand between the bars and gripped the Mexican by the front of his shirt, pulling him closer to the bars.

"I know nothing, *señor,"* quavered Jesus.

Burkitt's hands slid up and gripped the Mexican by the throat. His powerful hands closed on the thin throat. Jesus had no chance. His sandaled feet pattered on the floor. Then he was hanging in Burkitt's hands like a limp rag doll, his head lolling to one side.

Burkitt dropped the strangled man and padded back to Ray's room. The officer was still asleep. Boone took the cell keys and opened the door of Jesus' cell. Swiftly he untied the woven *faja* from about Jesus' waist. He dragged the little man to the window and noosed the *faja* about his neck. Then he looped the other end of the girdle through the bars of the high window and pulled it tight, pulling the body up so that the feet were free of the floor.

"Burkitt locked the cell, hung up the keys, and wiped his damp hands on his vest. He turned toward the door and stumbled over a chair.

"Who is it?" called Alex Ray.

Burkitt opened the outer door.

Ray's feet hit the floor. "Who in hell *is* that?" he called out.

Boone trotted swiftly up the street and turned off on Yucca. He vanished into the night as Alex Ray came out in front of the jail and looked up and down the deserted street. The big deputy shrugged and went back into the *calabozo* and back to sleep.

DADE AWOKE SHORTLY AFTER DAWN. He dressed and went downstairs, got a cup of coffee in the restaurant, and then went to the jail.

Ray was still asleep when Dade came in. Dade awakened him and sat down in a chair in the little room as Ray pulled on his boots. "All quiet?" asked Dade.

Ray nodded. He picked up his hat and walked out into the outer office. Dade followed him. "How about breakfast for the prisoners?" asked Dade.

"I'll have it sent in."

Dade looked at Jesus' cell. Then he threw his cigar on the floor and rushed to the bars. Jesus hung from his *faja*, his sandaled feet a few inches from the floor. "The keys!" yelled Dade.

Ray snatched the keys from the hook and unlocked the cell. Dade pushed past him and gripped the little muleteer. The man was hours dead. He looked at Ray. "Didn't you hear anything?"

"How did I know he would do this?" Dade cut the *faja* from the bar and lowered the little body to the bunk.

Ray stamped back into the office. "There'll be hell to pay for this," he said. "The Mexes will give us plenty of trouble."

Dade worked the noose loose from the swollen neck. Then he saw the livid fingermarks on the thin throat. He glanced back at Ray and then pulled the muleteer's shirt up about his neck. "Get Doc Safford," he said quietly.

Safford came in alone. He looked at the poor body. "He was scared to death, Dade," he said. "Poor no good. How'd he do it?"

Dade jerked a thumb at the *faja*. "Where's Ray?"

"Went to eat."

Dade pulled the loose shirt away from the throat "Look," he said quietly.

Safford examined the neck of the little man, probing with skillful fingers. He looked at Dade. "This man was strangled by hands," he said. "Powerful hands. The larynx is crushed."

Dade nodded. "Ray doesn't know," he said.

"What is it, Dade?"

"Damned if I know. It wasn't Ray; he couldn't fake his surprise that well."

"Then who "did it?"

"It's easy to guess. The man who killed Harshaw came in here, found Ray asleep, strangled this poor little Mex, then tried to make it look like suicide."

"*Who?*"

Dade lit a cigar. He said softly, "I'll bet this cigar against a drink that the murderer was Boone Burkitt."

Safford pulled the blanket over the still form. "What do you want me to do?"

"Keep your mouth shut about this. Write out a detailed report, stating the actual cause of death and keep it locked up."

"That's easy. I'm the county assistant coroner."

Dade smashed a fist into his other palm. "The one lead I had on the killing," he said. "Jesus never told me who it was he saw kill Harshaw. This is a dirty business, Doc."

Safford podded. "Maybe we'd better go fishing," he said and left the jail.

Dade walked down to Guthrie's cell. The foreman looked up. "Well?"

Dade eyed the sullen man. "That Mexican I brought in here last night is dead. Hanged himself."

"So?"

"He was the only man who saw Harshaw's killer."

Guthrie wet his lips.

"Did you see or hear anyone in here last night or early this morning?"

"No."

"Your breakfast will be in here shortly."

"Don't put yourself out, Lawman."

Miles Moilan came in at nine o'clock. "What's this about Jesus Madera?" he asked.

Dade jerked his head at the cell where the muleteer lay. "Hanged himself."

"I know that. But why?"

"How should I know?"

Moilan dropped into a chair and gripped his powerful hands together. Dade looked at the huge paws. Moilan was powerful enough to crush a man's throat in those hands.

"I've had three Mexicans in this morning," Miles said. "Jorge Amadeo. Tomas Chavez. Rodrigo Vaca. Believe me, Dade, they're riled up. Why didn't you stay here last night?"

"Ray is the boss here. He said he would."

Moilan sank down in his chair. "It's all over town. The Mexican quarter is seething. Jesus was a drunken quarreling no good, but now he's a martyr to gringo ways. The Mexicans say he was driven to suicide."

Dade scratched at the corner of his mouth. "Jesus wasn't driven to suicide, Miles; he was strangled to death. The killer looped Jesus' *faja* about his neck to make it look like suicide."

Miles paled. "You're sure?"

Dade nodded. "You can still see the finger bruises. The larynx was crushed. Took a powerful man, Miles. A man as powerful as you."

Moilan shot a frosty glance at Dade from under bristling brows. "Where was Ray when it happened?"

"Sleeping, I suppose."

"How about Guthrie?"

"He says he heard nothing."

Moilan scratched his jaw. "This is a stinking, dirty business, Dade. Tagger is riled. Now the Mexicans are talking war. Unless we square it with them, I'll lose their votes."

Dade eyed the big man. "Is that all you can think about?"

Miles flushed. "It's my business!"

Dade nodded. "How many funerals have you paid for in the Mexican quarter?"

"None of your business!"

Dade inspected his cigar. It was an old dodge with Anglo politicians. Pay for a Mexican's funeral and you had the love of his whole family. Buy a few pounds of sticky candy for the kids and you had their parents' friendship. Pay the rent for a crumbling adobe or a jacal, and you were like God to them.

Miles stood up. "Tagger wants Guthrie freed. The town wants Harshaw's killer. The Mexicans are up in arms because of Jesus' death. You'd better find a way out of this, Dade."

"I didn't kill Harshaw. Nor Jesus."

Miles spat. "You're in this thing now, Dade. Up to your neck. Think about it."

Dade watched the big man stamp out, of the office. Jimmy Harshaw came in, shamefaced as he greeted Dade. His face was white.

"Feeling better?" asked Dade.

Jim nodded. "I'm sorry about last night," he said. "It was the liquor."

"Learn to handle it or leave it alone."

Jimmy leaned against the wall. "I heard about Jesus. The Mexicans are surely riled, Dade."

"I know."

"There's about a dozen of them down in Bartolome's Cantina. Lefty Corse and Lanky Jones are down there, too, talking it up with them. I saw Boone

Burkitt heading that way. There might be trouble, Dade."

Dade grinned. "There's been nothing but trouble ever since I got off that train."

"You can deputize me."

"No. Go get Alex Ray."

Jimmy shook his head. "Alex left town half an homage."

Dade looked up. "Where are Tagger and his boys?"

"They went back to the ranch. Without Corse and Jones."

Dade stood up. "Tell Miles I'll need some help."

"Ok." The kid left the jail.

Dade placed his shotgun beside the front door, this was a new development. Corse and Jones were hardcases, and Corse had been riled the night before, not only at Dade but at Tagger for hitting him. Burkitt would see his opportunity. Dade walked back to Guthrie's cell. "More trouble brewing," he said.

"If I ever get out of this *calabozo,* I'll give you more trouble than you ever knew before."

"That's neither here nor there. The Mexicans are talking war. Alex Ray has left town. Burkitt is probably talking trouble with the Mexes right now. Lefty Corse and Lanky Jones are with them."

Guthrie looked up. "I don't know why Glenn ever kept those two *hombres* on his payroll. It cost him plenty to keep, bailing them out of here. He's well rid of them." Guthrie narrowed his eyes. "What makes you think the Mexes will come here?"

"They're riled about Jesus, as I said. Maybe your *amigo* Burkitt will use them to get at you."

Guthrie laughed. "You're losing your grip, Averill."

"Maybe. If they get in here past me, I wouldn't give a plugged peso for your chances of getting out of here alive."

Guthrie half-closed his eyes. "You can always spring me, Averill."

"And get a slug in the back from you?"

"When I shoot at you, Averill, it will be from the front when you've got a six-gun in your hand."

Dade walked back to the office and looked into the street. A cold wind swept up the street, driving dust before it. The sky was heavy with dark clouds. There was a feeling of rain in the air. There was no one on the street; there were no ponies standing hipshot in front of the saloons. It was like a ghost town, with the wind moaning through it

CHAPTER FIFTEEN

The rain began to come down before noon and by one o'clock the wide street was a shallow river. The rain was driven by the cold wind in billowing sheets. It darkened the wooden buildings and poured from the eaves and the flat roofs of the adobes in silvery sheets. Now and then, lightning forked across the black skies, illuminating the town in ghastly light.

Guthrie dozed on his bunk. Dade walked back and forth in the cold jail, now and then going to the door and looking up and down the steaming street. The town seemed deserted.

A little after three a lone horseman urged his steaming pony up the street. Dade watched him from the door. The *vaquero* reined in his roan beneath a ramada and slid from the saddle. The water glistened on his long poncho. He splashed toward Dade. Dade placed his hand on the Greener. The man raised his head. It was Slim Boyd. "Averill," he said, "I want to talk with you."

Dade jerked his head. Boyd came in, dripping water on the dirty floor. He took off his soaked hat and slapped it against his thigh. "Glenn told me to stay in town and keep an eye on things. I started for the ranch an hour ago, then I saw two Lazy T cayuses under the ramada near Bartolome's Cantina. I knew they was the horse's Lefty Corse and Lanky Jones used. Tagger had told me to pick them up if Lefty and Lanky didn't show up at the ranch. I was about to go into Bartolome's when I got to figgerin' I might get a hot reception from those two drunks. About that time a Mex comes out of the cantina and tells me Corse Jones and Burkitt are in there talking war with a dozen Mexicans."

Dade nodded. "I know."

The wrangler rolled a smoke. "You don't know all of it. The story those three have started is that Jesus was a witness against Guthrie and that Guthrie strangled him last night and hung him up to make it look like suicide."

"Guthrie's been locked up all the time!"

"I know that, but those people are taking on a bellyful of tequila, mezcal, and *aguardiente*. The more Burkitt talks, the madder they get. They're primed, Dade."

"Raise the mud, out to the ranch. Get Tagger and pound leather back here. I'm all alone here, Slim."

Slim sucked at his damp cigarette. "I won't make much time in this mud."

"*Vamonos* then! *Pronto!*"

Slim slapped on his soaked hat and left the jail. Dade walked back to Guthrie. He said, "Burkitt, Corse, and Jones are telling the Mexes that you strangled Jesus because he was a witness against you."

"This is loco!"

"I know it. You know it. But they're loaded with liquor."

"Give me a gun!"

Dade eyed the foreman, then walked back to the office and got Guthrie's gun belt, heavy with cartridges and Colt. He took the jail keys, opened Guthrie's cell, and handed him the belt. Their eyes met. "I'll leave the key in the back door," said Dade. "If they get in, you take off like a tall bird."

Guthrie grinned. "Don't worry."

Guthrie swung his gun belt about his waist and buckled it. He settled it about his lean hips and rested his hand on the butt.

"Head for the ranch," Dade said. "Slim Boyd went to get Glenn and some of the boys."

"Supposing I just keep going?"

"I'll come after you."

"I'd like that."

Dade took the cigar from his mouth. "I'll bet you would."

Dade went back to the front of the jail and looked out the door. The rain still sluiced down. A group of men stood at the corner of Main and Mesquite looking toward the jail. There was no mistaking the bulky figure of Boone Burkitt flanked by the shorter figure of Lefty Corse and the gangling figure of Lanky Jones. Behind the three men were ten or twelve Mexicans, the rain dripping from their huge steeple-crowned hats and ponchos.

Dade closed the door and leaned against the wall, waiting. It would take Slim forty-five minutes at least to get to the Lazy T. Another forty-five to round up enough men. Forty-five minutes to come back. Maybe they could be in Estanque in two hours. It would be a long two hours.

The men were plodding toward the jail now. There was no one else on the soaked street. He watched them cross the alleyway. Burkitt stopped at the corner of the jail. "Go ahead, Jorge," he said to a tall Mexican.

The Mexican came toward the door, his face set and hard beneath the shadowy brim of his hat. Dade stepped out and nodded. Burkitt wouldn't risk coming up against a scattergun this time.

Jorge stopped ten feet from Dade. "*Señor* Sheriff," he said quietly, "we want the man Chris Guthrie."

Dade leaned against the doorway. "Jorge," he said,

"this is a foolish thing. Those three gringos are out to make trouble. They are using you and your friends."

"One of our people was murdered in this jail last night by the man Guthrie."

"That is a foolish thing to say."

"No, Jesus saw Guthrie kill Sheriff Harshaw. Guthrie killed the only witness against him."

The rest of the men still stood in the alleyway watching Dade and Jorge. "The man who killed Harshaw was shorter and heavier than Chris Guthrie. Jesus himself said that he couldn't be sure that Guthrie had done it."

"That is easy to say. Jesus is not here to confirm or deny it."

"I swear it is the truth, Jorge."

The Mexican wiped the water from his face. "Let us have this man. We will settle with him."

"I'm sorry, Jorge."

Jorge spat. "We will attack the jail," he said.

"Men will get shot."

"*Señor*, you might be the one that gets shot. Come. Let us in. It is useless to resist."

"I have sent a man for Glenn Tagger and his men. If Guthrie is harmed, they will hunt you down and kill you."

Jorge's face creased into a smile. "The man you sent to get the Lazy T men is lying unconscious in the mud behind Bartolome's Cantina."

There was a cold feeling in Dade. The men at the corner had not moved. Then Dade saw that Lanky Jones was missing. He stepped back inside the doorway. "Jorge," he said, "I am closing this door. If you come at me with your men, I will shoot."

Jorge just stood there.

Dade reached for the door handle. Something rattled against the bars of a window set in the jail wall bordering the alleyway. Dade looked at the window in time to see a pistol barrel thrust between the bars. He hit the floor as the gun spat flame and smoke into the room. The slug smashed into the wall behind him.

Jorge drove a shoulder against the door, and it swung fully open, striking Dade on the shoulder, and driving him flat on the floor. Feet squelched in the mud outside the jail.

"Make your break, Guthrie!" yelled Dade.

Jorge kicked and his spurred boot raked Dade's face. He clawed for his Colt as a pair of Mexicans came through the doorway. Another boot drove against his head. The room whirled. Guthrie's cell door banged open, and a Colt barked twice. The Mexicans cursed as they dove for cover. Dade heard the back door crash open just as a wave of darkness poured over him, drowning him in a sea of ebony.

CHAPTER SIXTEEN

H e'll be all right," the voice said from a long way off. "He's got a hard head," another voice said. Dade opened his eyes. He looked up into the face of Doc Safford. Miles Moilan was behind him. Dade lay on the bunk in the first cell. Salford pushed Dade gently back as he tried to get up. "Take it easy, you got a bad crack on the head."

"Did Guthrie get caught?" asked Dade.

Moilan shook his head. "Chris made it. He winged Jorge and creased another man. No one else would close in on him."

"Where were you when I needed you?"

Moilan shrugged. "I didn't know anything was brewing.

"I sent Jimmy Harshaw for you."

"I was out of town."

Dade closed his eyes. "You and Alex Ray."

"I wasn't with him if that's what you mean."

Dade touched his bruised face. "I'm sick of the whole business. Damned if I know why I agreed to take on the job of deputy-sheriff in this place."

Moilan spat. "You've made a mess of it. Guthrie lose,

Jesus a suicide, the Mexes looking for Guthrie, and Tagger looking for the Mexes to keep them off Guthrie."

Dade sat up.

Miles clenched his fists. "And you... the lawman... lying here with a broken head. You know no more about Harshaw's murderer than I do."

Dade stood up, reeling a little. "I *told* you I winged the man who got Harshaw. Jesus knew it wasn't Guthrie who killed Gil! The doctor will tell you he treated Burkitt for a gunshot wound which Burkitt claimed was made by a nail. Guthrie's shotgun was missing from Mae Delano's place. Mae told me that Burkitt hinted Guthrie didn't kill Harshaw."

Moilan's eyes were half-closed. "So Mae told you?"

"Burkitt was supposed to come back there last night Mae said she'd work it out of him."

Moilan spat. "The damned fool! If Chris finds out you were in there and that Burkitt was in there, too, he'll come gunnin' for both of you."

"He heard I was there. I don't know who told him."

Safford looked up. "That's easy. Burkitt must have done it to turn Chris against you."

Moilan said, "That's it!"

Safford closed his medical case. "Something else, Miles. Jesus didn't commit suicide. He was strangled to death. Someone put the *faja* about his neck *after* he was choked to death."

"I know. Dade told me."

"Burkitt," said Dade quietly. "Burkitt killed Harshaw and tried to pin it on Guthrie. He must have come in here last night when Ray was asleep, saw Jesus, and knew that Jesus knew him. He couldn't take a chance on the Mex testifying against him."

He walked out of the cell. The floor was wet and stained with mud. The acrid odor of powder smoke still hung in the damp air. Outside, the rain slugged steadily down. It was almost as dark as night.

Dade unpinned the star from his coat and threw it on the desk. Safford looked quickly at him. "What's this?"

Dade turned. "I let Guthrie escape. I couldn't protect Jesus."

Moilan looked at the star. "You'll need it to get Burkitt"

"No," said Dade quietly. "I'll get him, but I'll do it on my own."

"You can get into trouble that way."

Dade looked queerly at the big man and then laughed loudly. "Sometimes you have a dab of humor, Miles. There are times when you really tickle me."

"That bump on the head did you no good, Dade."

"On the contrary, Miles. It did me a lot of good." Dade picked up his hat and placed it on his head. "Alex Ray can have his *calabozo* back. Empty. That seems to be the way he likes it." He walked out into the streaming rain.

Miles looked at Doc Safford. "Can you figure that out?"

Safford shrugged. "Don't worry. Averill is something we rarely find in this world. An honest man. He cannot wear that star and be an honest man."

"Poppycock!"

Safford's wise old eyes studied Miles. "Nor can he work for you, Miles Moilan, and still believe that he can be an honest man."

"Doc, sometimes you talk too much."

"I agree. But maybe the truth hurts you, Miles." Safford drew his raincoat about his thin shoulders and plunged out into the streaming rain.

Miles Moilan looked about the damp, deserted jail. Then he walked outside and closed the door, standing beneath the porch roof for a long time. *I've been angry with Dade ever since he came here,* he thought, *because he couldn't see his way clear to get mixed up in my political machinery. Maybe Dade's way is right. He was a little green when I*

*first knew him and he admired me for my qualities of strength
and courage. Maybe now I should admire him for his honesty
and courage. I thought I needed, his help. Now I know he needs
mine.*

Miles plodded down the street, heedless of the water
that ran down his collar and soaked his clothing.

———

DADE'S BAG was packed by a quarter-past five. The
Mogul passed through Estanque a little- before six. He
looked around the room once more and then put out the
Argand lamp. He left the room and walked downstairs.
The clerk handed him his bill and Dade paid it

The clerk leaned across the desk. "Some of us are
sorry to see you go," he said.

Dade picked up his bag. "I haven't met anyone in
Estanque who has said so."

"Estanque needs good citizens, Mister Averill."

Dade grinned wryly. "I hope they find them."

"I wish you'd reconsider staying, sir."

Dade shook his head. "Cump Sherman once heard
that all Texas needed was water and good citizens. He
capped that statement by saying that was all *hell* really
needed." Dade looked at the streaming windows. "You've
got your water." He left the hotel.

The street was inches deep in water, puddling greasily
on the high spots. Dade splashed across Railroad Street,
stepped up on the platform, and pushed open the door of
the station.

The station agent turned from a gloomy perusal of
the soaking night through a dirty window. He said,
"Another few hours of this and we'll have to get canoes to
get back and forth."

Dade nodded. "The train coming through?"

"Yes, surprisingly enough. I figured there'd be a
washout or two, but it's only half an hour late."

"I want a ticket,"

"Where to?"

"What?"

The agent looked curiously at Dade. "I said, *where to?*"

Dade hadn't really thought about that. "North."

"You'll *have* to go north. But where?"

"It doesn't matter."

"You can make a connection at Las Vegas."

"Ok."

The agent stamped the ticket, handed it to Dade and Dade paid him. The agent stoked up the stove. "I'm leaving," he said. "I want to get home before I have to swim."

Dade nodded. He bit the end from a cigar and lit it. The agent shrugged into his poncho and left the station. The telegraph clicked steadily and then stopped. The rain pattered on the roof and sluiced from the eaves. Outside, the signal light gleamed in the wetness.

Half an hour drifted past Dade drummed on the window with his fingers. His cigar went out. Twenty more minutes dragged past. The doorknob turned. Dade whirled, pushing back his coat The door opened and he saw the oval face of Lucy Harshaw. She closed the door behind her and leaned against it, her hands behind her back.

"Evening, Miss Lucy," said Dade quietly.

She eyed him steadily. "You're running out on us, Dade," she said.

Dade shrugged. "What have I done to run out on?"

She came forward. "Even those that dislike you admit that you have been honest."

"Honesty doesn't seem to be an admired trait around here."

"Since my father was murdered, they have been talking a great deal about what must be done in Estanque."

"Talk is cheap."

"Not many of them are people of action as you are."

Dade grinned.

"Please stay."

"No, I'm leaving. I've had enough."

She walked to the window and looked out into the streaming darkness. "You were the only man who made an effort to find the man who killed my father. You found Jesus. It wasn't your fault that he was murdered, too."

"Jesus was the one who could have placed the noose about the murderer's neck."

"You saved Jimmy from getting killed by Boone Burkitt. Saved him from fighting Lanky Jones. Changed him overnight. He admires you, Dade. Dad never had much control over Jimmy. He did until he became a political pawn here in the county, then Jimmy was ashamed of him."

"Thanks," he said quietly. "I'm proud of having helped Jimmy."

"He knows you are leaving. Now he knows he must find the man who killed my father. What chance does he have against men like Burkitt, Guthrie, Jones, and the others?"

Dade raised his head. Far down the line, he heard the thin whistle of the train. "Who sent you here?" he asked.

"I came of my own accord, Dade."

Dade took her by the elbows. "Tell me the truth!"

Her eyes were steady. "Miles Moilan came to the house and told me what had happened."

"Then it's more of his conniving!"

She shook her head. "Look at me, Dade! Do you think it was easy for me to come here? People know of your visiting Mae Delano. There are some stories circulating about the two of you. At first, I believed them. Now I don't"

"I knew Mae years ago. She wants to save Chris Guthrie. She was trying to help me."

"I realized that."

The whistle sounded again, much closer this time, above the lash of the driving rain.

"Will you stay?" she asked softly. She rested her head against his chest. "For me, Dade, only for me if you *must* have me say so."

The[7] sound of the engine came to them on the cold wind. Dade lifted her chin and kissed her wet lips. "You'd better get home out of this rain," he said.

Dade picked up his bag and took her by the arm. They left the station as the train rounded a curve and sounded its whistle. The locomotive's light showed the steely glitter of the driving rain.

They crossed the street as the train brakes shrieked in the night. The lights in one passenger car showed yellow against the darkness. The conductor swung down and waited on the soaked platform. He looked up and down the platform. "All aboarrrd!" he called out.

The conductor swung up on the open platform. The Mogul gripped the tracks and chugged off, leaving a low streamer of smoke hanging behind it.

Lucy looked back at the disappearing train. "I'm so glad," she said quietly.

Dade gripped her elbow. He felt as though he had just come home after a long trip.

The loneliest sound in the world carried to them on the wind, the whistle of a train across the night.

CHAPTER SEVENTEEN

At eight o'clock the wind was cold, but Dade felt warm from the arms of the woman he had just left. He whistled softly as he reached Main Street and turned toward the hotel. He looked back at the cheery lights of the Harshaw house, and a cold realization came over him that the real trouble was yet to come.

Dade walked into the hotel lobby. The clerk wasn't in. Dade took his key, signed the register, and walked upstairs. He let himself into his room and dropped his bag on the floor. He took out dry clothing and peeled off his wet boots and trousers. The rain rattled against the hotel walls.

Dade pulled on old trousers and his wet boots. He wasn't wearing the star now. He wiped his weapons and stowed them on his person, shrugging into his old leather coat. Boone Burkitt was still on the loose, possibly with his two new allies, Lefty Corse, and Lanky Jones. Maybe they had found Guthrie by now. That would settle the deal one way or another.

Dade reached for his hat, and something moved in the big closet. Then the door banged open, and Dade whirled, clawing for his Colt. Chris Guthrie stepped out into the room, his Colt at hip level, the thumb hooked over the hammer spur. "Don't draw, Averill," he warned quietly. "I'll drill you before you clear leather."

Dade slowly raised his hands.

Guthrie was splattered with mud from head to foot. His wet clothing hung on his lean frame. His eyes were cold in his pale face as he crossed swiftly to the door and turned the key, watching Dade all the time.

Dade felt the weight of his derringer on his left wrist, but the odds were too heavy against his drawing in time to outshoot Guthrie.

The foreman jerked his head. "Get over by the wall."

Dade moved. Cold sweat trickled down his sides.

Guthrie ran his free hand across his mouth. "Burkitt nearly got me," he said.

"You were loco to stay in town."

"Maybe. Burkitt is out in the rain looking for me with his two drunken *amigos*."

It had been shrewd of Guthrie to stay in town. Dade wondered where he had been hiding out. He would have avoided Mae Delano's.

Guthrie. shoved back his hat. "You're supposed to be a gunslick," he said. "I'm evening this up, Averill."

"How?"

"I don't doubt but what you've got a whole damned arsenal on you. Right?"

Dade nodded.

"Dump them! No tricks, mind."

Dade eased his hand into his left jacket pocket and threw the belly-gun on the bed.

"You've got a stingy gun, too."

Dade unclipped the derringer from his left wrist and dropped it beside the Colt.

"Where's your other Colt?"

Dade took it from the leather-lined pocket and placed it beside the others.

Guthrie looked at the trio of guns with sarcastic amusement. "Quite an arsenal."

"I've been forced to use all three of them at one time or another."

"Part of your dirty business?"

"Part of my *business,*" said Dade.

Guthrie jerked his head. "Put that single-action back where you keep it."

Dade slid it into his leather-lined pocket.

"No holster?"

Dade shook his head.

"You think you can outdraw me from that pocket?"

Dade eyed the cold-eyed foreman. "What do you mean?"

"I'll give you a fair shake. I'm going to holster this Colt, then we'll both draw."

"You're loco."

Guthrie shook his head. "No. Around here, I had the reputation of being the top gun until *you* came to town."

"Top gun, eh?"

Guthrie shrugged. "I don't give a damn about that you horned in on Mae, after sticking me in the *caldbozo,* Averill. I don't take that from any man. You promised to protect me until I was cleared. You didn't. Now it's between the two of us."

"This won't settle anything. You kill me and they'll really have a case against you. I kill you and that will do you and Mae a lot of good."

"You talk too damned much for a fighting man."

Dade raised his head. "We'll see," he said.

Guthrie stepped back, pinwheeling the heavy six-gun three feet into the air. The butt smacked into his palm and then he rolled it, sliding the barrel down into his Missouri holster.

Dade rubbed his lean jaw. "Very pretty," he said. "You must practice a lot, Guthrie."

"Yeh. Don't you?"

Dade shook his head. "This is a crazy business. Forget it, Guthrie. No good will come of it."

"*Nunca!*"

Guthrie poked two fingers into his vest pocket and brought out a coin. He balanced it on his left thumbnail. "When this hits the floor, Averill," he said, "we draw." Guthrie shivered a little in his wet clothing. He looked at Dade. "Ready?"

"As much as I'll ever be."

Guthrie snapped his thumb. The coin shot upward then dropped, and clicked on the floor. Guthrie's right-hand snaked down for a draw. Dade moved in one fluid motion, hunching forward, thrusting out his right shoulder, feeling his fingers curl about his own gun butt and trigger, thumb hooked over the hammer spur. The gun whipped up and forward at the same time his left hand shot out to block Guthrie's swift draw. Dade's muzzle jammed into Guthrie. The foreman's breath rushed out.

Dade looked into the wide eyes of the man he had outdrawn. "Well?" he said softly.

Guthrie raised his chin. "Shoot!"

Dade eyed the man for a moment and then stepped back, letting down the Colt hammer. "Maybe you'd like to try it again, Guthrie?"

Guthrie was struggling within himself, *wanting* to test the man opposite him again. A minute flowed past. "No," he said. "You had me cold, Averill."

"You're tired and wet. I had the edge."

Guthrie shook his head. Dade grinned and slid the Colt into its pocket.

Guthrie shivered again.

Dade took a bottle from his bag and handed it to the foreman, who took a deep slug. "I needed that!" he said.

Dade opened his bag and took out a clean set of drawers, a worn shirt, and a pair of levis. "Put these on," he said.

Guthrie stripped down, revealing his corded arms and

muscular upper body, dotted with goose flesh. He dressed swiftly and took another drink. "You're a man," he said to Dade.

"No more than you, Guthrie."

Guthrie grinned.

Dade handed the foreman a smoke. He snapped a lucifer on his thumbnail and lit the cigar. "You should have figured someone wanted us to hate each other, talking about Mae like that," he said quietly.

Guthrie's eyes half-closed. "What do we do now?"

Dade dropped into a chair and helped himself to a drink. "Burkitt aims to get you. Alex Ray feels the same way. They think you hate my guts. Burkitt, or Ray, has spread the story around town that you aimed to get me because of Mae."

Guthrie laughed dryly. "I did."

Dade relit his cigar. "Supposing word got around that you were coming into town for a showdown with me?"

"I don't get it."

"Supposing we were to shoot it out? Odds are that either one of us, or *both*, might get killed."

"Keep talking."

"Don't you think Ray and Burkitt would figure that as the answer to their problem? If I got you, Ray wouldn't have to worry about getting defeated for sheriff. If you got me, they'd frame you into a murder charge against me, or make it plain that you actually killed Gil Harshaw. It'd be the perfect deal for them."

Guthrie took his cigar from his mouth. "I don't get this clearly."

Dade hitched his chair closer to the foreman. "I'd be willing to bet they'd never stop you if you came into town. They'd be lying low waiting to see the outcome of our fight. Do you think they'd let either one of us walk away from that fight?"

Guthrie rubbed his jaw. He cursed softly. Then he looked up at Dade. "How do we work it?"

"No one knows about you coming here, do they?"

"No. I hid out in Moilan's Livery Stable after circling through the creek bottoms. I'm sure no one saw me."

"Bueno! You stay here. I'll get you a horse. You can get out of here tonight and lay low. I'll get word around town that you're coming in, and somehow I'll get the thought planted in their minds to lay an ambush."

"It's loco."

"What chance do you think you have if they track you down out in the hills?"

Guthrie downed a drink. "None."

"Then it's a deal?"

Guthrie looked up at Dade. "What's your real angle?"

Dade squeezed his temples with his hand. "I want the man who got Harshaw. That man is Boone Burkitt. And Ray is in with Burkitt."

"I know."

Dade pulled on his slicker. "Stay pat! Don't answer that door if anyone knocks."

"I'm not that stupid."

Dade left the room and walked down the back stairs to the alleyway and headed for the Harshaw house. Lucy Harshaw was in bed and Jimmy answered the door. He stood on the porch and listened to Dade as the rain dripped past them. "You can take my horse," the kid said. "People will think Guthrie stole it from me."

Dade gripped Jimmy by the arm. "You spread a story around town that Chris Guthrie is coming into town tomorrow night to gun me down. You think you can handle it?"

Jimmy grinned. "As a storyteller, I don't have to take a back seat to anybody, Dade."

"Where's the horse?"

"In the stable. The buckskin."

Dade stepped off the porch and made his way through the dripping night to the stable. He found the buckskin, saddled it, and led it through the alleyway to the hotel. He tethered it there and hurried upstairs. Guthrie answered the door when he identified himself.

Dade slapped the rain from his hat. "Jimmy Harshaw will spread the story that you're coming into town. Make it after dark, to give Burkitt and Ray time to plan their trap."

"I hope you're right about this thing, Dade. Sounds phony."

Dade looked quickly at the foreman. "It *is*."

"What do I do?"

"Come into town about seven. I'll be near Main and Mesquite. Leave your horse near the livery stable. I'll see you at Yucca and come to meet you. Challenge me. We draw. Start shooting."

"Who goes down?"

Dade thought. "Maybe it had better be me. They're more anxious to get you."

"Ok."

"Keep your eyes peeled on the building. If they are in ambush and I know where they are, I'll have Jimmy Harshaw at the livery to tip you off."

"And if they're not?"

Dade looked at the foreman. "They will be."

Guthrie thrust out his hand. "Good night, *campanero*."

"Go with God, *amigo*."

Dade heard him walking down the back stairs. Supposing Guthrie was still bent on revenge? It was a disquieting thought. But Guthrie was the kind of man who fought out in the open, with a fair shake. Dade would bet that Guthrie would act true to character.

CHAPTER EIGHTEEN

The rain had died out sometime during the gusty night, but low clouds hung over the countryside. The streets were puddled, and the mud was thick everywhere, churned into a greasy paste by the passage of wheels and hoofs. The cold wind swept through the town, swinging signs, and battering against the thin wooden walls.

Estanque was quiet except for the low-muttered talk in the saloons and the stores. Men came out of buildings, looked up and down the street, and then hurried about their business. There was a brooding tension about the town, for everyone knew by now that Chris Guthrie was waiting his chance to brace Dade Averill in the muddy streets.

Dade sat in the Bull's Head, playing poker with Joe Fettis and Krepps the barber. Doc Safford straddled a chair, watching the slow game. Krepps wet his thin lips. He said, "I'll be glad when I can get back to hair-cutting and shaving."

"Joe," said Doc Safford, "how come you're not at the stable?"

Joe leaned back and rolled a smoke. "I'm like everyone else in town," he said. "Can't keep my mind on my business." He looked at Dade. "You think Chris will actually come into town?"

Dade looked up. "The word has gone around."

Krepps pushed his cards together and shoved them to the center of the table. "I'm out," he said.

Safford laughed.

Harry, the bartender, came over to the table with a bottle. "Ready for more?" he asked.

Dade shook his head. Joe filled his glass and that of Krepps and Safford.

Harry looked down at Dade. "You won't be in here when he comes?"

Dade grinned. "You can always take the mirror down."

Harry spat. "I've done enough business this morning to pay for another mirror. Ain't anybody in this town minding their own business?"

"Roman holiday," said Dade.

Joe looked up. "Them Romans use six-shooters?"

"Knives," said Krepps.

Safford shook his head. "Dade means that the old Romans would have holidays when they went to the Coliseum to watch the gladiators fight and to see the Christians get fed to the lions."

"That a saloon?" asked Harry. "The Coliseum, I mean."

Doc shook his head.

Joe lit his smoke. "There useta be a Coliseum Saloon in El Paso."

"It's still there," said Dade.

Krepps stood up. "Damn. I can't sit here like this. Why don't you do something, Dade?"

"What, for example?"

Krepps shrugged. "Get outa town. Go look for Guthrie. Anything."

Dade shoved in his cards. "I'll wait," he said.

Krepps downed his drink and left the saloon.

"You want to play?" Dade asked Joe.

Joe shook his head. "I can't keep my mind on the cards," he said.

Dade walked to the bar and bought some cigars. He walked out into the cold street, stowing the cigars in his pocket. He walked toward Mesquite Street and saw Mae Delano come out on her porch. Her face was pale, and her hands shook as she looked at Dade. "Is he really coming?" she asked.

"That's what they say."

"Can't you stop it, Dade?" she asked desperately.

"No."

She came down to the fence. "What's going on?" she asked.

"Showdown, Mae."

"But why between you and Chris? Don't you see that's what they want?"

"Chris is safe from me."

"I don't understand."

Dade raised his head. "You will. Chris and I are working together. Keep your mouth shut about this, Mae."

She placed a hand at her smooth throat. "But what about the others? Burkitt, Ray, Corse, and Jones? What about the Mexicans? They'll kill Chris!"

Dade grinned. "You're not worried about me?"

"Of course I am!"

"*Gracias*. Stay in the house, Mae."

"You'll both get killed."

"Maybe."

"Look," she said quickly. "You leave town. I'll find Chris and get him to take me away."

"For a woman who has spent a great deal of her life in the company of men, you don't seem to know much about them."

"Maybe I've learned too *much* about men, Dade."

Dade shrugged. "You should have learned enough

about them to know they work these things out in their own way."

———

JIMMY HARSHAW CAME to Dade's room at four o'clock. He dropped into a chair and watched Dade cleaning his six-gun. "That's a beauty," he said. "I'd like to try it someday."

Dade looked up. "You can have it if anything happens to me, Jim."

"You? What have you got to worry about?"

Dade said nothing but wiped the gleaming barrel of the Colt and placed it on the bed. He picked up the ugly belly-gun and emptied the cylinder.

"I thought you said you had worked out a deal with Guthrie."

Dade began to clean the double-action. "I have. I wasn't thinking of Guthrie."

Jimmy shoved back his hat. "The story is all over town. Lucy is worried sick, Dade."

"About who?"

"You of course!" Jimmy wet his lips. "Burkitt and Corse are in Bartolome's Cantina,"

"So?"

"I don't like the looks of this, Dade. Alex Ray is in the *calabozo,* and he's got a bottle."

Dade worked on the six-gun, pushing a swab through the barrel. He checked it against the light. Then he wiped the gun with an oily cloth and followed it with a dry one. He slid the cartridges into, the cylinder and placed the gun on the bed. Then he took the derringer, the stingy little gun with the big bite, and emptied it. He cleaned it and reloaded it. Then he bit the tip off a cigar and lit it.

Jimmy shook his head in admiration. "My, but you're cool!"

Dade looked up. "What makes you think so."

"You act that way. Some day will you teach me how to draw and shoot?"

"Why?"

"To be like you, Dade."

Dade wondered if he should tell Jimmy about the six men he had killed. The men who sometimes came back to look at him with accusing eyes. The saddle tramp at Tascosa, his first. The greaser in Tucson who had gone after Dade with a *cuchillo*. The murderer who had refused to surrender in the Huachucas. The gambler in Mobeetie who had cheated clumsily. The Texas trail-driver who had killed the hurdy-gurdy girl in Hays and then had gone amok. The hardcase in El Paso who had bucked Dade as the man who had placed him in Huntsville for five years.

"Well?" asked Jimmy.

Dade took his cigar from his mouth. "All right," he said.

"Thanks, Dade." Jimmy stood up. "Anything you want me to do?"

"Keep an eye on Burkitt and Ray and keep me posted on their whereabouts."

"Sure, Dade."

Dade looked up. "Another thing. Don't get any ideas you're going to back me in gunplay. Keep out of the way."

Jimmy flushed. "It's maybe my chance to get my man."

Dade stood up. "You haven't a chance, Kid."

"With you there, I have."

"*Vamonos!*"

After the kid left, Dade walked to the window and looked down into the darkening street. They were all alike, wanting a chance to throw a gun against another man, to kill him, to prove they were better men. Until a better man came along.

Dade dropped on the bed and turned down the lamp.

He lay for a long time listening to the wind batter against the walls.

———

At half-past five, the street was empty of people. The lamplight glistened on the puddles. It was quiet! Too quiet. Not even the jangling piano in The Star of New Mexico jarred sensitive ears.

Dade walked down to the station. The agent was at his desk, nodding in the heat of the big stove. The wind picked up the smoke from the chimney and blew it down low against the tracks.

Dade walked east along Main, glancing in The Star of New Mexico. There was a poker game in progress. One man stood at the long bar. Burkitt was not there. Dade made the rounds to the end of Main and stood at the corner of Yucca looking off to the east toward the Lazy T. The road was deserted. He walked to Mesquite and stood opposite Bartolome's. There were no ponies standing hipshot at the rack.

He walked to the jail and tested the door. It was locked, the big *calabozo* unlit. He glanced in at the Bull's Head as he passed. Joe Fettis was at the bar. Moses Jaynes, the undertaker, was reading a newspaper at a table.

Dade walked to the Bee Hive. Kelly looked up at him from behind the bar and his face paled. "Lousy night," he said.

"Rye," said Dade. "Miles around?"

"He's over at the newspaper."

A rancher looked up from a table, downed his drink, and walked to the door. "Good night, Kelly," he called back.

"Good night, Cass. You're leaving early." Cass paused with his hand at the door. "I got a big day tomorrow," he said.

Kelly mopped the bar. "Cass usually gets likkered up before he goes home to face his old woman," he said. "She's a hellion. One of the Carter girls. They're all like that. Three of em. All three was married."

"*Was* married?"

"Yeh. Mary ran her old man off. She runs the ranch now. Thelma rode her old man so hard he went to Arizona and joined the cavalry. Apaches killed him. Maybe he was better off."

The door opened and Miles Moilan came in. He stopped beside Dade.

"Drink?" said Dade.

"I need it."

Kelly filled Miles' glass and then made himself scarce.

Miles downed his drink. "Ain't seen you around today," he said.

"I've been busy."

"Alex Ray left town two hours ago."

"That so?"

"You know damned well he wouldn't be around when trouble starts. Dade, why don't you pull out? I'll stake you."

"I'm sticking."

"Maybe Guthrie will kill you, Dade. He's good."

Dade said nothing.

Miles wet his lips. "What a mess I got myself into."

"Keep out of the way, then."

I aim to.

Dade walked to the Seeburg mechanical piano and dropped in a nickel. He walked back to the bar as the piano began to grind out an unsteady tune.

"Dammit," said Miles. "Do you have to play that thing?"

"You nervous, Miles?"

The big man turned on a heel and left the saloon, without a word.

Kelly ambled back. "Miles ain't himself lately."

Dade glanced into Kelly's bar mirror. The big wall clock hung on the opposite wall, with the numbers reversed so that a man could tell time without craning his neck over his shoulder. Saved drinking time. It was six-fifteen.

Dade stayed until half-past six, idly feeding nickels into the big Seeburg; then he walked out into the street. The moon shone fitfully between low, ragged clouds. The wind had died away.

Jimmy Harshaw appeared out of the shadows. "Alex Ray is out of town," he said. "Lefty Corse and Lanky Jones are gone, too. They took the north road toward Sand Creek."

"When?"

"About an hour and a half ago."

"Where's Burkitt?"

"I haven't seen him."

"Ok. Get off the streets, Jimmy."

"I'll stick."

"Get home!"

"All right. *All right!*"

The kid vanished down Ocotillo Street. Dade leaned against a post, smoking. A buckboard ground through the greasy mud. The driver looked at Dade and touched up his team.

Dade felt the weight of his guns. The single-action in its leather-lined pocket. The belly-gun in his left coat pocket. The derringer clipped to his wrist. It was like the night he had looked for Jonce Willis in the streets of Hays, years ago. Willis had sworn to gun Dade down for a buffaloing. A big man with a cross-draw. He had braced Dade. Dade's slug had smashed the thick forearm as Jonce had reached for his Colt. The big man had been game. He had managed to draw his cutter with his left hand and plant a slug in Dade's right shoulder, driving him back against a building. Dade had done the border shift in time to fire with his left hand and stop Willis with another slug through the left forearm.

That had been long ago. There had been other gunfights and other men. Dade looked down at his coat. This time, there was no star on his chest. He held out his strong, lean hands and looked at them. Killer's hands, Mae Delano had once told him long ago. He wondered how Mae was. How Lucy Harshaw was.

Dade looked up and down the quiet street. He didn't know where Burkitt and Ray were, nor Corse and Jones. Supposing they had thrown in with Ray and Burkitt? It would double the odds. The Mexicans would stay clear of the hassle. They knew better than to get mixed up in a gringo showdown.

The moon appeared and glistened on the puddles. A faint wind moaned about the buildings.

CHAPTER NINETEEN

Dade paced down to Railroad Street. A man watched him from the doorway of The Star of New Mexico and then went back inside. Dade opened the lid of his watch and held it close to his eyes. Quarter to seven. He wondered what Chris Guthrie was thinking as he rode into Estanque. Guthrie was fast, but it took more than that to make a man a gun swift. There had been fear in his eyes when Dade had jammed his Colt into him. Sick fear, but enough guts to tell Dade to shoot, knowing he had lost in the biggest game of all.

The whistle of the train sounded far off in the hills. Late again. Maybe Dade should have left Estanque when he had the chance. Lucy Harshaw had stopped him. *"Will you stay?"* she had asked. *"For me, Dade, only for me if you must have me say so."*

He wondered if she had really known what he would have to face tonight

The train was closer now, chugging through the low hills, descending to Estanque. Then it was in the station, puffing and panting. The conductor's voice carried to him, and then the train was gone on its way north. Quiet descended on Estanque again.

Dade walked east along Main. He remembered

Mexico and the starlit nights there. He mentally cursed the revolutionaries who had stopped the working of his mine. General Escopeto had offered Dade a thousand Mexican dollars a month to fight with him. Poor Escopeto's revolution had been short-lived. They had stood him up against a wall in Quatro Jacales and filled him full of slugs. The dreams Escopeto had had. To be *presidente*. A two-fisted *bandido* who had made a success out of his trade and then had been led astray by dreams of power and prestige.

It was seven o'clock by the clock in Jayne's Undertaking Parlor.

Dade paced slowly down to Mesquite Street and paused to light a cigar. He flipped the match into a puddle and heard it hiss. There was no sign of life.

Dade looked at the *calabozo*. There had been a faint flicker of light in one of the windows as though a man had lit a smoke. The thick door gaped open a few inches. It had been locked before. He knew now where at least one of them was.

Dade stepped into a doorway and scanned the far side of the street. Not one window showed light on that side. A dog padded through the mud, looking for scraps. He paused at an alleyway and growled deep in his throat. Then he tucked his tail between his legs and trotted off, satisfied that he had shown he wasn't really afraid. Dade snubbed out his cigar against the door behind him. There was another of them over there.

He looked at the jail, quiet and unlit. The alleyway was almost directly across from it. Crossfire.

Dade looked up toward Yucca. A lone horseman just beyond the livery stable drew rein and looked up the street. Then he slid from the saddle and led the horse to the rack in front of the livery. He tethered it and then settled his gun belt about his lean hips. Chris Guthrie.

Dade let his breath out softly and eased the derringer in its wrist clip.

Guthrie was standing in front of the livery stable, looking up the silent street. He felt in his pocket and drew out his makings. Deftly he rolled a smoke one-handed and touched it off with a match. The brief light showed his lean face and then was gone.

The moon drifted behind clouds. All that Dade could see was the intermittent darkness and brief spot of light as the foreman drew on his smoke.

A door banged far up the street and a man stepped out into the mud. He paused and looked up and down the muddy thoroughfare and then plowed across to the Bee Hive. The Bee Hive door opened and closed behind him. Silence again. A brooding silence that caused the cold sweat to trickle down Dade's sides.

Guthrie flipped away his cigarette, passed a hand along the neck of his horse, and then walked fifty feet toward the center of town. He stopped and looked from side to side.

Dade waited. Guthrie walked out to the center of Yucca and then stopped again. The moon drifted behind the ragged clouds again, plunging the town into dimness.

Dade looked at the jail and then across the street, Guthrie came on. Dade took a deep breath and stepped from beneath the darkness of the porch roof into the greasy mud. It squelched beneath his boots.

Guthrie walked on down the middle of the street, turning his head to one side and then the other.

A cold, disquieting thought came to Dade. Supposing Guthrie took the long chance and shot to kill? He dispelled the thought. Guthrie wouldn't live a minute in that muddy street if he shot down Dade.

Dade walked out into the middle of the street with a crawling sensation down his back. He was presenting a broad target to whoever was in the *calabozo* and across the street, but he couldn't let Chris Guthrie walk into a crossfire of which he was ignorant.

Dade wondered how many men were watching from

unlit doorways and windows. How many were peering into the implacable darkness of the street, waiting for the deadly flash of gunfire? How many friends? How many enemies? How many men who didn't give a damn *who* got it that dark night in the mud-choked streets of Estanque?

Guthrie was a hundred yards away now, standing plumb in the middle of the street, His fingertips brushed the butt of his Colt as his head turned from one side to the other, looking into the shadows, trying to see what awaited him.

What was going through Guthrie's mind? thought Dade.

Then Guthrie saw Dade. He tensed and then relaxed. There was no going back now.

Dade waited, with the wind flapping the long black coat against his back.

Guthrie moved forward. Fifty yards. Forty yards. Thirty yards. He stopped.

"Are you looking for me, Guthrie?" called out Dade. *How many waiting men had heard him?*

Guthrie raised his head. "I am," he said loudly.

"I'm waiting, Guthrie."

Chris Guthrie raised his lean hands to grip the front of his loose gray coat. "You've thrown your weight around, Averill. Maybe you'd like to try me?"

Dade glanced sideways. The alleyway was fifty feet behind him. The jail seventy-five feet at the most. He called out. "Where do you want to end? In the alleyway with a slug in your gut? Or in a cell in the *caldbozo* where you belong for killing Gil Harshaw?"

Guthrie nodded.

"You're yellow, Averill. Hiding behind those guns and a star."

Guthrie closed the gap and stopped twenty feet from Dade. The moon came out and shone on him.

"Make your play," said Dade harshly.

Guthrie slapped down. Dade jumped sideways, trying to keep an eye on the alleyway as he whipped out his Colt.

Guthrie fired. The booming echo slammed back and forth between the false-front buildings. Dade fired twice, just over Guthrie's head. Something moved in the alleyway. Guthrie cursed and fanned his hammer back with a cut off his left hand. He fired. Dade staggered and turned. The jail door had swung open. The moon gleamed on a rifle barrel. Dade plunged to the cold mud and jerked spasmodically.

"He got him!" yelled Burkitt from the darkened alleyway.

Alex Ray jumped out on the stone slab in front of the jail and raised his rifle. Guthrie fired twice, the heavy slugs smashing into Alex Ray. Ray pitched forward, the rifle muzzle driving into the mud.

Burkitt jumped out into the street and raised a shotgun, his face set and cold over the twin barrels. Dade rolled over in the thick mud and fired from the ground. Burkitt's scattergun roared. The shot threw mud up into Dade's face. He got to his knees and clawed at the mud as Guthrie fired at Burkitt. Burkitt's gun flamed again. Guthrie cursed and ran toward Burkitt. The killer threw the shotgun at Guthrie and jumped back into the alleyway, clawing for his twin Colts.

Dade jumped to his feet. His Colt was plastered with mud. He dropped it and freed his belly-gun. Feet pounded in the alley. A man yelled up the street as Guthrie sprinted after Burkitt. Dade raced down Main toward Mesquite, hoping to cut Burkitt off. He slipped as he reached the corner. Burkitt came from the alley, looking back over his shoulder.

Dade raised the double-action. Two men appeared across the street. "Hey, Burkitt! Didn't you get them?" yelled Lefty Corse.

Burkitt ran into the middle of the street as Chris Guthrie appeared. Burkitt snapped a shot and Guthrie staggered as he fired his last shot Lanky Jones whirled. "He got me!" he screamed harshly.

Jones and Guthrie were down. Corse turned toward Dade, fifty feet away. Dade dropped, thrusting forward the double-action and pumping the trigger three times. Corse grunted as the soft slugs ripped into flesh and bone. He folded over, with a gush of blood pouring out of his slack mouth.

Burkitt hurdled Jones and whirled, thrusting out his six-gun for a shot at the writhing Guthrie. Guthrie raised a white face. Dade fired as the Colt settled for the shot Burkitt grunted and stepped back. He dropped the Colt fumbled for its mate and got it free as Dade rose from the mud. He fired as Dade did. Burkitt's slug whipped through the slack of Dade's coat. Dade's slug smashed into Burkitt's gut. Even as the killer went down, he had the strength to rip out one more shot which sang harmlessly up into the clouded sky.

Dade wiped the cold sweat from his face. Powder smoke swirled low in the street. Jones raised his head and then dropped it. He rolled over, throwing his arms wide, to look at the sky with glazing eyes.

Dade reloaded his belly-gun with shaking hands. It had been a near thing. Five men downed in the pasty mud in less than five minutes. Estanque would never have another day like that.

Burkitt groaned and moved a little, scrabbling in the mud with clawed hands.

Dade knelt beside Guthrie. The foreman's face was racked with pain. Dade lifted his head. "Where is it?" he asked.

"Left shoulder. Up high. Bone's broken."

Dade ripped back the shirt and pulled a handkerchief from his pocket. He wadded it against the bullet hole. "You'll live," he said.

Guthrie winced in pain. "We showed em," he said with a tight grin. "We showed em, Dade."

Men gathered in the trampled street looking at the

carnage. One of them said, "Corse, Jones, and Burkitt are dead!"

Dade stood up. "Carry Guthrie to Doc Safford's office," he said. "Take it easy with him. He's got a broken shoulder."

Miles Moilan pushed his way through the crowd. Krepps and Jaynes were behind him, carrying shotguns. Kelly, the bartender, had a pistol in his hand. Miles stopped beside Dade. "What the hell is this?" he asked.

Dade wiped the mud from his face. "Guthrie and I faked that meeting, figuring they'd lay for us. They did."

Miles wiped his broad face and swore softly. "Alex Ray is dead in front of the jail."

Burkitt raised his head. "Gather my friends around me," he husked.

Some of the bystanders carried Guthrie down the street. Dade stood over Burkitt. The killer's head rested on Jaynes' knee. "Burkitt," said Dade, "who killed Gil Harshaw?"

"Go to hell!"

"You're dying," said Moses Jaynes.

Burkitt closed his eyes.

"Who killed Harshaw?" asked Dade.

Burkitt opened his eyes. "I'm through," he said faintly.

"Make it easy on Guthrie," said Dade.

Burkitt nodded. "It was me. Alex Ray planned it." He coughed bloodily and tried to wipe the pink froth from his thick lips. Jaynes wiped the drawn face with his handkerchief.

Burkitt opened glazing eyes. "I backed the wrong play. I... *backed*... *the*... wrong... *play*" He sank back.

"He's gone," said Jaynes.

"That clears Guthrie," said Moilan.

Hoofs thudded in the mud. Glenn Tagger appeared at the corner followed by a dozen of his *corrida*. Miles spat.

He slid back his coat. Tagger kneed his horse forward. "Where's Chris Guthrie?" he asked.

"He's alive," said Jaynes.

Tagger looked at Dade. "Thanks," he said.

Miles shook his head. "Averill and Guthrie worked together. Ray and Burkitt tried to dry-gulch them, with" Corse and Jones to back them."

Tagger looked at the sprawled bodies. "They got all three of them?"

Miles nodded. "And Alex Ray."

Tagger looked at Dade. "Him?"

Dade slid his gun into his pocket. "Guthrie is clear," he said. "Burkitt has admitted that he killed Gil Harshaw."

Dade walked away from the gaping crowd. He reached Main and walked toward Mae Delano's house. Jimmy Harshaw was standing with the crowd in front of the jail. Alex Ray lay where he had died. Jimmy handed Dade his Colt. "Is it all over, Dade?" he asked eagerly.

"Yes." Dade slid the six-gun into its leather-lined pocket.

"You're all right?"

Dade nodded, turned away from the kid, and walked to Mae Delano's house. He rapped on the door, and she opened it. Her face was chalk-white. "Where is he?" she asked.

"At Doc Safford's."

"Oh, no!"

He placed a hand on her shoulder. "It's just a wound, Mae. He'll be all right."

She threw a shawl about her shoulders. "Can I go to him?"

"He'll want to see you."

She stepped out on the porch. Dade followed her. "Guthrie has been cleared of the murder charge. Tell him that. He'll want to hear it from you."

She came close and kissed him quickly.

"Mae, get him out of here after he recovers. Marry him. Go somewhere where neither of you are known. Start over."

She touched his face with cool hands and then hurried across the street.

Dade walked past the gaping townsmen and into the hotel. The clerk eyed him as he went upstairs. Dade slammed the door behind him and peeled off his muddy clothing. He washed and changed.

He was cleaning his Colt when someone tapped on the door. Miles Moilan came in, followed by Glenn Tagger. "You all right, Dade?" asked Miles.

"Yes."

They watched him as he worked on the gun. Miles lit a cigar. "Tagger and me have been talking," he said.

Tagger leaned on the end of the bed. "You helped Chris," he said. "You cleared him. I won't forget it, Averill."

Dade shrugged.

Miles wet his lips. "We've got a deal for you."

Dade looked up quickly. "Leave me out of deals," he said.

"You might at least listen to what we have to say," said Miles.

"Shoot."

Miles inspected his cigar. "There's no good candidate for sheriff now," he said. "How about you taking it on? I can get you in."

Dade stood up. "That's the trouble, Miles. You can get me in."

Miles flushed.

"Listen, Averill," said Tagger, "I'm with Miles on this. The ranchers will listen to me, too."

Dade cut a hand sideways. "No deals!"

Miles placed a heavy hand on Dade's shoulder. "Where are you going?"

"I don't know."

"Stay here, Dade. We need you."

Dade rubbed his jaw. "You'll get no favors from me. Neither one of you."

"We don't want any," said Miles. "It's worth it to both of us to have you in office."

Dade laughed. *"Both* of you? You know what Doc Safford told me? That Gil Harshaw had once told him what a sheriff was."

"So?" asked Tagger.

Dade eyed them both. "A sheriff is an officer who represents the administrative power of a state within one of its counties; an officer who executes the mandates of the courts of record within a county; the *chief* ministerial officer in a county."

Miles looked at Dade through narrowed eyes. "We understand, Dade. Will you run?"

"I don't want it."

Tagger walked to the door. "There's someone here to see you," he said quietly. He opened the door. Lucy Harshaw came in and hurried to Dade. Tagger walked outside.

Miles grinned. "Talk to this idiot, Lucy," he said. "We want him for sheriff."

Miles closed the door behind him.

Lucy looked up at Dade. "Well?"

"I want no part of politics."

She rested her head against his chest. "Don't you see?" she said softly. "That's exactly why they want you."

He lifted her chin with his hand. "What about you, Lucy?"

Her eyes held his. "It wouldn't be any use trying to place you on a ranch or in a shop."

"I'm sick of killing, Lucy."

"My father never killed a man in the line of duty, Dade, but he was a good sheriff until he listened to men like Miles Moilan."

The wind sighed about the window. Dade kissed her.

She clung to him. He was glad now that he had come to Estanque.

"I'll never kill another man," he said quietly as he drew her close.

And Dade Averill, professional lawman, never did.

TAKE A LOOK AT BARRANCA AND BLOOD JUSTICE:

Two Full Length Western Novels

Gordon D. Shirreffs, Spur Award and Owen Wister Award winning author, tells the tales of the old west as they were meant to be told—with no holds barred action and adventure.

In *Barranca*, a dying blind man vows to reveal the site of a lost silver mine to two Civil War vets, but only if they will help him see through the quest. He knows he won't live long enough to enjoy the spoils, but he wants to die at least having the knowledge that it was found. The unlikely trio must deal with arid desert heat, hostile forces, crooked Federales, and treacherous cliffs to discover the lost valley where a silver treasure beyond their wildest imaginings awaits.

In *Blood Justice*, Jim Murdock had left Ute Crossing seven years before, with a posse hot on his heels and thirsty for blood. Now, he'd arrived back just in time to see another lynching. The three men who were supposed to have murdered the town's leading citizen were removed from the jail at midnight, taken to a hill, and hanged by their necks until dead. Someone was too anxious to get them out of the way, and Jim Murdock was going to find out why. He was going to track down the truth—and the real killer or killers—even if it meant putting his own neck in a noose...

"The joy of reading Shirreffs' work is in his mastery of pacing and his tough, gritty prose." – James Reasoner, author of *Outlaw Ranger*.

AVAILABLE SEPTEMBER 2022

ABOUT THE AUTHOR

Gordon D. Shirreffs published more than 80 western novels, 20 of them juvenile books, and John Wayne bought his book title, Rio Bravo, during the 1950s for a motion picture, which Shirreffs said constituted *"the most money I ever earned for two words."* Four of his novels were adapted to motion pictures, and he wrote a Playhouse 90 and the Boots and Saddles TV series pilot in 1957.

A former pulp magazine writer, he survived the transition to western novels without undue trauma, earning the admiration of his peers along the way. The novelist saw life a bit cynically from the edge of his funny bone and described himself as looking like a slightly parboiled owl. Despite his multifarious quips, he was dead serious about the writing profession.

Gordon D. Shirreffs was the 1995 recipient of the Owen Wister Award, given by the Western Writers of America for "a living individual who has made an outstanding contribution to the American West."

He passed in 1996.